Sherlock Holmes
The Adventure of
The Pigtail Twist

By M J H Simmonds

Copyright Page

First edition published in 2018
© Copyright 2018 Matthew Simmonds

The right of Matthew Simmonds to be identified as the author of this work has been asserted by him in accordance with the Copyright, Designs and Patents Act 1998.

All rights reserved. No reproduction, copy or transmission of this publication may be made without express prior written permission.

No paragraph of this publication may be reproduced, copied or transmitted except with express prior written permission or in accordance with the provisions of the Copyright Act 1956 (as amended). Any person who commits any unauthorised act in relation to this publication may be liable to criminal prosecution and civil claims for damage.

Although every effort has been made to ensure the accuracy of the information contained in this book, as of the date of publication, nothing herein should be construed as giving advice. The opinions expressed herein are those of the author and not of MX Publishing.

Paperback ISBN 978-1-78705-304-5
ePub ISBN 978-1-78705-305-2
PDF ISBN 978-1-78705-306-9

Published in the UK by MX Publishing
335 Princess Park Manor, Royal Drive, London, N11 3GX
www.mxpublishing.co.uk

Cover design by Brian Belanger.

For Henry and Ania

With all my love

Introduction - June 1884

The summer of 1884 was so abominable it was barely worthy of the name. A band of low pressure had settled stubbornly to the west of Ireland and spread its cold misery eastward throughout the entire month of June and beyond. The rain pelted down through the murky grey streets of London and the wind blew it into swirls that left no surface dry and many a hardy soul with a limp and a shattered umbrella.

Sherlock Holmes, lacking for a case or any other intellectual challenge, was the very mirror of this foul presence. A hawkish, dark and moody doppelganger, taken to rapid pacing followed by hours of lethargy and cadaverous stillness. Neither pipe nor newspaper gave him relief and his eyes were increasingly drawn from the silk Persian slipper beside the firedog to that small coffin shaped box that sat above the gently crackling fireplace.

At the time, I was happy and content just to be indoors catching up with my reading and indeed putting some of Holmes' recent exploits down on paper. Any lengthy exposure to the cold and damp would certainly inflame my old war wound - the throb from the old Jezail bullet was already noticeable. My suggestions for topics of conversation were met with silence or, at best, a curt grunt of disagreement. His face was drawn, and he appeared even thinner than usual, I could not recall seeing him take any solid sustenance for several days. Holmes' ennui had now set in to the point where I could no longer see any way of stopping him reaching for his syringe.

Although it now felt like an eternity, it was, in fact, a mere three weeks since Holmes had astounded myself, most of Scotland Yard and half of England with the most amazing and sustained display of his talent for deduction and creative reasoning I think I have ever witnessed. Over the course of six days he had solved six crimes and even hinted at the presence of a seventh, yet undetected, felony.

Part One

It had all begun on a fine, if still rather chilly, May morning with a visit from Inspector Lestrade. He arrived at our Baker Street rooms looking particularly agitated. His face was flustered, and he twitched and flinched even more than usual. His clothes were ruffled and unkempt as if from a sleepless night and the dark shadows that had formed below his eyes seemed to confirm this. Despite the early hour, I immediately poured him a large brandy and motioned him to take a seat by the fire to which Holmes added fuel and prodded to encourage into greater activity.

"I see that you are quite overcome by your recent case volume," announced Holmes with his back still turned.

"Why, yes I am. But how…?" stuttered Lestrade

"Your atypical appearance married to the veritable crime wave being reported over the last few days," he gestured languidly at a disordered pile of recent local and national newspapers, "points towards friend Lestrade's present state of duress."

He turned slowly, and I imagined for a second that I could see the faintest hint of a smile appear and then vanish as he sat himself down in his musty old armchair.

I offered Lestrade a cigar, which he gratefully accepted, as Holmes gently emptied his favourite caliginous clay pipe into the fire before refilling, tamping and lighting it in his well-worn morning ritual. The smoke produced from this first pipe of the day was, as always, dark, acrid and pungent. It swirled around, quite overwhelming the lighter, finer smoke from our cigars. It was almost as if even his tobacco was asserting its total superiority over us mere intellectual mortals.

Although Lestrade was, at that time, still deeply suspicious of Holmes' abilities he had, by now, witnessed the efficaciousness of his methods at first hand and a grudging respect was forming beneath his surface layers of scepticism.

"It is not the cases themselves, you understand," began Lestrade, his composure restored by the warming golden liquid. "It is the sheer number of them. Mounting up more quickly than anyone on God's earth could possibly solve them. Truly, I feel like Sisyphus himself".

"Well I am rather busy myself," lied Holmes, quite brazenly, gesturing towards his copious files, "but I will see what I can do to lighten your load," he added, noncommittally.

I knew he had recently solved a rather unpleasant poisoning case involving a wine merchant, a chemist and a dissolving cork and was looking forward to a new challenge.

"Well, so far, I have a murdered flower girl in the Old Nichol, a rogue cabby at large, a jewel theft, a violent conflict of wills, a spate of suspicious deaths in Hampstead and a bookmaker beaten to death outside his own front door," Lestrade disclosed, flicking through his leather-bound pocket notebook.

"I am aware of a number of these cases already and the remainder hardly appear to offer much more of a challenge either," Holmes responded, casually. "But please let us start with the first, the poor flower seller."

Case 1: The Flower Girl - Monday 12th of May 1884

"As you know the Old Nichol is the very worst of the East End, both in terms of poverty and crime, a place to be avoided even at the best of times, if you get my drift," began Lestrade, leaning forwards to emphasise the seriousness of his statement.

"We were called to St Leonard's Church at around eight o'clock last Friday evening, after someone reported seeing a man attacking a young lady who was selling flowers outside the church. When we arrived, her stall was wrecked, and she lay dead among the detritus. A sad sight it was, her lying amongst all those broken stems and colourful petals, considering that's probably more flowers than she will see even at her own funeral."

Lestrade paused for a moment. I often forgot that he was from, and empathised with, a far lower social stratum than Holmes or I, and had worked his way up through the force by sheer ability and persistence alone. This only rarely manifested itself, and almost always when dealing with the suffering of one London's poorest creatures.

"She had been strangled and it appears her takings stolen, as she had not a coin on her."

"We have arrested three suspects. Two are local ne'er-do-wells, the other is the son of the local verger. All were seen hanging around the church before the poor girl was attacked. All three fit the descriptions of the witnesses, but as it was already getting dark when they were seen, the actual descriptions were pretty vague to say the least."

"Was this her usual spot? Or did she move around to ply her wares?" asked Holmes.

"I believe she was regularly outside the church, according to the witnesses anyway," replied the Inspector.

"The verger's son?" I questioned. "Is he really a likely suspect when you are also holding two miscreants who are already well known to the police?"

"Evidence, Watson. Discount no one until you have data. But I believe I have a fairly good idea of how to obtain it," was Holmes' curt reply.

"We shall see you at the Yard this afternoon then, say, midday? I wish to see the suspects."

Holmes rose suddenly and gestured towards the door. Lestrade put down his now empty glass, bade farewell and uncertainly shuffled his way out and down the stairs.

"You already know who did it, don't you?" I asked, slowly shaking my head in disbelief.

"I have a hypothesis that needs testing, but I am confident the matter will be resolved either way in time for a late luncheon in town".

At half past eleven, we took a Hansom from Baker Street and made for Scotland Yard. The journey was fairly short and uneventful, taking us down Oxford and Regent Streets then across Piccadilly Circus. Holmes seemed to be in a good mood for once and began a short discourse on the relevance of pipe shapes to character and crime.

"A man who smokes a Bulldog or Rhodesian can always be trusted. But beware the man who smokes an overlarge bent Billiard. A voluminous sagging bowl indicates a lethargic personality. A man lazy enough to wish to fill his pipe as few times as possible is not one who should be tasked with any great responsibility. Whereas, the smoker of a Lumberman has made a deep conscious decision to…" However, we had arrived, and I never did discover the deep decision made by the Lumberman smoker.

Once inside, Lestrade greeted us and took us to the holding cells deep within the building. The three men were lined up before us, and I have to be honest here and admit that I saw little in their appearance to change my mind as to whom I would have suspected of having committed the ghastly deed.

The locals appeared to be of the low criminal kind, dressed in old, slightly tattered but basically clean, working clothes. Their faces were prematurely aged by days spent outside in all weathers and stuck in a perpetual half grimace of either pain or scorn, I could not tell which, probably a fair bit of both.

The verger's son could not have looked any more different if he had just arrived from a far distant country. His eyes were red and swollen from weeping and he visibly shook as we studied him. His clothes were neat and well kempt, his shoes regularly shined but showing scuffs from recent heavy use.

To my great surprise, Holmes took only a cursory look at the two rogues and not much longer at the quaking young man.

"Hold out your hands," he ordered.

Holmes' manner could be so compelling that often those he commanded simply obeyed him without a second's thought. All three instantly stretched out their hands towards him.

"I've seen enough," he announced, "return them to their cells."

"Well? Does Mr Sherlock Holmes have the solution then?" asked Lestrade, with more than a hint of a sneer, as the men were led away. His confidence seemed to have returned since his morning visit. His conceitedness too, sadly.

"Oh, I am so sorry, Inspector. I thought you knew. It is, after all, rather obvious is it not, Watson?"

As he spoke, I thought I spied the flickering return of his smile - but it was gone again in an instant.

"Oh, is it? Erm... maybe?" I stumbled, but the truth was that I was no further along with my reasoning than I was before we arrived at Scotland Yard.

"The verger's son is the killer, that much is blindingly obvious." We both stared at him but said nothing. "Whether it be murder or manslaughter will be up to a jury to decide."

I slowly began to see the logic behind Holmes' pronouncement.

"If the motive had been common robbery, the victim would have simply been punched or hit with some kind of weapon," Holmes explained. "These types of criminals have no wish to hang for the sake of a few pennies. They would not have killed her and then wrecked her meagre stall for no personal gain. This was a crime of passion, gentlemen. Despite what you may have read in some sensational fiction, strangulation is a very personal business, intimate, close up, face to face."

"I strongly suspected that the two knew each well, as they would have from being in such close and regular proximity. The verger's son must have had designs on the poor girl and been spurned when he declared his feelings and intentions. I doubt that even in his wildest imaginings he could have believed that she, a mere flower seller, could ever reject him, an educated young man with real prospects. He snapped, smashed up her stand and killed her in a fit of madness".

"But the hands, Holmes? What was the significance of examining those?" I asked.

"What is almost everyone's favourite flower, Watson? One she would sell every day, far more than any other? One that begins to bloom in early spring"

"Why, roses of course!" I exclaimed. "Roses with thorns. If he swiped the stock off her stall with such ferocity that she was covered in broken stems and petals, then he would surely have also have been caught by many thorns in the process."

"I saw the unmistakable prickles and punctures caused by their barbs all over his hands. It was really just the final confirmation of what I already suspected."

"What about the missing money then? Just vanished did it?" Lestrade interjected, sarcastically.

"Why do you think I sent all three back to the cells? A simple case of opportunism after the event, as distasteful as it may seem. They saw the aftermath of the crime and quickly rummaged around, located her purse and ran off with it. If we are lucky, we will find it back at their lair, but I fear they have disposed of it already. In that case I cannot see any charges sticking, and you'd do as well to keep them locked up for as long as you legally can as this is the only punishment they are likely to receive."

There is not much to add regarding this sad case. The two ruffians were never charged, just as Holmes predicted. The verger's son narrowly escaped the noose, thanks in no small part to the surprise testimony of my friend Mr Sherlock Holmes, who showed then, and continues to show, a deep and sympathetic understanding of human nature that belies his seemingly cold and uncaring exterior.

Case 2: The Rogue Cabman - Tuesday 13th of May 1884

The next day began early. I was woken by the sound of voices, orders being given and received, it seemed to me. I dressed and made my way to the sitting room where I just caught sight of the back of one of Holmes' young 'Irregulars' as he retreated from the room.

"A bit early for young Wiggins, is it not?" I yawned.

Looking at the mantel clock, I saw that it was just after half past six. The day was bright but crisp and I was glad to see that Holmes had already lit the fire.

"Almost all great work is achieved before midday" Holmes replied, brightly. "I promised to help Lestrade with his burden and help I shall".

"So which case it today, then? If you're going to work through them in the order given to us by Lestrade then it would be that business of the rogue cabman. It has been in all the papers due to some pretty high-profile victims."

"Indeed. A cabby who takes your fare and then your valuables and wallet too. It may only be a matter of time before he also takes your life."

Holmes chose a dull brown Bulldog briar for his early smoke, filled it with the previous day's dottles and cigar ends, packed them in gently with a slim thumb and then lit them with a taper, which he pulled from the fire.

"How do you expect to catch this rogue cabman? Surely, he could be any one of hundreds operating in the city, maybe thousands." I was now addressing a dark smog that almost totally obscured my friend.

"Not at all," Holmes gesticulated with his empty hand, clearing a small opening in his personal black cloud. Well here is the silver lining coming, I chuckled to myself. "The carriage is a Hansom, black with blue trim and dark leather seats inside."

"Which currently describes several hundred cabs in London right now," I complained. "Surely even you cannot find such a needle amongst the smokestacks."

Holmes raised a critical eyebrow at what I thought was a rather clever little updating of the adage.

"Not only do I believe I will solve the case, but I shall do so by lunchtime. Without leaving this chair. Everything is set in motion, all we need do is wait," Holmes paused, before adding, "and smoke".

Holmes seemed to be grinning. I suddenly realised that he was turning this into an intellectual exercise. The case, though totally baffling to me, was not enough to challenge him, so he had set what I thought were impossible boundaries to make the problem even harder to solve.

After only a short while the noxious atmosphere of the sitting room became too much for me, so I escaped outside into the low early morning sunshine and spent a couple of blissful hours strolling through The Regent's Park, returning only when the throbbing of my old wound moved from a distraction into actual discomfort.

I returned to Baker Street shortly before nine, and on my way inside greeted Mrs Hudson. I ordered rashers, eggs, toast and coffee for two to be sent to our rooms, knowing with absolute certainty that Holmes would not have eaten. I climbed the familiar stairs to our rooms, opened the door and stepped inside.

Holmes was sprawled strangely in his old armchair. He appeared not to have moved at all, he was still wrapped in his shapeless mouse brown dressing gown. He continued to puff upon the old brown Bulldog briar, the Persian slipper being within easy reach.

I took his extended limbs to be some sort of Eastern exercise to stave off discomfort from his self-enforced immobility.

"I know it is early days, but have you made any progress?" I genuinely worried that this time he had surely promised too much.

"Nothing at all, my dear friend," he replied, but added "Don't worry, the truth is always singular. However, its arrival time can be neither predicted nor guaranteed.'"

I must say that I took less notice of Holmes at that moment than I did of the spectacular breakfast being laid before us by the inimitable Mrs Hudson.

We took our breakfast, and I have to admit to also having eaten at least half of that allocated to Holmes who, of course, left it almost untouched, as he was always wont to do when working a case. I say almost untouched as this was one of the very few times, when on a case, he did indulge in eating along with the rest of us, the great unworthy. He simply leaned forwards, picked up a soft-boiled egg, carefully removed the shell, and devoured it in two bites. This seemed to suffice, and he returned to his pipe with renewed gusto and indeed, gusts.

At a little after eleven o'clock, Inspector Lestrade of Scotland Yard arrived in full-on bluster mode, with added pompousness. He somehow had got wind of Holmes' boast that he could solve the case by midday and without leaving Baker Street. Holmes was, as always, courteous in his welcome and gestured to Lestrade to take a seat and await further developments.

Less than ten minutes later, a stocky boy of about twelve or thirteen years appeared unannounced at the sitting room door, he seemed to have learned well the discipline of stealthy movement and entered the room entirely silently. He stood to attention and offered up a quick salute. He held in his chubby right hand a sheet of paper. It was dark, faintly lined, frayed and appeared to have been torn from an anonymous exercise book. This he handed directly into Sherlock Holmes' long, bony fingers.

"Thank you, Wiggins, you have all performed excellently." He gestured towards a small leather pouch on the sideboard. "Please distribute as per usual – there is an extra shilling in there for you and one for the boy who found it."

Wiggins turned, grabbed the small coin purse and left in some haste.

"Ha-ha!" Holmes snorted, as he gazed upon the tatty missive. "Just as I thought. Well Inspector, you can rest easy now for I have the name, and indeed address, of this present-day highwayman." Holmes handed the grubby note to Lestrade.

"Well, I suppose I'll send some men round, sure enough, but how on earth did you come up with this fellow?" Lestrade's mouth was almost hanging open in surprise.

Holmes leaned back, took a long drag on his pipe, savoured the taste of tobacco in his mouth and across his tongue, and finally exhaled it into a huge cloud.

"Knowledge plus data, Lestrade. It was really rather simple. I have a vast knowledge of criminals, and a fairly good knowledge of London's cabs and their drivers. One thing I do know, for certain, about our cabmen is that they keep their carriages spotless. It is their source of income and indeed also a source of great pride. You will never see a dirty or unkempt cab first thing in the morning as they invariably attend to them, meticulously, at the end of every shift, then cover them to protect from the weather overnight."

"A criminal, however, is inherently lazy and would make only the smallest effort to maintain the outward appearance of his cab. A quick wipe down at the end of the day would be enough to make it look respectable to the casual observer. So, in light of this, I employed some very detailed observers and set them a simple task, to find my data."

"I told them to examine all the cabs operating in well-to-do areas this morning. Look at the wheels and, in particular, the spokes and undercarriage. Report any that have clearly not been cleaned for at least two days."

"It is testament to the London cab driver that only one dirty carriage was found amongst the many hundreds they inspected."

"Well, we shall see, will we not?" Lestrade looked resigned to the fact that Holmes appeared to have solved the crime in the exact manner that he had predicted. "I have doors to knock upon. Good day gentlemen."

I followed Lestrade out onto the landing, pulling the door half closed behind me. The Inspector appeared tired and impatient to take his leave.

"I am far from convinced that these cases are doing anything other than fuelling his already inflated opinion of himself," he growled, in a low voice.

"I fear he is not himself," I whispered.

"He is taking short-cuts, relying on the belief that his intellect alone can solve any puzzle, rather than fully investigating the matter himself. This is a dangerous, unpredictable path. If he continues to solve these cases with such ease, or fails to find a genuine challenge, he may well return to the drugs that he increasingly craves. The alternative might be even worse; he makes a catastrophic error, one that damages both him and his reputation beyond repair."

Lestrade shrugged, "Perhaps he will find something more deserving of his talents in the morning," he replied, obviously still irked by Holmes' arrogance.

I bid the Inspector a good afternoon and returned to the sitting room.

"There is a fine line between confidence and hubris you know, old man," I warned, but Holmes' interest in the matter had already passed.

He rose, stretched and picked up his battered, black violin case. He thoughtfully applied rosin to his bow. I was optimistic that his mood would be positive after the day's success and I might, for once, be treated to an evening of pleasant melodies and not a cacophony born of frustration.

The next day's newspapers confirmed Holmes to have been correct in every detail. That Lestrade accepted the credit seemed, to me, to be fair recompense for Holmes' questionable treatment of the good-intentioned Inspector.

Case 3: The Hobnail Boots - Wednesday 14th of May, 1884

The Chelsea jewel theft of May 1884 was highly unusual in that it was a case that had to be first unsolved before it could finally be truly solved. Lestrade had positively beamed with delight when we met him at Scotland Yard on that sunny Wednesday morning and proceeded to inform us that the case had already been solved, the jewels recovered and the suspect in custody.

"All rather straight forward, I am sorry to say, Mr Holmes. Shame that you came all this way for nought".

My first instinct was to complain that Lestrade had failed to send a telegram to inform us of his success, but I held my tongue for the sake of diplomacy.

"Yes, a passing mendicant had spotted an upstairs window left open and thought he would chance his luck by shinning up the drainpipe and seeing what he could pinch. We caught the man from his footprints, you see. He was wearing a pair of hobnail boots, ones that he had clearly repaired himself, several times. The nails were all over the place, not at all evenly spaced, as a real cobbler would have nailed them. The heel iron looked like it was made from a small horseshoe. So, all in all, he had left a pretty distinctive impression in the flower border by the downpipe."

"Well done Inspector, nothing more for us to do here then, I gather." Holmes' smile was a little too broad to be genuine. "But may I just trouble you for, perhaps, one small favour, Inspector? We have travelled all this way," Holmes pleaded, as fawningly as he could muster. "Could I please see the suspect? For a brief moment, no more. It would just put my mind at ease."

Lestrade gave his assent and nodded towards the Duty Sergeant who gestured that we should follow him down to the cells. As we moved into the depths of the building, the brightly painted plastered walls gave way to bare brick and then finally naked stone as we reached the holding pens.

The Sergeant brought out the suspect and he stood before us. I looked at him, then at Holmes and finally back to the man in front of us.

"Do you deny all knowledge of this crime?" demanded Holmes, unexpectedly. The man nodded. He seemed confused and I wondered if he was even mentally balanced.

The man was much older than I had expected. I know that a life on the streets prematurely ages, but I am sure he had seen at least sixty winters. His clothes were old and threadbare and hung off his spare frame, much in the manner of a scarecrow that has lost its stuffing. His head had but a few patches of spiky white hair and his thin face was covered by a beard, which was unevenly trimmed and stained yellowish from tobacco. He certainly did not look like a man prone to shimmying up drainpipes. However, as I looked downwards, I saw that on his feet were, indeed, a pair of old black hobnail boots.

"Sir, please try not to worry, for I fully expect to have you out of here before the day's end." Sherlock Holmes spoke these words in his most sincere and comforting tone.

The old man gave a gentle smile and managed a quiet "Right you are, sir," as a response, before being led back to captivity. Holmes turned on his heels and left at an electric pace.

I struggled to keep up. "This is monstrous, Holmes. That man could not possibly have climbed up a drainpipe and stolen those jewels. It is preposterous. His age, his condition. It would be difficult for a young man, let alone a sexagenarian."

"Well done, Watson. You are quite right, but for mostly the wrong reasons."

We left the Yard and Holmes ordered me to try to flag down a cab on the increasingly busy street. He announced that, in the meantime, he would visit the nearest post office and dispatch a telegram. When he returned to our waiting cab, two minutes later, it came as no surprise that he ordered the driver to take us the three and a half miles, or so, to Chelsea.

Whilst we headed along the King's Road, he expanded upon his earlier comment.

"The age of the man is irrelevant, and his physical condition is masked by his ragged clothing. I have known men far older who have been capable of amazing physical feats. Remember 'The Great

Giuseppe'? Still performing as a trapeze artist well into his seventies."

"And still just as capable of murder, as I recall," I added, remembering the case from the previous summer.

"Exactly, Watson, but I also believe that you did notice the most important detail. How could you miss it, after all, Lestrade has made it the very heart of his case?"

"The hobnail boots, of course!" I exclaimed. "I must admit that when he first mentioned them I did think they were an odd choice of footwear for a dangerous climb up the outside of a house. But I just assumed that, as a beggar, he simply had no others and had to make do. Maybe, he simply left them behind altogether and chanced it without any footwear."

"Very good reasoning, my dear friend, but I do not believe that any of the theories we have, so far, heard are as simple, or as obvious, as the actual truth."

"Which is?" I asked, encouragingly, but we had arrived at the leafy street where the robbery had taken place. Ignoring my plea, he sprang from the cab and skipped towards the house.

Holmes knocked sharply on the large black front door while I stood back a few yards and surveyed the house. It was a typical Chelsea villa. Recently built and quite handsome, in a familiar kind of way. I made a special note of the high wall, which surrounded a smallish garden giving a good level of privacy to anyone living within. Only the lack of mature bushes and trees allowed anyone to see into the grounds at all.

A young man answered the door. He was dressed in the casual, modern style of a sportsman, white shirt and trousers with an old striped school tie worn as a belt, and lightweight shoes. He was of average height, slim with a good bearing. His most distinguishing features were his jet-black hair and dark eyes. He had a long fringe that dropped so often before his deep-set eyes that his habit of continual brushing it away with his fingers made him appear rather dismissive to any enquiries.

"Mr Pemberton Lythe?" inquired Holmes, politely.

"Ah, no sir, sorry. I am his nephew, Galton, Samuel Galton." He replied, with a slight air of disinterest. "My uncle is bed-bound these last few years and sees no one outside the immediate family."

"I am Sherlock Holmes, consulting detective, and this is my colleague Dr John Watson. We are here regarding the recent theft of items from this property. Although we understand that the matter has been resolved to the contentment of Scotland Yard, you would be doing me an enormous service if you could let us have a look around the grounds for just ten minutes, or so."

"I am not sure what that would achieve. The matter is closed and besides, we have important business of our own to attend to within."

He swiped his errant hair away yet again as he spoke, his air of indifference had not lessened upon hearing our request.

"I do understand, good sir, but I promise that I am asking this favour simply to keep my own personal records up to date. My livelihood depends on gathering details of all notable and singular criminal activity. Just five minutes, we can enter and let ourselves out through the side gate." Holmes gestured to the dark red wooden gate at the side of the house, which gave access directly to the garden.

Holmes' politeness and persistence were paying off. After a short pause, Galton acquiesced. "Alright then, but be quick. I have important legal papers to sign."

He stopped speaking abruptly and just a hint of reddening appeared in his cheeks. It seemed to me that he may well have said a little more than he intended. With a curt "Good day, gentlemen" he closed the door and left us alone on the doorstep.

If Holmes had also sensed anything in Galton's manner, he kept it to himself as he strode directly to the gate. For one moment, I thought it might be locked and that even now Galton may be inside laughing at having put one over on us, but Holmes simply lifted the latch and entered.

The garden was simple and neat. A well-kept lawn was bordered on one side by a small vegetable and herb garden and some young-looking fruit trees to the other. Holmes, of course, gave this picture-perfect English kitchen garden not a single glance as he had not moved from the right side of the house, less than twenty yards from the gate where we had entered.

Silently, he began his examination. He searched both the flowerbed that ran the full length of the house and the yard or so deep ribbon of grass that lay between the border and the path, which led from the gate to the garden. Occasionally, he dropped to his knees for an even closer inspection.

After a few minutes had passed, I felt I had to say something.

"Found anything?" I asked, rather redundantly.

Holmes sprang up like young buck and looked skywards. There was the drainpipe, and it did indeed pass close by a second-floor sash window, which was, on this occasion, firmly shut.

Feeling rather foolish for not having even thought of examining the drainpipe I looked at it as closely as I could.

"I am not sure I would trust that pipe to hold my weight, not even in my significantly lighter army days."

Holmes smiled, but he let any jibe on my weight pass without comment.

"You may well be right, Watson," he stated, but offered no further elucidation. "There is nothing more to be learned here for now."

"I now have nearly all of the pieces I require, but the last few will be difficult to obtain."

Holmes was being as enigmatic as usual, as we sat in the carriage on the way back into town.

"I fear that, whilst I have to all intents and purposes solved the case, there is little I can do to bring the actual perpetrator to justice. I know what he did. I know how he did it. I may also know why he did it. But there is insufficient evidence to make an accusation let alone convince Lestrade to issue a warrant for arrest."

"So, what can we do now?" I asked, now totally bewildered. "We cannot simply give up, surely?"

"I will just have to tell Lestrade all that I know and hope to heavens that he takes it in. He is many things, the Inspector, but he is not a total fool."

We arrived back at the Yard shortly after one o'clock in the afternoon, via a quick stop off at Baker Street where Holmes picked up what I assumed to be the reply to his earlier telegram. The sun was high and the day had warmed sufficiently to have made the journey back from Chelsea a rather pleasant one. Despite being completely in the dark about the case, I felt better than I had in a long while, the warmth spreading through my bones and soothing my old injury. Even the fact that Lestrade was busy, and we had to wait a good hour to see him, did little to dampen my spirits. Instead, we headed over the road for a light lunch of poached fish and vegetables. Holmes refused to discuss the case, instead he insisted upon detailing, and planning for, the forthcoming summer concert season.

By the time we returned, Lestrade was waiting for us in his office. It was a plain, sparsely furnished room with a desk, three chairs, a large filing cabinet and a bookshelf filled with many hundreds of files. It spoke of a man who performed his job upon his feet, it appeared very much to be a room in which he liked to spend as little time as was humanly possible.

"My apologies for keeping you waiting, gentlemen", said Lestrade, his tone unusually serious, with none of the sneer or sarcasm with which we had become accustomed, "but something has occurred to make me wonder if this case might not be quite as black and white as I had previously thought."

"Has it really? Oh, do pray tell, Inspector," asked Holmes. He seemed to come back to life in that instant and was suddenly as keen and eager as he had been first thing this morning.

Lestrade smiled, without much humour.

"I think I would rather hear what you have been up to since you left this morning in such a hurry. I cannot be giving it all to you on a plate, can I?"

"Very well, Inspector. I had already told Watson on the journey over here that I was prepared to share with you all that I have learned and so I shall."

"The solution, as I told Watson as we were examining the property of the alleged victim, is remarkably simple. So simple, that even I almost overlooked it." Holmes spoke confidently, but with no hint of superiority.

"I first became aware that something was not as it seemed when we were shown the alleged burglar. Although, unlike you Watson, I was not entirely surprised by his physical appearance, we did both notice his singularly inappropriate footwear. How could a man climb a drainpipe wearing such heavy cumbersome shoes? You had the beginnings of the solution when you suggested that he may have left them behind altogether. However, you failed to take this theory to its ultimate logical conclusion."

"You see, my dear friend, you were quite correct when you suggested that the shoes never left the ground, but then neither did anything or anyone else!"

I was both taken aback and puzzled by Holmes' exclamation.

"I could see quite clearly, even from ground level, that the pipe was perfectly straight, the paint unmarked and not a single screw had been pulled from the wall," explained Holmes.

I was gobsmacked. "I don't understand. Then how were the jewels taken?" I implored.

"They never were, there was no burglary, was there?" interrupted Lestrade. "But if that is so, then how do you account for the evidence, the footprints?"

"All part of an elaborate set-up, Inspector, designed to allow a quite separate nefarious act to occur unnoticed. Did the countenance of our poor accused not strike you in any way as unusual? Doctor, surely, you must have suspected something?"

Holmes looked upon me with barely concealed disappointment.

"Confusion, lethargy, lack of coherent communication? I could go on."

"Of course, he was drugged! I am sorry, Holmes, it has been a long time since I practised medicine, but there is no excuse for missing those symptoms."

I felt my face redden and anger grow from deep within. What a fool I had been. I resolved, then and there, to get back up to speed with my much-neglected profession.

"Whatever he was given, it must have been pretty strong to still be in his system this morning," I added, trying desperately to be helpful. "Whoever is responsible is fortunate not to be looking at a murder charge."

Holmes nodded his agreement and continued. "The poor man probably came to the side gate of the house hoping for charity from within when he was accosted. His boots were then taken and used to create the impression that he was standing below the open window. Then it was simply a matter of taking the unconscious man to a quiet place nearby where he would not easily be discovered."

"But what of the jewels, Holmes?" asked Lestrade. "We found them secreted on his person."

"A calculated risk was taken here. The man had been hidden and the jewels placed deep in the pockets of his old trench coat. The assailant now had to lead the police to the criminal at precisely the right time, long enough for him to have at least begun to regain consciousness, but not so long that he might wander off, never to be found. I suggest he achieved this by keeping the poor beggar under surveillance, while also giving ever-growing hints to the police to guide them closer to where the faux intruder was slowly waking. That he managed both, speaks of a man of extreme intelligence, cunning and resourcefulness."

"Couldn't he simply have kept him secured at the property and taken him outside once he had begun to recover?" Lestrade asked.

"Quite possibly, Inspector, but adding the risk of him being discovered at, or around, the house by a member of staff, to those already being taken would surely be too much and also leave absolutely no room for an innocent explanation, if he were to be discovered."

"I see, it appears that we are now, if not quite on the same track, then at least moving in the same direction, approaching the same destination," replied Lestrade, somewhat confusingly.

"Without having access to your new information, I have to, grudgingly, conclude with speculation, rather than fact," admitted Holmes, candidly.

"There can be but one suspect. Samuel Galton is the only person capable of perpetrating this deceit but, alas, I have to yet to obtain absolute proof of his guilt or indeed his motive. Of the latter, though, I do have considerable suspicions."

"Well, I understand how he might be responsible, Holmes, but I fail to see a motive," I admitted. Lestrade and I both looked towards him for expansion.

"It has been argued that there are only three possible motives for any one crime. Love, money or power. This must be about money. Well, that's enough from me for now, I feel we would now be better served by hearing the Inspector's contribution rather than any more of my aimless conjecture."

Lestrade straightened up, looked briefly at the first page of a small pile of papers before him, and began.

"Very well. What I am sharing with you now is an incomplete and unconfirmed report, so be prepared for details, even major ones, to change at any time."

"At around ten o'clock last night, there was an 'accident' at the electrical supply plant at Holborn Viaduct. It seems that one of their top engineers spilled a large amount of water onto a live electrical cable and, well, I think you can imagine the results."

"How ghastly, the poor fellow," I remarked. Electricity was a modern wonder, but certainly not without its dangers.

"Yes, indeed, but it is the identity of the engineer that is of interest. His name was Rufus Pemberton Lythe. The younger brother of a certain Mr Edgar Pemberton Lythe of Chelsea. Well, what do you make of that?"

Holmes raised an eyebrow, paused for a few seconds to ponder this new revelation, and then spoke.

"It seems that this case may be darker than we had imagined. But it does at least confirm what I suspected, young Galton seeks control of the family fortune."

"Earlier today, I made some discreet inquiries into the state of the Pemberton Lythe family finances," Holmes continued. "What I discovered is that a considerable amount of money has accumulated in a charitable trust. This pays out to good causes, on the approval of its two trustees."

"Sounds like perfectly normal and decent behaviour from an old and well-respected family," I commented.

"Indeed. Both brothers had added considerable sums to this trust, as both had been successful in their chosen fields; Edgar in banking and his younger brother in engineering. However, neither man had married, so there appeared the thorny issue of inheritance. At present, the fund is designed to default to the state upon the death of the last trustee. Young Galton clearly has his beady eyes set upon the trust fund. He appears to be rather profligate and careless, prone to wasting large sums on gambling and questionable women."

"But if the money is in trust, how could he gain access to it?" asked Lestrade.

"I believe he saw his ailing Uncle as his way in. If he could persuade him that he was no longer fit and able to look after the trust, then he might pass his authority over to the younger man. It is a quite straightforward procedure, it simply requires his retirement from the trust and the drawing up of a new deed of appointment."

"And he attempted to do this by faking the burglary, to shake up the poor sick old man," Lestrade added, taking up the narrative. "He thought the shock would make him more amenable to an offer, to lighten the burden of his responsibilities. Good heavens, he might be working on his Uncle even as we speak."

"He did say he was busy with important legal matters when we visited earlier, I thought he was just being short with us," I suddenly remembered.

"Of course, there was still the issue of the younger brother - he would have, in effect, a total veto on any decision Galton may try to make regarding the trust," said Holmes, sombrely.

"And, as a decent man, he would never allow Galton to syphon off any funds for his own lurid activities," I added. "So, he needed him out of the way, permanently."

"Precisely, Watson. And this, it appears, is just what he has done."

"It certainly seems that way," agreed Lestrade. "But how did he do it? Electricity is tricky and volatile, how could he ensure that he would not also be electrocuted?"

"Here we are back into the realms of conjecture, but I do have a theory that fits all of the known facts. Watson, do you remember Galton's footwear?" asked Holmes.

"Why yes, they were those new athletic shoes, the ones with - of course - the ones with the rubber soles! He knew enough about electricity from his uncle to know that he would be safe standing on an electrified wet surface as long as he was separated from it by a layer of rubber."

"The Liverpool Rubber Company has actually been manufacturing rubber soled footwear for over ten years," Holmes corrected, "but otherwise you are quite correct, old friend."

"Well, bravo, Mr Holmes, Doctor Watson. On this occasion I can honestly say we have all had a hand in solving the crime," Lestrade beamed.

"But to what effect?" Holmes' face took on a very serious aspect. "He has, I fear, achieved his aims and we do not have a shred of real evidence against him. No proof at all. Any half-decent barrister would have the case thrown out within a day. And then sue, successfully, for damages to his reputation too, I venture. No, he has beaten us, for now, but we must keep a close watch on this young fellow. He will either rise quickly in the criminal underworld or be brought sharply to his end by it. Which one of these comes to pass will, at least, be of some interest to me."

"Well it is late enough in the day for a drink. Would you gentlemen care to join me?" Lestrade stood up and gestured to the door. "Tomorrow I will see what I can do about releasing the beggar. I think a few hints that we are onto him might make Galton more sympathetic to a dropping of the charges."

Holmes declined Lestrade's offer, stating that he had other business that needed his attention. I, however, was happy to join the Inspector for a pleasant hour in a nearby public house. The place appeared to be wall-to-wall police, and Lestrade was clearly at home here, something of a big cheese, holding court amongst his colleagues. I imagine his regular patronage here was the perfect antidote to a day spent in the perpetual shadow of the intellect of Sherlock Holmes.

Postscript

You will be pleased to know that, under Lestrade's pressure, all charges against the poor beggar were dropped. In fact, to his credit, the Inspector even went so far as to get the old fellow some light work at reasonable rates. Galton never faced any charges for his wicked crimes, but he may well have had to face a far higher authority, shortly after.

Holmes kept a keen eye on Galton's activities from then on and announced, only three months later, that he had sailed to America. Holmes contacted the local authorities to warn them of his diabolic character. The reply was as singular as it was unexpected. The passenger manifest confirmed him as having boarded in Southampton but no one of that name had disembarked in New York. At first, we suspected some subtle subterfuge, but nothing further was ever, officially, heard of Samuel Galton. The trust remained untouched and was dissolved some years later, its wealth going, as was always intended, to the state.

Case 4: A Clash of Wills - Thursday 15th of May 1884

I slept late into Thursday morning. The activities of the previous day had left me exhausted. When I finally rose, I found that I was alone, so called down for a very late breakfast. By the time I had finished what I believed to be a very well earned meal, it was already well past eleven o'clock.

As Holmes had left no note or other instruction, I decided that the day was my own, so I mentally planned the simplest of afternoons. I dressed and left for a walk in the nearby Regent's Park. The sun was already near its zenith and, though it was still unusually cold for May, the sunlight warmed my face and eased the sense of disappointment and failure that I had felt regarding the previous day's adventure.

It was mid-afternoon by the time I returned to Baker Street. I climbed the stairs and entered the sitting room to see the familiar figure of Sherlock Holmes sitting in his usual armchair. His knees were raised so that his feet perched on the edge of the chair cushion. He had replaced the long dark coat he wore outside with his comfortable mouse-brown dressing gown. He was deep in thought and appeared not to notice me as I entered and divested myself of my hat and coat. He had in each hand a piece of paper, about eight by twelve inches in size. The paper looked to be of a good quality, heavy in weight and buff in colour.

"Legal documents?" I ventured, breaking the silence.

"Very good, Watson. Yes, and indeed, no. Legal, or not legal, is the precise question I have to answer."

Holmes failed to elaborate on this, so I poured us both a drink and sat down opposite.

"These must be the wills mentioned by Lestrade on Monday, that much is clear," I stated. "But I have to ask, in what way is this Police business? Any argument over the validity of a will is up to the civil courts to decide, not a Scotland Yard Inspector, surely."

Holmes stopped staring at the sheets, looked up, and smiled.

"No, but the breach of the peace these two little documents caused was quite within his remit. Apparently, some pushing and shoving amongst rival family members escalated into a veritable free-for-all when the family solicitor discovered that two opposing wills existed."

"So, one must therefore be a fake or forgery, but how did you come by them?" I asked.

"Friend Lestrade asked me to take a look to see if I could ascertain which was the imposter. And, if forgery it is, then we are firmly back into the realms of the criminal."

Holmes put the paper aside and reached for his stygian clay pipe, filled and lit it. Large plumes of tobacco smoke filled the air.

"It was an interesting challenge, while it lasted, but now I have nothing left to do but report back to the good Inspector."

"Do you mean you have solved it already? In that case, I cannot imagine that the forgery was of a very high quality. Would you mind if I took a look?" I asked, grinning.

Holmes ignored my mild teasing and handed both pages to me.

I examined each, carefully, trying to spot any tell-tale signs of foul play. The wording of the wills themselves was fairly standard, both seemingly being based on a popular legal template. The main difference between them was, of course, the list of beneficiaries. What stood out most plainly, was that not one name appeared on both lists. This troubled me and I said as much to Holmes.

"Good old Watson," he replied. "You see the first major clue. Now, can you find the others?" he challenged with a faint smile. I was now the one being teased.

I studied the papers intently for a further ten minutes or so. I rose and moved closer to the bay window to utilise all of the available light before giving them a final close-up examination with the aid of Holmes' magnifying glass. I passed them back to Holmes who raised an eyebrow and awaited my conclusions.

"The signatures do appear to be almost identical at first glance, but when you look closely at this one," I pointed to the paper now in Holmes' right hand, "it appears to be less distinct, somewhat fuzzy around the edges, as it were. And if you look very closely, the ink seems to be denser in the centre of each individual stroke, as if someone had gone over the letters with a very fine-nibbed fountain pen, probably one of the recent American models. In fact, if you angle the document to the light you can see that the only actual impressions onto the paper are the extremely fine marks scratched by this thin instrument." I felt rather pleased with myself as I was certain that I was on the right track and looked to my friend for confirmation.

"Watson, well done old chap, your abilities increase daily," Holmes declared. "I cannot fault your observations so far, but can you deduce the rest of the process used to create this, really rather amateurish, fabrication?"

"That is where I think a better mind than mine will have to step in." I sank back into my chair and sighed, resignedly.

"But this time it really is child's play, almost literally in fact," laughed Holmes. "When you were a young boy did you never paint or draw in ink then fold the page over to create a mirrored double of the image?"

"Yes of course, how simple," I exclaimed, but I was halted by a thought that occurred almost immediately. "But that would not work, the signature would be back to front, a mirror image as you said. And what about the witnesses? Surely they would notice papers being folded and pressed."

"Yes, but if you add some cunning, practice and a degree of resourcefulness, it becomes possible to imagine how this little imposter could have been created."

"Imagine a rocker blotter, quite normal in appearance to the casual observer, but with the thick absorbent blotting paper replaced with a thinner slightly glossy sheet. Add the darkened room of a dying old man and a fountain pen tampered with to increase the flow of ink. It would take a little practice to master the routine, but once perfected it would be almost impossible to detect."

"Using a sharp blade, it is possible to prise open up the two parts which form the very tip of the nib of a fountain pen," continued Holmes. "This increases the flow of ink. Trial and error would ascertain the ideal level. The genuine will would be presented for signature in the dull candlelit bedroom. The will would be signed and no one present would bat an eyelid at the careful blotting of the wet writing. Neither would they notice the peculiar way in which it was returned to the writing desk, placed down firmly, rocked from left to right. This would leave a very convincing copy of the signature at the bottom of a completely blank page, the rest of which was hidden beneath the many other documents which covered the desk."

"But it seems that on the day the plan was not quite as successful as they had hoped," I added. "Hence the need to improve the forged signature afterwards. It was too faint, they must have made an error with the ink flow."

"Very enterprising, I am sure, but the results were really rather amateurish in the end. I have no illusions as to my own abilities, yet even I saw that something was amiss with the signature," I declared with some satisfaction.

"Most certainly, my dear Watson, but think upon this: would you have challenged the will had there not been a contradictory document present itself almost simultaneously?"

"I suppose not," I admitted, with a sigh. Holmes was quite right, of course. Unless there is a specific reason for doubt, we do accept all manner of signed documents to be genuine without a moment's thought.

"Well, in this case, at least, we can reveal a falsification and endorse the opposing will as genuine." I tried to sound upbeat despite Holmes' continued dark countenance.

"And that is where you fail, sadly, my dear friend. You have examined only a part of the picture, but once you discovered an anomaly, you made the worst possible mistake. You stopped looking altogether."

"Well, what more do you expect?" I replied, feeling somewhat put upon. "Surely the matter is resolved."

"How about this then?" Holmes waved the second will in a thin, white, bony hand. "You have yet to inform me of your observations upon this document."

I shrugged. "Other than a few drops of wax towards the bottom, it seemed perfectly normal - a clear, crisp signature, no obvious signs of foul play."

"Did anything strike you as odd regarding the wax droplets?" Holmes asked, clearly enjoying himself.

I asked for another look under Holmes' glass and, after a few minutes examining the page, I suddenly announced, "Some of the drops are not complete. They have a sharp, horizontal upper edge as if something has cut through them. They appear to be," I lay a ruler across the page, "and indeed are, in a perfect horizontal line about four fifths of the way down the page."

"Caused by?" Holmes asked, patricianly.

"Something else covering the page? Wait, I have it Holmes!" I declared. "Another sheet of paper was laid over this one. It must have been the text of the original will. In the candlelit gloom, the old fellow and the witnesses would not have noticed that he was, in fact, signing a completely different sheet of paper. As the old man struggled to read in the half-light, a candle was brought closer and the wax has dripped on the area where the two sheets met. They were quickly pulled apart once the signature was completed and, as the wax was still soft, this left a straight edge to the top of the droplets that remained. Why, it is an even simpler subterfuge than the first fabrication."

I was momentarily shocked by the ramifications of our discoveries, but soon composed myself.

"So they are both fake, how extraordinary. I suppose the poor old fellow was too ill to realise much of what was going on and simply signed whatever was put before him. What a contemptible bunch of relatives he had." I shook my head, disgustedly.

"Greedy, duplicitous and very much the masters of their own downfall," added Holmes, with a glint in his eye.

"How is that? They very nearly got away with it. If we hadn't been called into investigate -" I stopped, suddenly, the light beginning to dawn. I began to laugh, long and loudly.

"Indeed, dear Watson. If only some of them had not been so avaricious then they would probably have got away with the deception. But they were all covetous of the inheritance and formed two groups, each without knowledge of the other. They used whatever artifice they could muster and each produced a will favouring their own interests. Once satisfied with their spurious documents, they each deposited them in the family safe, completely unaware that a competing party was doing exactly the same."

"Once the two contradictory wills were discovered, it was inevitable that they would be investigated and subjected to extreme scrutiny, far more so than had there been only the one. As they would both bear a very similar date, there was no way that they could be mistaken for a will written some years earlier and a later one that superseded it,"

Holmes continued. "One simply had to be a fake. That, along with the abominable behaviour of the beneficiaries, alerted the police and, ultimately, ourselves to their little chicanery."

"Hoist with their own petard?" I ventured.

"See, sons, what things you are,
How quickly nature falls into revolt
When gold becomes her object," Holmes concluded.

Case 5: *"Cura te ipsum"* - Physician, Heal Thyself - Friday 16th of May, 1884

By the time I had risen and dressed for breakfast the following day, Holmes had already visited Scotland Yard, learned what he could about his next challenge and returned to Baker Street. He threw off his hat and coat and sat down with me at the table, which had already been set and was awaiting our presence.

"Well, this is a problem with a little more substance." Holmes declared, after we had called down for coffee for the both of us, along with rashers and eggs for myself. There was little point in wasting good food by ordering it for Holmes when he was so deeply immersed in a case.

"Two suspicious deaths, Watson, alongside two burglaries. For once, Scotland Yard do already have a suspect in custody, however, they are struggling to build any sort of case against their captor. With no physical evidence of any kind, they will shortly be obligated to release him."

Holmes looked gaunt after the week's exertions but his eyes shone brightly with fierce determination.

"Well, regardless of any help Lestrade may require in this case, I would prescribe complete rest for yourself for at least a day or two, but you seem quite determined to drive yourself to a breakdown. The best I can hope for is that you will solve this case as quickly as you have the previous ones this week. Then you can eat some proper food and put your feet up for a while," I snorted, as discouragingly as I could manage.

I deliberately avoided direct eye contact with Holmes, as I was certain he would see that I was, of course, secretly loving every minute of these investigations.

"A time for everything, Watson. Now is the time for dissemination and reflection upon what I have so far learned. Would you be good enough to sit with me, share a pipe and give me your thoughts?"

We moved to more comfortable seating, filled our pipes and Holmes began.

"Even by the standards of central London, Belgravia and its surroundings are home to a measure of such wealth it is almost impossible to calculate. However, its affluence does not make the area immune to crime, the very opposite in fact. The risks may be high, but the rewards available to a skilled and determined criminal must be very much greater, indeed."

"You mentioned murder, that's about as temerarious as you can get," I interjected. "But, one moment Holmes, I do not recall hearing of any murders in Belgravia recently, and certainly not of any double murder. Surely such an event would be national, nay international, news for the area is home to numerous foreign embassies and high commissions."

"Quite correct, Watson. The murders have yet to be publicly reported as such and as things stand, at this moment, are unlikely ever to be so described. I believe the Duke, himself, has made it very clear that unless, and until, charges can be levelled with a realistic chance of conviction, any suggestion of murder in this case will remain resolutely unreported."

"Luckily, our old friend Lestrade was more than happy to share with me all of the known facts, such as they are," he continued. "Two elderly, wealthy, men have been found dead in the past month. They both appeared to have died during the night, and each was pronounced dead before nine the following morning. In the first instance, the exact cause of death was never determined and it was simply put down to old age, in fact, very little detailed examination of this body was carried out."

"That is certainly not unusual in cases where the patient was of advanced years," I concurred.

"It was only later, when some extremely valuable pieces of jewellery were found to be missing, that suspicions were raised. After hearing of the second death, a friend of the family made contact with the family of the second victim. They soon realised that the circumstances were remarkably similar in both cases. By good fortune, this friend was a former officer in the Mounted Military Police and he quickly and ably informed Scotland Yard as to the details of the situation."

"In both cases the elderly victim had been visited on the fateful night by the same Doctor. A minor ailment was diagnosed and a sedative was administered to aid the patient's sleep. The next morning, the patients were found to be unresponsive and a physician was quickly summoned. The victims were pronounced dead shortly after the doctor's arrival. It must be noted that, in both cases, the physician who attended in the morning was not the man who had treated the patient the night before."

"I don't like the sound of where this is leading," I admitted. "A doctor gone rogue is a terrible danger to anyone around him. I take it that he is the man in custody. What do we know about this egregious fellow?"

"His name is Ambrose Wormwood, no criminal record, not much record to speak of at all. Studied medicine at the Université de Poitiers in France, graduated in seventy-seven. Moved to London four years ago and joined a practise as its junior doctor, covering mostly late night call-outs. His colleagues all speak well enough of him, although due to his unsociable hours they have had precious little direct contact with the fellow himself."

"What did you make of him, yourself? I am sure that you persuaded Lestrade to let you speak to him."

"Indeed so. He is still a young man, maybe four and thirty years of age, of average height, clean shaven with slicked-back jet-black hair. He was wearing exactly what you would expect from a doctor: black frock coat, dark trousers and white shirt. His ascot tie was fixed in place with a gold tiepin. He has dark, deep-set eyes, which reveal little expression even when questioned at length. He speaks clearly and crisply, when he speaks at all. He is extremely reluctant to engage with his interrogators, save to protest his innocence and the unlawful nature of his detention."

"Sounds like a man with something to hide," I concluded. "But I do have one question, Holmes, was the doctor who called the following morning the same man both times?"

"Indeed he was, and that is also something worthy of note, I am certain of it." Holmes exhaled a swirl of blue-grey smoke, which coiled and lingered in the air.

"Now, let me tell you how they came to arrest this Wormwood character," Holmes continued. "Lestrade, after being told in no uncertain terms to be discreet in his investigations, had formulated a really rather ingenious little scheme to catch the villain in the act. He had ordered that the doctor, that is Wormwood, be followed. He also had his surgery closely observed, especially so in the evenings and at night. When the doctor was called out late, they followed him from a distance until they discovered his destination. Of course this was not always such an affluent address as Belgravia and when arriving at such locations, they held back and watched from the shadows."

"Then, one night, when Lestrade himself was following the physician alongside a plainclothes sergeant, they saw their man enter a luxurious apartment block on Park Lane. They followed him inside and identified themselves to the concierge who confirmed that an elderly resident had indeed been taken ill and had called for a doctor about an hour earlier."

"So, they caught him red-handed, bravo Lestrade!" I declared, rather prematurely.

"They caught him, alright, he was in the very act of injecting a unknown substance into the poor old man's arm when they burst through the door. They immediately arrested and handcuffed him, shouting down to the concierge to call for another doctor. But it was too late, the old man was already unconscious. Lestrade waited until the replacement physician arrived and then left in a Black Maria with the suspect. They interrogated him overnight but he never once strayed from his story. He was an innocent doctor who was simply helping a sick old man to get some much needed sleep."

"A ghastly tale of a learned man gone badly wrong," I sighed, sadly. "But surely Lestrade has his man, what is the problem?"

"The problem, my dear fellow, is what raises this case from the mundane, though unpleasant, to the singularly intriguing." Holmes' eyes twinkled with excitement.

"At three o'clock the following afternoon, the victim awoke from his sedation, seemingly none the worse from his ordeal. At around the same time, confirmation was received that the drug administered to the victim was nothing more than what Wormwood had claimed it to be, a standard tranquiliser, used the world over. The house was carefully examined and nothing of value was found to be missing. A thorough search of the doctor and his medical bag revealed nothing out of the ordinary and, more significantly, nothing that might be used as a poison. What's more, even after his house had been almost torn apart in a search for the items that had been stolen previously, the police found nothing at all to show for their efforts."

"Well, I'll be," I began, hardly able to take it in. "I see now exactly what you mean. Poor Lestrade, he must be desperate. But, for the sake of fairness, I must ask, could this man actually be innocent? Could it all just have been a series of improbable coincidences?"

"Much as I hate to admit it, it is a possibility. It is certainly not impossible, so it cannot be ruled out entirely. But every fibre of my being cries out in protest against this hypothesis. Coincidence? If coincidence it ultimately proves to be then, my dear Watson, I will retire immediately to the South Downs, where I shall keep bees!"

I could not help but release a roar of laughter at this totally unexpected outburst of humour.

"Watson, really, this is a serious matter," scolded Holmes, but he could not completely hide a subtle smile.

I recovered enough to give voice to a thought just occurred, "What if he knew that the Police were onto him? Maybe he had realised that he was being surveilled. I mean Lestrade is one thing, but how do we know that the other officers were as discreet in their pursuit?"

"Again, Watson, you make a good point, but Lestrade was adamant. He had used only his very best men, those with prior experience of surveillance operations. He also swears that the doctor appeared to be genuinely shocked when interrupted and certainly panicked when they rushed in to arrest him. The doctor also then increased the pressure upon the syringe to ensure the complete transfer of its contents into the patient. No, we must proceed under the assumption that he was not expecting such an intervention."

"Then we have reached an impasse." I stretched, then inhaled and tamped at my pipe, reinvigorating its burning heart.

"Not quite. Would you care to join me in a brief sojourn?" asked Holmes. "I would like you with me when I question the doctor."

We flagged down a Hansom in Baker Street and set off through the busy lanes towards the river. I was surprised to hear Holmes give our destination as Kennington Lane, Vauxhall.

"I thought we were going to see Wormwood?" I asked.

"I said we were to interview the doctor, you concluded too quickly as to which doctor," Holmes corrected.

Our cab made its way along the fine avenue that formed the border of Westminster and Pimlico until we reached the Vauxhall Bridge, the first iron bridge to be built over the mighty River Thames. We continued for a further fifteen minutes or so before finally alighting on a pleasant side street in the shadow of the great Oval Gasometers. Holmes paid the driver an extra shilling to wait for our return.

A small, white haired lady of advancing years in a grey dress, wrapped in a white apron, answered the door and led us silently to a small sitting room where we waited to see the doctor. The room was furnished with good quality matching mahogany furniture, several decades old judging by the style, but all in excellent condition. On the walls were various paintings of landscapes from around Europe. I recognised the Matterhorn and what looked like the Swiss or Italian lakes. After a few minutes, a distinguished looking gentleman entered the room.

"Doctor Armoise, delighted to meet you," Holmes began. "I am Sherlock Holmes and this is my colleague Doctor John Watson. We are currently helping Inspector Lestrade of Scotland Yard with his inquiries regarding the Belgravia incidents of the past few weeks," Holmes continued quickly, before the Doctor could reply.

"We wondered if you might take a few moments from your understandably busy schedule to answer a few simple questions?" He sounded almost casual. "Splendid," he announced, again before Armoise could answer. "Do you mind if we take a seat? Excellent."

Holmes sat down on the nearest chair and gestured that I should do the same. The now puzzled looking doctor moved behind his desk and seated himself in front of us.

"How can I help you, gentlemen? I have told the Inspector all I know which was, quite frankly, not very much." The man was approaching his sixtieth year but straight-backed with a healthy looking, slightly olive, complexion. His hair had once been black but was now streaked with grey and high at the temples where it had begun to recede. He wore it quite long, swept back until it reached down several inches below his collar. He was dressed in a dark morning jacket and grey trousers. Around his neck, he wore a rather exuberant cravat of multi-coloured silk held in place with a gold tiepin bearing a simple but unfamiliar crest.

"I was called that morning to attend an unresponsive patient. Sadly, by the time I arrived, he had passed away. I simply informed the family as compassionately as I could and reminded the servants of the procedures that should be followed in events such as these. After that, having seen no evidence of anything unusual or any sign of foul play, I completed the death certificate and left."

"Was it the same for both cases?" Holmes inquired. Armoise nodded. "At what times were you called out on each occasion and when exactly did you leave? Please be as precise as you can," Holmes asked with a thin smile.

"Oh, it was early the first time, maybe seven o'clock. I left around nine to nine-thirty, I think. The second time was later. If I recall correctly, I was called shortly after eight and didn't leave much before eleven."

"Why were you there so long on the second occasion? Why, that's almost three hours?" Holmes had subtly increased the tone of his questioning from purely friendly to one bordering on the belligerent.

Armoise clearly did not appreciate the rise in temperature.

"Mr Holmes, I have no more answers for you. I have told you clearly that I carried out my duties regarding these matters as courteously and professionally as I could, given the circumstances. I was in no position to rush anyone or anything and it was certainly not the time, nor the place, to be impatient. I left as, and when, my obligations were fulfilled." He stood up. "Now please, I am a very busy man and have patients to attend. Gentlemen?" He gestured to the door.

Holmes sprang up. "Thank you, sir, for your cooperation. We will show ourselves out."

And with that, he swooped from the room, his black coat billowing up behind him. I had to move at a fair pace myself, just to keep up.

Holmes almost jumped into the waiting Hansom and we swiftly set off back into town. Holmes spent the forty-five minute journey in virtual silence. He spoke only once, to explain that he needed to return to Baker Street in order to consult his files.

Holmes' 'library' consisted of papers, folders, files and boxes, containing the most eclectic collection of information imaginable. From the most innocuous looking article in a local newspaper to the most obscure and outré scientific studies. However, the vast majority consisted of reports of crimes from around the world, their perpetrators and the methods they had employed. Holmes' esoteric collection was ever growing, but only rarely curated, so it often appeared to resemble a waterfall of paper, cascading down from the shelves and onto the floor.

As soon as we reached Baker Street, Holmes bounded up the stairs, threw his hat and coat to the floor and began to energetically search his records. I removed my own coat and hat more carefully and sat down in my armchair. With Holmes, it was impossible to predict how long he might take in such a search so I lit a small cigar, feeling that a full pipe might be wasted if he discovered his objective too soon.

After what was, indeed, an unexpectedly short exploration, Holmes took a deep breath and loudly exclaimed, "Ha! Just as I thought."

Unexpectedly stentorian vocal pronouncements were one of Holmes' great endearments, and they almost always signalled a breakthrough.

"You've solved it, haven't you?" I asked, failing to conceal my surprise.

"I do not have enough data to yet be certain, Watson, but I am beginning to make definite inroads" he replied.

Holmes then looked at me with a most serious expression. "This is the moment, Watson, the watershed. Very rarely do we see it at the time. Once a case is over, one can look back and see the pivotal point, the decision, the action or the discovery that swings the balance. But right here and now we are on the very fulcrum itself. Which path we now take will determine whether we succeed or fail. Which path to take?" It was clear that the final question was meant just for himself.

"Well unless you share your revelations, you will get no advice from this, or any other, quarter." I tried to sound helpful, hiding the terrible frustration I felt inside.

Holmes paused, then stared at me with wide eyes. "Share! Of course! Watson, you have done it again. Dear old Watson, my lightning rod, bringing the wild untameable spark of knowledge safely to my feet. We must contact Lestrade, immediately."

"Of course, if you say so. However, I do have to ask one thing? Which path *have* you chosen?"

"Why, both of them, of course, my dear old chap."

I was totally baffled by Holmes' enigmatic reply, but recognised the urgency in his voice. We then set off for the nearest post office where Holmes wired an urgent message to the Inspector.

"And now we must wait for Lestrade's reply," Holmes said, as we strolled back to 221B.

"Well, maybe now you will share something of this opaque mystery with me. After all, you did state that I had helped you solve it, even if I have no idea of exactly how."

"Very well, but it is almost teatime and you must be ravenous old chap. Let us see what the inestimable Mrs Hudson can muster up and, while we wait to hear from our friend the Inspector, I shall try to answer some of your questions," Holmes said, somewhat condescendingly. He seemed to be enjoying my inability to comprehend his deductions, but I refused to rise to his bait.

In no time, we were back in our Baker Street rooms. I was soon eagerly tucking into the early supper that Mrs Hudson had conjured up, seemingly in moments. Holmes sat in his chair, the only thing that had passed his lips was the dirty brown stem of his rancid clay churchwarden.

"Watson, what we are dealing with here is not, of course, four separate crimes. Put most simply, we have two murders and two thefts. I am sure that it is perfectly obvious to you that all four are connected. The problem is, of course, finding that connection."

"The solution seems indisputable at first," Holmes continued. "Young Doctor Wormwood had treated both patients the night before they died. He had administered some poison that led directly to their deaths, sometime between him leaving and the discovery of their bodies the next morning. After injecting them, he had somehow committed the burglaries before leaving. This theory forms the basis for his arrest and current incarceration."

"However, this was all blown apart when the potential third victim recovered fully from Wormwood's attentions. Add to this the fact that the substance he was caught injecting was nothing more than an ordinary, everyday sedative, administered in an amount that would cause no lasting effects."

"Yes, that much is clear," I agreed. "So therefore, unless he was warned in advance of Lestrade's ploy, which both you and he appear to believe inconceivable, then he must surely be innocent. But, if Wormwood is not our man, then who else could it possibly be? The only other person present at both locations was Doctor Armoise, but he was present only in the morning when the poor victims were already dead."

"Watson, you see only what you are supposed to see. Look at the facts. Only two men could have committed these murders. Wormwood is one. If it could not have been him then it must have been the only other suspect. The killer must have been Doctor Armoise."

"I understand your reasoning, Holmes, but I just don't see how he could have done it. Not to mention, how he could have possibly arranged for the victims to conveniently fall ill beforehand so he could be called in to attend them?"

At that moment, we heard the bell downstairs. "Ah, news from Lestrade I believe," declared Holmes. A minute later, a liveried boy appeared at the door to our rooms.

"Urgent telegram for Mr Holmes," he announced. "To be delivered to his hand only," he added, holding the envelope close to his chest.

"I am he," Holmes announced loudly, before taking the message from the now-startled young man. He quickly read the missive before handing a shilling to the boy and waving him away. "No reply required, thank you."

As the boy left, Holmes reached for his coat. "Come Watson, Scotland Yard awaits. We can talk on the way."

We quickly procured a cab and headed for the Yard. The early evening light bathed the stone-faced buildings in a warm sandy glow. London in the twilight is a magical place, the grime and poverty temporarily washed away by the gentle golden rays of the late spring sunshine.

Holmes' voice dragged me back to reality. "What most people simply fail to realise is how much time, effort and ingenuity some criminals are prepared to put into their schemes. Forget the stereotype of the lazy burglar. Forget the idea of the opportunist robbery. This case is of the very highest echelon of criminality, possibly the greatest I have yet encountered." I was so intrigued to hear more that I very nearly let my lit cigarette drop from my now half-open mouth.

"Connections are the very heart of this case. What connects the Doctors to the crimes? What connects them to the victims? But most of all, what connects them to each other?"

"You mean they were working together? But even if this was indeed a nefarious partnership, I still cannot see how they carried out the murders and the thefts, not to mention how they outwitted Lestrade over the third attempt." My personal fog was far from lifting.

We arrived at Scotland Yard before Holmes could continue further. Lestrade greeted us warmly and led us to his austere office.

"Well Holmes, we have done exactly as you asked. Three cells are now occupied. Now, for the love of all that is holy, please tell me you have the solution." Lestrade seemed to know as much, or as little, as did I.

"Logic, my friends. Ignore your emotions and expectations. Recount, precisely, everything relevant that has happened, as simply as you can." Holmes was as infuriating as ever, but I acquiesced.

"Very well. Let me see. A doctor makes a late call, prescribes and administers a sedative. The next morning the patient is found dead -" but Holmes interrupted.

"Wrong, Watson. We must be exact. How was the patient found to be?" he demanded.

"Unresponsive," I suddenly remembered. "Wait a minute, I think I am beginning to see it." The fog had thinned a little, right there in front of me.

"Unresponsive, yes." Holmes continued. "But not dead. The poor victims were still alive when Armoise arrived, it was he that administered the fatal blow. As a doctor, he would know of several poisons and methods that would induce a quick death, leaving little or no trace."

"That much could certainly be true, I can think of several chemicals that have just those properties. However, the simplest method would be to simply inject some air directly into the patient's veins. It would induce heart failure within seconds."

"With no need to carry any tell-tale poisons which might incriminate him if caught," added Lestrade.

"Why, Watson, Lestrade, I never dreamed that you had such murderous expertise. Remind not to cross you in future." Holmes' smile came and went swiftly, but was most welcome.

"Of course, this also explains how they managed to outmanoeuvre the police," Holmes continued. "I had no reason to suspect that the operation you carried out, Inspector, was anything less than professional and discreet." Lestrade nodded at this rare acknowledgement of his competence from Holmes. "But being followed, or indeed detained, was never something that Wormwood was ever overly concerned about. This was the genius of their plot, you see, for if Wormwood was arrested then no murder or subsequent theft would have taken place. Nothing incriminating would be found on Wormwood and, as it appeared that no crime had been committed, he would have to be released without charge."

"And by the simple fact that Wormwood hadn't returned home on the night of his capture, his accomplice would know that the following day's evil mission was cancelled," concluded Lestrade, rather admirably I thought.

"So, if I understand you correctly, and the doctors were indeed working together, then Wormwood's entire role was a blind, Holmes! But how did they arrange the late night visits? Surely they couldn't have engineered the victim's illnesses?" My head swirled with the possibilities.

"This is where we would enter the world of speculation and conjecture. No, it is now time to interview the chief architect of this most elegant, but deadly, plan. Lestrade, would you be so good as to ask the Duty Officer to bring out Doctor Armoise?"

A burly sergeant with a magnificent red beard escorted the older doctor into Lestrade's office. His face was expressionless but his eyes shone with defiance. The sergeant bustled him into a chair.

"Doctor Hugo Armoise," Holmes began. "I know almost everything. I cannot save you, but if you cooperate with me I promise I shall do everything within my powers to spare your son from the gallows."

As an opening statement, it was stunning and I could see from his face that Lestrade thought the same.

"So, you think you know something, but you have no proof that I or this other gentleman, whoever he should be, have committed any crime. Please feel free to huff and puff but eventually you will have to let me go." The doctor appeared to have nerves of steel.

"Very well. Let me tell you exactly what I know and then I will again make my offer, one last time." Holmes' voice was expressionless, his eyes ice cold.

"You and your son are scions of Poitiers. Your family was once high born but when the revolution came, like many others, you had to hide, give up the family name along with its money, land and privileges. The final insult was having to leave France and escape to the land of your hated rivals, there to live in relative poverty. After all, what else could have driven you to such jealousy and contempt towards those who still had all that you had lost?"

"Your family could not, however, break all ties with your homeland and, once it was safe to do so, sent its sons back home to study in the family tradition. As you did yourself, followed by your son."

"Nothing of which you can remotely prove," Armoise responded, coolly.

"Are you quite certain of that? We have your son's medical degree certificate and even now, the authorities in France are looking into a request from the good Inspector here. Namely, who paid young Wormwood's university fees? I believe we already know the answer."

"Your son is facing capital charges, I will not make this offer a third time," Holmes finished with quite some menace.

"How did you know?" Armoise' face slackened as his resistance failed.

"Your tie pin sir. A lion rampant beneath three Fleurs-de-lis. The ancient coat of arms of Poitiers. That, along with a generally familial appearance would have been enough to connect you but then there is also, of course, the matter of your names, or rather, your assumed names"

"Their names?" Interrupted Lestrade. "What about them?"

"Wormwood? Armoise? Please, doctor, you do not have to be a horticultural expert to see the connection there. What was it? Some family joke?" Holmes asked.

Armoise shrugged subtly, his pertinacity all but gone. "We were never a conventional family, even before things went rotten in our homeland. One of the things we were most famous for was our Absinthe, the first in all of France. So, wormwood, mugwort or armoise, call it what you will, was always a part of our lives even if we were no longer distilling *'la fée verte'* ourselves."

"I now need only to confirm a few details from you and my case will be complete." Holmes had visibly relaxed, now firmly on the finishing straight. "How you chose your victims and why were they chosen, how you arranged for the late night calls and how you perpetrated the thefts?"

"Knowing a little of your history it seems likely to me that you would target victims sharing the characteristics of those that you now hated the most. Not wealth accumulated nobly over generations by titled families, like yours, but those whose wealth was more recently acquired. The merchants, the bankers, the industrialists. What you might call the *'Nouveau Riche'*."

"This new class is often guilty of less than subtle public exhibitions of their wealth. Their ostentatious displays of gold and jewellery adorning their bodies like trophies have been seen at many an event and function throughout the city. During the course of your many visits over the years to these wealthy households, you heard your clients boast about their collections of valuables and, crucially, about where they were kept. It was also useful to know who had bought which latest fabulous creation in order to outshine his peers. This, I believe, answers the how and the why the poor souls were chosen, am I correct Doctor?"

Armoise nodded. "Correct in every detail, I am astounded sir," he agreed meekly.

"The late night calls were, I believe, simply a matter of being patient," Holmes continued. "To induce an illness would add an unnecessary risk to an already complex scheme. You would have known from past experience which of your patients would be most likely to fall ill and simply waited for the timing to be right. And, in any case, I am sure that you had identified several targets over the years. This way, the chances of one of this group of aging men eventually falling ill, during the night, would have been higher than you might think."

"Now all was set. Wormwood had visited, administered a higher than usual, but not fatal, dose of a common sedative and had departed, leaving the patient sleeping but, importantly, still alive. The next morning's evil drama would unfold, you would inject the coup de grace and declare your poor victim dead. Amidst all of the shock, chaos and confusion, you would simply slip away unnoticed to wherever the jewels, or other valuables, were secreted. You had, of course, chosen targets who did not take the security of their valuables seriously enough - I myself am still astounded by how many wealthy people fail to own even a safe and simply lock up their precious items in drawers or jewellery boxes. Once you had located and acquired your plunder, you returned to the centre of activity where you completed the death certificate and left. Would I also be right in thinking, from the extra time taken during the second incidence, that you either had trouble obtaining the jewellery, or that you were disturbed at some point?"

"Both," admitted Armoise. "Firstly, I had devil of a time breaking into a small wooden chest, which turned out to be reinforced with iron rings. Then, unexpectedly, I had to justify my presence in the deceased's office. My explanation, that I was looking for some ink with which to complete the death certificate, was perfectly plausible and was accepted without question, although it did take a while for the elderly butler to search the office and finally locate some."

"And so we come to the final irony. A plot born from decades of resentment and planned meticulously over many years was thwarted for a lack of the one thing that you seemed to have in spades. Patience." Holmes now looked triumphant, as energised as I had ever seen him. "You had waited months for the right set of circumstances to fall into place. A late night call was received and your plan went ahead, flawlessly. How could you have imagined that, just two weeks later, the exact same set of variables would again slip into perfect alignment?"

"This one time you chose greed over caution. You were so confident from your earlier success that you failed to see the one thing that would cast suspicion on your whole pernicious plan. Coincidences in life are rare. Coincidences in crime are a shining beacon of suspicion. If you had left it another six months, I am certain no one would have ever made a connection, but two weeks? Even the simplest observer could see that something foul was at work here."

"Well that's quite remarkable, Mr Holmes," remarked Lestrade, finally. "But what about the occupant of the third cell? What should we do with her?"

"Her? Who is this, Holmes, another associate?" I asked.

"Sometimes, even I make erroneous assumptions, Watson. What we took for a servant at Armoise' house was in fact someone much closer to him."

"Do you mean a relative, like an aunt perhaps?" I guessed.

"Possibly even his mother. But Lestrade can ascertain that little detail. What is important is that I believe that she is the key to finding the lost jewellery - find the property that I am sure she owns and there you will find the stash."

Holmes stood up. "Well, I think we can leave the rest to you, Inspector. Come, Watson, we must return you to your rooms, you look like you could do with some rest," he grinned.

By the time we arrived back at Baker Street the sun had almost set. Just a few red veins of wan light traced the underside of the low-lying clouds as the inky blackness descended upon London. We ate a light supper then settled down for a quiet smoke before we took to our beds.

"Holmes?" I asked, breaking the silence. He looked up, accepting the interruption. "Can you explain these paths that you had to choose from? And how could you have chosen both?"

"Oh, that is quite straightforward, my good fellow. I had just learned, at that point, that the two doctors were related but I had yet to decide upon which one to concentrate, Wormwood or Armoise, who was the most likely to be the killer?"

"So what did I do to help, exactly?" I asked, still somewhat perplexed.

"Not did, Watson, said," Holmes answered with unusual warmth. "You admonished me for not sharing my theories and suspicions.

This formed a connection in my mind. What if the two doctors were themselves sharing? Could they be working together? Then, like an avalanche, the rest of the evidence fell into place. Therefore, I had to pursue them both equally, I had to take both paths."

Despite Holmes' best efforts, both doctors were found guilty of premeditated murder, conspiracy and theft and thus sentenced to hang. Their mother, as the old lady indeed turned out to be, escaped the rope, but I am still not sure if sparing her might, in fact, have been the cruellest punishment she could have received.

Case 6: The Unfortunate Bookmaker or The Wrong End Of The Stick - Saturday 17th May 1884

I was woken by a bright shaft of light, which seemed to be aimed directly at my face. I could see nothing, save for its glare, searing my waking eyes, until I had moved sufficiently away from its blazing rays. I looked up, gingerly, to see that my bedroom curtains had been partially and, it seemed to me, deliberately opened.

A gap had been precisely left, but not in the middle where one might have expected. The left hand drape had been bunched up so that it covered only the first twelve inches or so of the window. Then there was the wretched gap, no more than two inches wide. The right hand curtain was stretched as far as it could be, further even, for there was an inch or two of glass on the right hand side that was now uncovered. This was clearly of little importance, as the sun breaking through here lit up nothing more than my dull walnut wardrobe. I sighed as I realised who was undoubtedly responsible and dressed resignedly for the day.

"Seven o'clock and 10 minutes," declared Holmes, as I entered our sitting room. "A little off, but a reasonable effort given the tools I had to work with."

"Did you really calculate the path of the rising sun with such a degree of precision that you used it to wake me at a predetermined hour? How on earth did you determine where the gap in the curtains should be? To be honest, Holmes, I was rather irritated at first, but now I must confess to being rather impressed, old man." I smiled and sat down at the breakfast table.

"A field compass and a few simple equations were all that I required," Holmes explained casually, and with more than a hint of false modesty. "If I hadn't been working in the dark at the time, I believe I could have done better."

"The Sherlock Holmes Patent Silent Alarm Clock!" I chuckled. "Fascinating and ingenious, but not much of a market for it outside of 221B Baker Street I would wager."

"But anyway, Holmes, why the early *réveille*?" I inquired as I poured myself some dearly needed coffee. "You already look exhausted man, this marathon crime-solving mission that you insist upon is doing you real harm. When did you last sleep or have a decent meal?"

"That is of no relevance, Watson, what matters now is the work." Holmes sipped at his coffee, his eyes dark and deep-set, his face cadaverous and his lips all but devoid of colour. "And anyway, in this case we literally have no choice but to act immediately."

"What is so pressing that it cannot wait until Monday? At least take the weekend off, for the sake of your health, and mine too for that matter!"

"We must visit the morgue this morning Watson. The body is being released to the family at midday. I estimate that we can reach

Scotland Yard, once you have had an adequate breakfast, before nine, so that leaves us about three hours in which to examine the corpse and question the officers involved."

"The morgue? What body? I am sorry, Holmes, but we have dealt with so many cases this week that I am afraid I simply cannot recall which crime it is that you are currently referring to. I had hoped, in all honesty, that you had solved the lot of them by now and we could finally take a day off." I made no attempt to hide my petulance.

"I am not expecting this to be a difficult case so fret not, Watson. Why, we may even be finished in time for a late luncheon in town."

Holmes moved to his armchair, lit his nasty black clay with a twig from the fire and waited for me to finish eating. I am slightly ashamed to admit, now, that from that moment I was deliberately somewhat more than leisurely in consuming my repast.

The journey to Scotland Yard was unremarkable. Holmes was unprepared to speculate about the case, so my complete ignorance of the circumstances continued as we passed through the quiet Saturday morning streets. The sun was bright but the air was still chilly and we appreciated the blankets provided in the open-fronted Hansom.

After about twenty-five minutes, we pulled up outside the familiar building, standing upright and sturdy as always against the ever-rising tide of London crime. We entered and headed straight for the morgue.

"The Inspector will meet us there as soon as he can," informed Holmes, when I asked why we had not first stopped at Lestrade's office.

The room was whitewashed and brightly lit, a welcome change from the dark horrors of the charnel houses I had endured whilst in service. The body had been laid out on a mortuary table awaiting our inspection. This was a man in his mid-forties, I would estimate, average in height and of a stocky build, rather heavy around the waist. His hair was dark and slick, combed back from the temples and held in place by the heavy application of pomade.

Holmes got to work straight away, examining the body closely, at first with his naked eye, then after with his magnifying glass. After only a few minutes, he stopped, stretched his long, lean frame and moved his attention to the victim's clothes and belongings, which were strewn untidily upon the adjacent table. I now had my first close look at the body.

Even from a distance, it was clear that the poor man had been beaten viciously to death. His body was covered in ugly dark welts and bruises, and it was clear that several bones in his arms and legs were fractured, along with numerous ribs. Up close, the injuries were nothing less than horrific. His head and face that had been subjected to the most sustained and brutal assault. The nose was smashed flat, cheekbones shattered and all of his front teeth were missing. His left temple had been hit so violently that it was now a three-inch concave depression. Undoubtedly, this was the blow that had killed him.

"A frenzied attack with a heavy blunt weapon," I stated, finally breaking the silence. "A monstrous assault. This was vicious, Holmes. It must have been personal or otherwise the work of a madman."

"Very good, Watson, but I think in this case your first instinct is the more likely."

Holmes turned to address me directly.

"This is a refreshing challenge, Watson. Almost a blank sheet, nothing for us to work with but physical evidence. We know but two things. The victim was a bookmaker and that he was beaten to death. However, both are facts and indisputable. No unverifiable and unreliable witness statements, no crime scene trampled by over-eager constables. Just what we have here, before us."

"Well I am glad that you are happy, but I see nothing but a poor victim of a terrible assault, a pile of his clothes and a few sad belongings," I countered.

"So, what do you make of his clothes and belongings then, Watson? What do they tell you?"

"The suit is of a very good quality tweed, traditional country style but recently tailored. His boots and gloves are of similar quality and vintage. This was a successful man, as is attested by the contents of his wallet, no less than forty pounds in notes. Well at least that means we can eliminate robbery as a motive for the murder."

Holmes nodded his silent approval.

"He was also carrying a few coins in change, a fine gold half hunter pocket watch, two keys and a silver hip flask with a matching cup, also of silver. These usually sit upturned on top of the flask, a stirrup cup I believe it is called. These last two seem to have taken a fair few blows. The cup has been beaten almost flat."

Holmes smiled, "Well said, and now, I think, I hear the unmistakable approaching footsteps of our good friend, the Inspector."

A moment later, Lestrade appeared looking flustered and impatient.

"Make it quick please, Holmes. If you somehow know the identity of the killer, please share it with me."

Lestrade paused, composed himself and took a deep breath before continuing.

"No, I am sorry, I apologise. After all, you have done for us this week I have no right to make such demands of you. But what am I thinking, I haven't even shared the details of the case with you."

To my astonishment, Holmes casually announced, "Do not worry Inspector, I already have the solution. But I'll leave the minor details, such as the murderer's identity, up to you to ascertain."

Lestrade was understandably flabbergasted, as was I.

"Come on, Holmes, this is no time for your twisted sense of humour. A man has been horribly murdered and our friend here needs your help," I admonished.

"A thousand apologies, my dearest friends, but I meant no joke," Holmes declared, most earnestly. "I merely wish to pass onto friend Lestrade that which I have discovered."

Lestrade sighed, and then smiled. "Even if what you now recount is fevered nonsense brought on by overwork and lack of sleep, it will not change the fact that you have helped us in solving five cases in as many days. I am ready to listen, Mr Holmes."

I nodded in agreement, already regretting my outburst.

"We thought that the killer had left no trace of himself, nothing to identify him." Holmes had clearly been unaffected by our doubt-ridden interruption and continued his summation untroubled. "On closer inspection of the evidence, I have determined that this is not the case."

"Look at the victim's belongings. Watson listed them as well as any casual observer might have," Holmes continued. "I, however, examined each of them in as much detail as, is here, possible and I discovered something curious."

"Well, go on, Holmes, don't keep us in the dark now, for heaven's sake. The victim's family will be here shortly and the morticians still have to dress and make the body presentable," Lestrade entreated.

Holmes moved to the table where the poor man's clothes and chattels lay. "The answer lies here amongst the sad detritus of this poor man's life. At first impression, it appears to be a collection of goods that any well-to-do man might have carried. I had closely inspected all of the items, but kept being drawn back to the silver stirrup cup. Something about it troubled me. Once, twice and finally a third time I studied the flattened silver cup with my glass. Then, I finally saw what had subconsciously raised my suspicions."

"Go on, Holmes, what was it?" I urged.

"The hallmarks Watson, the hallmarks." he declared, triumphantly.

"What about the blessed hallmarks, Holmes?" Lestrade pleaded, fatigue again wearing at his patience.

"They do not match!" Holmes declared. He picked up the battered silver flask and motioned us to come closer.

"This flask was manufactured in Birmingham, the anchor is quite clear, by Josiah Holt and Co." Holmes held up the flask. "The year was, let me see, lower case 'd', ah yes, eighteen seventy eight, some six years past." He lowered the flask to the table and picked up the flattened cup. He took out his pocketknife, opened the shorter blade, and began to prise apart the sides of the battered object where it had become folded flat.

"Ah yes, that's better," he said, after having worked the little cup into a more three dimensional state. "Now we can see the hallmark, here. London, capital 'A', eighteen hundred and seventy six. The maker's mark is unclear to me due to some damage sustained in the attack, but I believe an expert could still identify it from what remains."

"But what does that mean?" I asked.

"It means one of three things, gentlemen. One, the flask and cup were matched together by the retailer, who then sold them as a set to the victim. Two, the victim himself came across the items separately and combined them himself. Or three, the two items do not belong together at all."

"But that would surely be an unimaginable coincidence, would it not? A man dropping his own silver cup at the scene of a crime where he himself has battered his victim's silver hip flask? That cannot have happened, it is incredible, preposterous even." Lestrade shook his head, clearly disappointed with Holmes' reasoning.

"Almost, Inspector, but not quite. You see, now that I had suspicions about this cup, I examined it in minute detail with my pocket lens. Two things became apparent. Firstly, the lip of the cup is rather rough for a drinking vessel. It would not cut you, but you would certainly notice its slightly uneven edge against your lower lip when drinking from it. Secondly, it has two very small indents, one on either side, about three quarters of the way up the side. These are too small, and too even, to have been formed during the assault."

"So, what does this mean, Holmes?" I asked. "Are you suggesting that the cup may not actually be a cup after all? If so, then what on earth could it be?"

"The answer is in the hallmark. Once you have found an expert to identify the manufacturer, Inspector, then you will have definite proof, but I think I can be confident in my prediction of what that answer will be." Holmes was now smiling.

"This is not a cup at all, you are quite right, Watson," he announced with considerable swagger. "This is a ferrule from a walking stick. A stout and heavy stick, almost certainly freely adorned with silver decoration. Ebony would be my guess, the weight of which would certainly account for the destruction it inflicted. During the furious attack the ferrule was dislodged."

"Do you mean the metal fitting at the bottom of a cane?" asked Lestrade, incredulously. "Well it is the right shape, and if the bottom of the stick was stout enough it would closely resemble a small cup."

"The lip of which would not need to be as fine or smooth as a cup," Holmes furthered. "The marks on the side are from where a blunt nail has been hammered in to help fix the ferrule in position."

"It would be a very expensive stick to have had a silver ferrule fitted. There cannot be many manufactured in London and, of course, we know the year it was made. If we can ascertain the maker's name we might be able to track down the very man who commissioned it," I added excitedly, finally realising where Holmes' deductions had been leading.

"Can we leave this with you now, Inspector? I am sure you will feel happier now that you can inform the victim's family, when they arrive, that Scotland Yard is hot on the trail of his killer and close to making an arrest."

Holmes smiled, doffed his hat to the Inspector and prepared to leave.

"Why thank you, Mr Holmes," replied a slightly stunned Inspector Lestrade, before making an admirably quick recovery. "I am sure we can take it from here. I'll let you know when we have our man, it will not be long now you have pointed us in the right direction."

Holmes was already at the door as I bade farewell to the Inspector. I followed him through the corridors of the venerable home of the Metropolitan Police and out into the late morning sun. As I felt the warm sun on my face, Holmes turned and spoke.

"It is almost midday, Watson, and we are but ten minutes' walk from the Strand. Lunch at Simpson's?"

At that place, and in that moment, his suggestion could not possibly have been bettered.

Postscript

Lestrade did get his man, a fellow bookmaker no less. A dispute over territory had escalated into a full-blown feud in which neither man would back down. A one-to-one meeting was arranged, supposedly to calm the situation, but this failed disastrously. As he was leaving, suddenly realising that they were alone and there were no witnesses, the assailant grabbed the opportunity to settle the score once and for all. When he was found and arrested by Lestrade's men, he was holding a stout ebony stick dressed with silver adornments. Its ferrule was missing.

Part Two

Tuesday 3rd June 1884

The rain hammered mercilessly against the windows and the wind blew its contempt around the dark grey streets of the greatest city in the world. Outside, hardy folk braved the elements on their way to and fro, not letting the squall keep them from their business.

If only my friend were currently so occupied. When involved in a case, nothing could keep him from following it through until its end, however complex or dangerous it transpired to be. Yet now, as I look at the pale, pathetic figure curled up in his armchair, I see the opposite. Holmes, when not retained upon some mystery or other, was a sad sight indeed. Thin, gaunt-faced, barely eating or drinking and drawn ever closer to the enslaving syringe.

The exploits of the previous month now seemed like a lifetime ago. The good weather had gone and taken with it Holmes' health and caseload both. I had even taken to visiting Lestrade alone, to ensure he was keeping no cases of interest from us. The Inspector had profited well from Holmes' Herculean successes in the preceding weeks, but despite my disloyal thoughts, it transpired that he was himself also actively searching for a case worthy of our friend. He had seen the change in Holmes first hand, and it troubled him as much as it did me.

Even when we bullied, shamed or even forced him to take on a lesser case, he resolved it without engaging even a fraction of the great intellect we know him to possess.

One morning, during a brief lull in the turbulent weather, we were visited by a young lady. She was of maybe four and twenty years, and fairly attractive in a commonplace way. She worked in town as a sales assistant in a well-known ladieswear store and spoke well, rather better than her background might have suggested.

The case was simple and quite pathetic. Her cat had gone missing. She suspected her husband, a carpenter, of having disposed of the poor creature, but had no proof. I heard the details myself as Holmes had yet to rise that morning. I was just in the process of trying to explain, as kindly as possible, that Sherlock Holmes did not take such cases when a disembodied voice called out. "Trousers Watson, ask about the trousers."

"Excuse me," I addressed the young lady more than a little embarrassed. "What about whose trousers?" I hissed back at Holmes.

"The young lady's husband of course. Shoreditch, I believe. The accent, that is. Much worked upon, but still just apparent," came Holmes' casual reply.

"What about them? This is insufferable, Holmes." My face was as red as a Guard's jacket.

"Does the gentleman wear turn-ups?" He asked. I looked at our client and gave an apologetic shrug.

"Why yes, yes he does," she replied, somewhat bemused.

"Very good," answered the unseen detective. "When you arrive home, check inside his turn-ups. If you find a light-coloured sediment, heavy with grey clay, then I am afraid your cat is dead."

Holmes volunteered no further explanation or indeed anything at all. I led the confused client away as politely as I could, gently explaining that Holmes was suffering from nervous exhaustion and was not quite himself.

Once she was safely outside 221B, I rounded on Holmes, banging on his door.

"Really Holmes, this will not do. Teasing a poor client like that, not to mention what she will tell her friends and customers. You have a certain reputation that you must uphold."

There was a considerable pause followed by what sounded like weak laughter. "Fear not, dear doctor, I am not yet for Bethlehem," Holmes said, weakly.

"Then how can you excuse such behaviour? That poor woman has lost her cat and you have sent her home to examine her husband's trousers?" I asked, incredulously.

"The case is simple, Watson. These animals, the ones people keep for affection, vanish by the thousand each year. They are stolen, killed, trapped, poisoned and drowned for numerous reasons. I saw one other possibility. If it turns out to be correct, she gets her explanation and my reputation is enhanced. If I am wrong, then I believe we will never know what happened to the creature and I fear that, in future, I may find little work in Shoreditch."

"Well, it is good to see that your twisted sense of humour is still present, but please explain about the trousers," I implored.

"The Thames, Watson. Old Father, Mother and bastard child of London. The banks and shore around Shoreditch are mostly sticky grey clay. What would this distinctive alluvial matter be doing on a carpenter?"

"I have no idea," I admitted.

"It could only have got there if he had recently walked upon the shores of the river, and what reason could he have had for doing so?"

"Of course. What a cad, killing his wife's pet and throwing the poor thing's remains into the river." I shook my head in disgust.

"We shall see, Watson, for this may not be quite as you imagine. But no matter really, the odds are several to one against my theory and we will probably hear no more of this matter."

However, the very next morning, to my considerable surprise, we received a note from our client. She thanked us for our help in solving what she had believed to have been an impossible problem. She had done exactly as requested by Holmes, found the soil and confronted her husband. He immediately admitted disposing of the animal's body, but explained that he had found the creature in a terrible state, dying from multiple wounds, the result, it seems, of a vicious feline battle for territory. He could do nothing but end the poor creature's suffering. Wanting to spare his wife's feelings, he removed the body and denied all knowledge of the sad incident. Though sad at the confirmation of her pet's demise, she was nonetheless happy to discover that her husband was not at all the violent, spiteful man she had begun to fear.

I was impressed, as anyone would have been, but Holmes merely shrugged off any compliment with a languid wave of his hand. His only comment on this, or any other minor case brought to him at the time, was to simply convey an estimation of how small a percentage of his brainpower he had used in solving such meagre pickings.

"About twelve per cent," was his desultory approximation of the above case, one unique, in that he had solved it without ever leaving his room and having never actually met his client.

The days passed and still no case worthy of the great detective knocked upon our door. It was now Monday, the ninth of June and finally, so it seemed, the weather was beginning to change for the better. I awoke to an unfamiliar crescent of bright sunlight breaking through the edges of my bedroom curtains. I dressed and made my way to the sitting room, my mood improved by the subtle warmth that was already radiating its warm fingers through the city. Holmes was sitting in his chair, early morning sunlight streaming through the windows. For the first time in weeks, the fireplace was empty and unlit.

"Well this is a bit more like it, old man. The sun is out, one can almost feel the damp being steamed out of the city. I am sure this must be a good omen," I ventured, as cheerily as I could muster.

"Has it stopped raining? I hadn't noticed." Holmes looked up and saw the bright morning sunshine cascading into our rooms as if for the first time. "Sadly, Watson, it will take more than sunlight to stop me from rotting away." He sighed and settled back to his morning pipe, its hideous smoke curling and twisting like a cursed wraith dying in the bright early rays of the new day.

As I sat down to another fine breakfast prepared by Mrs Hudson, I was surprised and excited to hear the ringing of the front door bell.

"Well, this must be a case, old man, who else would call at such an hour?" I questioned, enthusiastically. Holmes barely shrugged.

About a minute later, Inspector Gregson appeared at the door. His tall, slightly stooped figure peered into the room. "I hope I am not disturbing you, gentlemen, but I find myself rather lost and incapable. I have a problem that I think only you, Mr Holmes, could ever make sense of."

I looked towards Holmes and saw a momentary flash of pleasure sweep across his face before turning a serious glance to Gregson. "Pray, tell me your story. Be precise, leave out nothing."

I smiled and offered Gregson a seat and warm coffee. Inside, I felt relief and elation that my friend might have finally found a case that could challenge him. As Gregson began his tale, there was little to suspect that this would turn out to be one of the most labyrinthine and saddest cases of his entire career.

The Pigtail Twist

Chapter One - Beda's Hurst Hall

Monday 9th June 1884

"Bedhurst Hall is a fairly obscure country house in rural Bedfordshire. It is owned, or rather, was owned, by a Mr James Harrison. Last night he was murdered in a house full of guests. No one could have entered the house and nobody left. We know that he was strangled, but have found no murder weapon. We have searched the property and all of those present, but have found no clues or evidence, whatsoever. We are at a complete loss, Mr Holmes. I beg you to help as you have done in the past."

Gregson's big blue eyes were wide open and pleading, his scruffy blonde hair only adding to his almost childlike appearance.

"Bedfordshire, you say?" Holmes leaned forwards. "There is an hourly train from St Pancras, we shall meet you at Bedford station at midday and share a cab to the Hall."

Holmes turned away, dismissively. Gregson knew it was time to leave, but as he passed me, he nodded and I could see that he was greatly relieved that Holmes was now engaged in this mystery.

"Well, what do you make of this then, Holmes?" I asked.

"Probably a simple matter, but there may just be a few points of interest," was his less than enthusiastic reply.

"Oh come on, old man, show a bit of ardour. It certainly sounds like a real puzzle to me. I am going to pack a bag as I am guessing we may be there a day or two."

"Don't forget your service revolver," Holmes replied, rather to my surprise.

"Whatever for?" I asked, but received no reply, as Holmes ignored my inquiries and retired to his room to dress and prepare for the journey.

We took a cab from 221B and journeyed through the welcome sunlit streets to the magnificent station of St Pancras. We alighted in the finely jagged shadow of Gilbert Scott's great gothic Midland Hotel and made our way inside, past the ticket offices and into the cavernous iron-beamed Barlow train shed, its roof the largest without support in the entire world. Even after numerous visits, I still had to pause to take in its scale and geometric beauty, a miracle of engineering and mechanical artistry. Beams of light streamed in and where they met smoke and steam they were bent, twisted and diffracted in a magical dance of light and dust.

"Wake up Watson, you old dreamer." Holmes grinned as he, almost playfully, nudged me with his overnight bag. I grunted myself out of my daydream and followed Holmes into an empty First Class carriage.

The short, hour-long journey passed quickly with little conversation. The train slowed as we passed the Britannia Works and halted a few moments later at Bedford station. Gregson was there, waiting on the platform, his tall form and blonde hair fluttering in the breeze, were unmistakable.

A four-wheeler awaited us and we climbed aboard, beginning the six-mile drive to the village of Bedden. On the way, Gregson gave us a short history of the Hall.

"The village was originally called Beda's Dene, dene being Anglo-Saxon for a small valley. The house itself was built on a wooded hill, a hurst, so was known as Bedashurst Hall, later contracted to Bedhurst. Similarly, the village is now known simply as Bedden," he recounted, most keenly.

Holmes appeared to be dozing, so I nodded at the appropriate points and feigned interest in Gregson's local knowledge.

We headed northwest through gently undulating farmland until we descended into a small hollow where about a dozen small houses and a handsome inn announced that we had arrived in the village of Bedden. A small green with a closely cropped cricket square along with a regulation duck pond completed this most quintessentially English village. We stopped briefly at the inn to take rooms and unload our bags before continuing through the village and following the road, which soon became wooded and began to slowly climb. The trees suddenly gave way and we caught our first sight of

Bedhurst Hall, a quarter of a mile away, sitting proudly atop the highest ground of the parish.

The Hall was not particularly large or grand but was finely proportioned and set among neat, well-kept gardens. The house appeared to have originally been of ruddy-brick Tudor origin, but had been extensively, but sensitively modernised. I instantly approved of this clever method of both conserving the historic Hall and bringing it up to date without losing what had made it so attractive in the first place.

Holmes was still silent. I imagined he was studying the house and grounds with a very different eye. I attempted to do the same. I could see that the open ground, which surrounded the house, would make it very difficult to approach or leave unobserved. I mentioned this to Holmes, who nodded, but said nothing.

A constable was waiting at the front of the house and he saluted Gregson as he jumped athletically from the carriage.

"Has all been left exactly as I ordered?" he asked.

"Yes sir, but it is getting harder to keep the guests quiet and all in one place. They are complaining with ever increasing regularity, sir."

"I will have a word with them, presently. A murder has been done and no one is leaving until we have answers." His confidence and mood had clearly been improved by Holmes' presence.

He turned to us, "Would you like to meet the guests?" he asked.
"Soon, but first the scene of the murder, I think. I suppose the body has been removed?" Holmes sighed, without optimism.

"Certainly not, sir. I insisted that it was left exactly as it was found, just as you have wished it in the past." Gregson's eager face looked at Holmes for approval.

"I will save my praise until I see what the local constables have left me to work with, I can already see their heavy footprints in the gravel, obscuring all others," Holmes replied, rather brusquely.

We followed Gregson into the Hall. The inside was much like the exterior, a mixture of traditional dark mahogany panelling and plain white plaster walls, giving the Hall a sense of space and light, but also of warmth. There were surprisingly few paintings, and all of these were quite shockingly modern - bright, crude and rather vulgar. We passed by a large wooden staircase, turned right and through a sparse parlour, into a similarly unpretentious dining room. There was little in the way of decoration, the walls were painted in simple uniform bright colours and the occasional shelf and table held little more than a handful of drinks bottles, a large humidor and a collection of tribal looking statues and masks. At the rear was a set of glazed double doors in the French style, these were both wide open and through them we could see into a large greenhouse or conservatory. Once inside, we could finally appreciate the size of the glasshouse. It stretched twenty yards ahead of us and was almost as wide as the house. It was filled, from floor to twenty-foot high roof, with exotic plants, flowers, ferns, bushes and trees. Hundreds of glass panels, each about three feet square, were held in place by a latticework of white-painted iron, creating the impression of a vast spider's web, dripping with condensation from the humidity created by the massed flora below.

We walked forward, then left, right and right again. It appeared that the layout of the paths had evolved in a manner as unplanned and organic as the plants themselves. We eventually reached the far end of the structure. Looking through the windows, we could see a neat garden, after which, the ground fell away leaving a huge stretch of blue sky interspersed with occasional fluffy clouds. I estimated the view faced somewhere between southwest and west, some truly beautiful sunsets must have been observed from here. It was with this thought that I noticed the wooden bench, positioned just for such occasions, and also the slumped figure, thereon.

The attending constable stood to attention, then stepped back to allow us full access to the wretched scene. Harrison was still half-upright but leaned dramatically to the right. His head was turned upwards and his face told me a simple and terrible tale. His skin was dark, blood vessels burst all over. The eyes were wide and bloodshot, almost protruding from their sockets. A black tongue stuck, out surrounded by a pair of light purple lips. He had been strangled to death.

Holmes began his examination. He removed his lens and studied every inch of the dead man in minute detail. From head to toe, he looked in every pocket, turn-up, fold and crease of his clothes. He even checked the undersides of the poor man's soles before inspecting the surrounding area. After twenty minutes, he straightened.

"Of course, I may wish to examine the corpse in more detail at the morgue. Make sure all of his clothes and their contents are present," he ordered.

"Now, Watson, what is your medical opinion? Take your time, old friend, for I believe we have only just begun to gently stir these stygian waters, and they may well be very deep indeed."

Holmes' ominous tone could not fail but affect me as I made my examination. I checked the head and chest for other injuries, but there was nothing to suggest that there was any cause of death other than the one I had immediately posited. I pulled down his collar and saw just what I had been expecting, the bruising and tearing caused by the contraction of a ligature. From what I could tell, it was roughly half an inch in width and had left a faint black, oily residue.

"Strangulation," I announced. "By means of a rope or cord, less than an inch in diameter. There are traces of a black oily substance, so we should maybe be looking at a maritime connection. Has the Hall been searched for rope or any similar cable that might have been used?"

"From rafters to cellars", replied Gregson. "The only rope we have found was either far too long to have been of practical use or so old that it was covered in green mould, none of which has been rubbed off the rope or found anywhere on the body. We did find several finer cords, but none of these fit the pattern or size of the wounds."

"The guests have all been searched, I presume?" I asked.

"Yes, we even called in female staff to check the ladies, nothing we found matched the injuries, not belt, tie or garter."

"Well done, Watson, Inspector, a perfectly credible account. Do you have a list of everything found upon those present at the Hall, Inspector?" Holmes asked.

"Yes, of course, everything found about the guests' persons is listed in their witness statements," replied the efficient young detective.

"Now what about the larger scene, Doctor?" Holmes gestured from left to right encompassing the area surrounding the body and bench.

Reluctantly, and cursing somewhat under my breath that this was his rather than my domain, I got to my knees and examined the ground.

"The paths, being inside, are dry and hard so there is not much in the way of footmarks. The ground is scuffed up immediately before the victim, caused no doubt by the poor chap's desperate final struggle. There is some tobacco ash, the end of a cigar, stubbed out, so we know he finished his cigar before he was attacked. There are also some black flakes here." I picked one up and put it to my nose. "Pipe tobacco, a dark Virginia. As there is no pipe found at the scene and

Harrison carried no pouch, I think we might deduce that it came from the murderer. Do we know which of those present smoked a pipe?"

"At least four of the gentlemen guests were pipe smokers," replied Gregson.

I stood up gingerly, careful not to inflame my old wound, feeling rather proud of my deductions.

"Why, Watson," commented Holmes, "you have learned so much in so short a time. Aside from missing a couple of clues of vital importance, you seem to have observed most everything else of interest."

"Damned with faint praise," I chuckled quietly to myself.

"The cigar is a Havana, an unusual size, rather large in girth but short, less than five inches, and wrapped in a dark Maduro leaf. This is the smoke of a connoisseur, the large girth encourages flavour onto the palette, the shorter length prevents a sticky build-up of tar. I am certain we will find more of its companions in the ebony and cedar wood humidor in the corner of the sitting room."

"I am sure it will prove necessary to try one, purely in the name of research," I grinned.

"Merely to compare and confirm the ash of course," Holmes replied with inscrutable sincerity. "The tobacco flakes are indeed dark Virginia, not a pre-packed brand but one bought loose by the ounce.

The exact identification of these proprietary tobaccos is made particularly difficult by the scent and flavour being fundamentally altered by the length and method of storage used by each individual tobacconist."

"Well, Bedford has a tobacconist of national renown, on the High Street, I believe. That would be an errand I would happily volunteer for."

"Their house blends are indeed famous throughout the southern counties but this is certainly not one of them. Maybe we can pay a brief visit before we leave but not just yet, Watson, for now we must establish the security of the house and the order of events of last night. Gregson, in what state was the house when the first constables arrived? Doors, windows, everything."

Gregson had been watching in silence, still rather in awe of Holmes. He reached quickly into his pocket, withdrew his notebook and located the relevant entry.

"The alarm was raised at around twelve thirty. An attendant ran to the stables and rode to the village to raise the local policeman. He sent word to Bedford and followed the servant back to the hall. All doors and windows were locked and bolted from the inside, save for the front door, which the servant had unbolted to leave but had locked behind him. In fact, this had been done as early as eleven, which was the usual procedure. A few of the guests had even remarked that it was rather warm and were surprised that no windows were open. Once reinforcements had arrived, they checked all of the doors and windows a second time and confirmed that all were securely fastened."

"The local Doctor quickly confirmed the apparent cause of death and we began a thorough search of the house, but with no immediate results," he continued. "All of the servants and staff are accounted for and none of the guests have left. At first light, two constables and I walked around the outside of the Hall looking for any signs of entry or exit. We carefully examined the paths, grass and flowerbeds but found nothing, no footprints or other suspicious marks, such as those that might be made by the use of a ladder for example. All window sills and frames were clean and well-secured."

"It appears that you have not been idle, Inspector, well done. You will excuse me if I take a look for myself later? Just for my own satisfaction, of course," Holmes smiled, graciously. "But now we must meet the protagonists. Gregson, do you have a list of all those present last night?"

Gregson handed Holmes a sheet of paper, which he examined for about a minute. "Good. Names and professions. Much better than just going in completely blind. Thank you, Inspector."

Holmes returned the page to the Inspector, who pocketed it before leading us back into the Hall, through the dining room and the spartan parlour, across the entrance hall and into the opposite front room. This proved to be the formal drawing room and, unlike the rest of the house, was decorated in a far more traditional style. Seated on various armchairs and settees were four ladies and five men. A sixth man was standing, looking out of the front bay window. As we entered, he approached Gregson.

"When will you and your men be finished, Inspector? We have been cooped up here like poultry since last night, the poor ladies are very shocked and tired and I now have a mountain of things to attend to."

He stopped and looked at Holmes and I. "And who are you two? More police, I do not doubt. Well, we have made our statements, I fail to see what further help we can be."

His face was lined with worry, his eyes dark from lack of sleep. I could see that this was a normally calm and polite gentleman, struggling to cope in a desperate situation.

"Colonel Fauwkes, this is Mr Sherlock Holmes, consulting detective, and his colleague Doctor John Watson. They are here to aid us in unravelling this terrible mystery. I know you have spoken to myself and others but please be patient a while longer and cooperate with Mr Holmes in whatever way that he requests."

Gregson then gave way to Holmes, who bowed slightly, before addressing the room.

"I would like to ask each of you a few simple questions, if you would be so kind. I shall take interviews in the parlour. Inspector, please, a word?" Holmes led Gregson back into to the entrance hall, with an added gesture that I should also follow.

"Send them to me in the order that you have written down. Couples can come together." Holmes spoke quietly, looking back at the drawing room door seemingly suspicious of being overheard. "Do you have the statements already provided?"

Gregson smiled and handed over a thin folder containing about a dozen sheets of testimony. Holmes ran his eyes over each sheet, reading at an impossible speed, before taking a seat.

"Send in the first witness," he ordered.

Chapter Two - Questions & Answers

Holmes sat in a plain cream armchair, to his right was a small table on which the folder containing the statements taken by the police lay open. I sat on a straight-backed chair with my back to the bay window in an attempt to appear as inconspicuous as possible and allow me to observe the witnesses as closely as possible without distracting them, my notebook on my lap.

The first to be interviewed was a Colonel Ephraim Fauwkes.

Col. E Fauwkes

"Colonel, my sincerest apologies for this continuing inconvenience. You reside here at the Hall, and I think it is well known that you are the closest friend of the deceased. Yet your statement indicates that your knowledge of him is rather limited. Why should this be?"

The Colonel shuffled, uncomfortably. He was in his late fifties but lithe, spritely and as healthy as anyone twenty years younger. His hair was thick and dark with flashes of grey at the sides. His eyes were a bright steel grey and a thin moustache sat below a noble nose. He wore a suit of fine bottle green tweed and looked every inch the archetype of a handsome, middle-aged English country gentleman. He thought long and deeply before he finally answered.

"James Harrison was the greatest man I ever met. Generous, intelligent, kind, gentle and wise. But, he was a man of secrets. To be his friend, he asked but one thing. Never inquire after his past. In everything else he was an open book, but his life before he returned to England could never be discussed."

"So, he had left the country at some point earlier in his life and returned at a later date?" I interceded.

Fauwkes shrugged, "That is as much as I have ever known. We met in '78, when I returned from India."

"I also served, in Afghanistan. All too briefly though, as a Jezail bullet ended my military career rather earlier than planned." My revelation that I was a fellow former soldier seemed to relax the Colonel, slightly.

"Sorry to hear that," he replied. "Somehow, I passed through every skirmish, melee and even major encounter without a scratch, while better men than I will ever be fell at every side of me," he added, with a note of sadness and regret.

"And then you met Harrison?" Holmes gently moved the conversation forwards.

"Yes, we met in London, where at the time I had modest lodgings. He had made a fortune on the railways, backing the lines into the centre of the city, you know the Metropolitan over and underground lines. His financial acumen helped turn my modest pension into a decent income for a gentleman. We became good friends and one day he confessed to me his deep loneliness and wondered if I might be willing to take a room in his otherwise largely empty Hall. I argued hard to make him accept any form of rent and soon after I had moved in and I can honestly admit to never having been happier. I make this point most strenuously and wish nothing more than for all of this awfulness to have been but a foul dream, and to return to my life as it was before, here with my friend." I could not fail to see that his once cold, grey eyes were now red-lined and glassy.

"So, moving on to last night," said Holmes, seemingly oblivious to Fauwkes' suffering. Can you describe the events of the evening? Actually, why don't you start with the reason for the gathering?"

"Once a month we hold, or held, a dinner up here at the Hall." Fauwkes began, after composing himself. "The guests varied slightly in their make-up, but the core was always the same. Harrison was, of course, the host, I just helped out as best I could."

"The vicar had a standing invitation, he and Harrison enjoyed a friendly, but unusual relationship. Harrison is, or rather was," he hesitated, "a confirmed atheist. The vicar, St John Beekey, was nonetheless determined to win Harrison back into his flock. It became a running topic of debate, always passionate but never unfriendly and always delivered with great humour on both sides. I wonder if he now knows who was right?" he trailed off sadly.

"The other regular guests were Joseph Banks-Wells, a local farmer who owns much of the surrounding countryside and more than half of the village, along with his wife Eleanor. The local Magistrate and lawyer, the Hon Rodney Wulf Fessington, his wife Mrs Catherine Fessington plus Doctor and Mrs Ernest Pace completed our cabal.

The remaining guests were all present at the Hall for the first time," Fauwkes added.

"What can you tell me of the newcomers?" Holmes offered Fauwkes a small cigar from his monogrammed silver case, (the monogram not being his own, and if ever identified and made known publicly, had the power to bring down two western governments) but he declined.

"Unfortunately, not a great deal, I am sorry to say Mr Holmes," he admitted. "The widow Clarity Fairchance had finally taken up her long-standing invitation and was accompanied by a man who was renting her summer cottage, a Mr Jude Wergeld. I do not think that a word was spoken between them all evening, now I come to think of it. The final guest was a real mystery. Professor Jacob Seaworthy. Harrison never explained exactly how they met or what their relationship was, but he was a fine enough guest, knowledgeable on many subjects, but rather cold and precise with it."

"Thank you, Mr Fauwkes, your testimony has been refreshingly precise. Now, can you please recount the events of the evening in as much detail as you can remember?"

Fauwkes spoke at length about the fateful evening, the time and order of arrival, the drinks reception and the four-course meal that followed. Harrison came across as a genial and entertaining host. He sparred with the vicar on religion, discussed the harvest prospects with Banks-Wells and bemoaned the petty crime caused by drunkenness with Wulf Fessington. He engaged occasionally with the Professor on scientific subjects, particularly astronomy, but could remember no direct interaction between Harrison and the remaining pair of guests, other than general pleasantries.

"After dinner was concluded, the men retired to the greenhouse for a glass of port and a smoke, the ladies to the drawing room. You have seen it, it is rather a maze, so we all wandered where we pleased, chatting in pairs or sitting on benches enjoying the warm evening, such a change after the recent inclement weather."

"You saw all of the male guests in the greenhouse? Nobody was missing? Did you see anyone else, a servant perhaps?" asked Holmes, his fingers now arched, papers fallen to his lap.

"Yes, all were there and I saw no one else. The greenhouse was locked, the only way in or out was through the dining room. We smoked Harrison's Hoyo De Monterrey Maduro Especiales, that he had specially imported from Cuba through H&S in town and, after about an hour, we began to leave and re-join the ladies in the drawing room."

"In what order did you arrive in the drawing room? Please be precise here, it is imperative."

"When I reached the drawing room, the Doctor and Magistrate were already there. Directly behind me was the vicar, followed shortly, maybe five minutes later, by Banks-Wells and Wergeld together. The professor arrived a little later, I cannot be exact as we were all, by then, conversing. I think I noticed his presence maybe ten minutes after the last of the others had arrived."

"Most illuminating, sir. Now I have to ask who discovered the body or, rather, who first noticed that Harrison had not returned?" Holmes' eyes were bright and alive, a heart-warming change from just hours earlier.

"That would have been the Doctor's wife, Grace, a usually quiet and timid lady. She mentioned it to her husband, who then asked me. At the time we made rather a joke of it, I am sorry to admit, something like 'what kind of host misses out on his own finest brandy?' that sort of thing. So I sent the butler, Greaves, to look for him. He returned ashen-faced only a few minutes later. He is a fine man, Greaves, a former sergeant in the Rifles, not easily shaken, and he knew well enough not to disturb the scene."

There was a short pause before Holmes stood up and held out his hand, which Fauwkes nervously shook. "Thank you, sir, for your time, your testimony has been invaluable. I promise that I will do everything in my power to ensure that the murderer of your friend is brought to justice."

"I hope so too, but do you really think you can untangle such a puzzle? It could be anyone present, after all, even myself I suppose. No one has an alibi, except the ladies."

Fauwkes looked tired and desperate, wringing his hands nervously before composing himself. "Who would you like to see next?" he asked, seemingly grateful for this simplest of tasks.

"Please send in the vicar, the Rev St. John Beekey, I believe."

Rev. St. J. Beekey

Holmes wrote a few notes before there was a light tap and the vicar poked his head around the door. Approaching sixty, the vicar's hair was thick and white, either side of a large domed hairless forehead so smooth it actually reflected the sunlight. He had a large nose but small piggy eyes, which hid behind brass-rimmed pince-nez that seemed several sizes too small. His mouth, though, had many laughter lines on either side and he showed every sign of a man more used to smiling than scowling. His clothes were rather old fashioned and showed signs of both wear and repair, this was clearly a priest who thought little of worldly wealth.

"Good afternoon, gentlemen." He smiled broadly, as we made pleasant introductions. "Why Mr Holmes, what a terrible business, I am sure. The good Lord has taken home a fine man. Judge not, I say," he paused, and for a second looked very old and very sad. "But an earthly judgement must come to the fiend who ended my friend," he declared, waving a finger in the air.

"But I know you will prevail, for I have read your accounts, Doctor Watson, and Inspector Gregson has since confirmed to me their veracity. I believe God himself has brought you here to solve this mystery."

"No pressure then," I muttered under my breath. "Please share all you know with my colleague and I can guarantee that he will not rest until he has solved this terrible crime," I added, most presumptuously. Holmes, though, refused to be riled and merely raised an eyebrow.

The vicar talked at length of the evening, confirming all that Colonel Fauwkes had said, adding much local lore and gossip, but little actual detail, to the night's events. He was affable, learned and on any other occasion, I would have genuinely enjoyed his company. The more he talked, the more evident it became that his unlikely friendship with Harrison was real and built on genuine respect and affection.

Mr. & Mrs. J. Banks-Wells

Once the Vicar had left the room, I stretched my limbs and awaited our next witnesses. Joseph Banks-Wells and his wife Eleanor were the local landowners, their marriage had united the east and west sides of the valley to create a larger and more efficient estate. This had led also to several workers losing their jobs and a sense of resentment in the village. We had learned all of this from the vicar, for the Banks-Wells' proved to be dull, unimaginative and somewhat unreliable witnesses. Their accounts generally matched those we had heard so far, but they struggled to recount even the simplest detail. Holmes dismissed them well before they had finished their full account.

"Well there we have it, old boy," I chuckled as the door closed behind them.

"Have what?" Holmes asked looking unusually puzzled.

"They are clearly the culprits. They bored him to death," I sneered, most inappropriately.

Holmes stared daggers at me before breaking into a wide smile. "Watson, please remember where we are," he scolded, with mock sincerity.

Hon. R. & Mrs. Wulf Fessington

The local magistrate and his wife were much more congenial. The Hon Rodney Wulf Fessington was a bright legal mind from one of England's oldest Anglo-Saxon families. His wife was similarly interesting, a gifted musician and a member of the then nascent women's rights movement. He was tall with wild black hair and beard, she was blonde, slim and elegant, her small frame in contrast to her strong, fiery disposition.

They were most keen to discuss the case. They had managed to put together nearly as much information as ourselves, via the other guests and some less than discreet constables.

"So, we are really dealing with two problems here, aren't we?" Wulf Fessington spoke, but both he and his wife together leaned forward eagerly, hungry for any new information.

"Who committed the murder and how it was done?" added Mrs Fessington. "The who I am sure you will determine, but how on earth was it done? Strangled with a rope or cord, which then disappears? Has everywhere really been searched thoroughly? What about the glasshouse? Has every inch been searched?"

"Inspector Gregson assures me that it has and the search is indeed continuing over old and new ground, even as we speak," Holmes confirmed, before adding, "There are actually three problems. You have overlooked the most important question of all. Why was he killed? Know this and everything else should simply fall into place."

Despite their keenness, the Fessingtons added little additional detail, save confirming the returning order of the men to the drawing room and adding a little more precision to the timings of each.

After the Fessingtons had returned to the drawing room, Greaves the butler kindly appeared with a tray of cooked ham, cheese and bread followed by young lady bearing cups, milk and, of course, a steaming pot of tea. My face lit up, but Holmes was singularly unimpressed.

"Watson, we have no time for interruptions, we must hear from all of the witnesses while their memories are still fresh and clear. Every hour that passes will blur and alter the witnesses' recollections as surely as any bribe or threat."

Dr. E & Mrs G. Pace

Grudgingly I put aside thoughts of refreshment and asked the serving girl to send in Doctor and Mrs Ernest Pace. Doctor Pace was in his fifties, below average height and slightly rotund. His face was quite large, a wide nose above a small mouth. His hair was brown but streaked with much grey, large side whiskers completed a three-sided frame that gave the impression that he was always peering out of a sort of window. His wife was petite, dark haired, with small, pale features and arrestingly black eyes. She wore her hair up, held tightly in place with myriad pins. Despite her elegant dress, she looked uncomfortable and sat nervously with her hands tightly gripped together.

"Good afternoon Doctor Pace, Mrs Pace. I hope you can help us by answering a few questions and giving as fine an account of the evening as possible," I asked as graciously as I could, despite having asked the same question numerous times already.

"Well, myself and my wife, Grace," began the doctor, "arrived shortly after seven. We were met by our hosts and shown to the parlour where we were offered a glass of champagne, Pol Roger I believe, a '78."

However, I heard little else he said, as I had, I am mortified to admit, been struck by a fit of childish giggles over the poor lady's name. Grace Pace. I picked up a napkin to cover my mouth and attempt to pass it off as a bout of coughing. I was growing rouge and close to bursting when Holmes showed, again, just how gallant and charming he can be if needed.

"Aha I see," he exclaimed with apparent delight. "A match made in heaven if ever there was one. Ernest Pace married Grace, an inspired and most poetic sounding match." He beamed at the couple, allowing me to regain such much-needed composure.

Mrs Pace was quiet, nervous and shy by nature, and I am sure that she cringed internally whenever reminded of her unfortunate name, but Holmes' seemingly warm and genuine compliments seemed to put her at her ease and defused an otherwise embarrassing situation.

I silently vowed to gift Holmes an ounce of his choice for saving me, and sat back to listen to Doctor Grace's account. He was a wonderfully precise witness and seemed to know everyone's movements down to the exact minute, but despite this we learned little new except for the fact the all of the previous witnesses had told the truth and had been as accurate as they could. The doctor also insisted on engaging me on topics ranging from my military service to the latest developments in surgery, a subject where I, shamefully, had to bow to the knowledge of a much older man, a country GP at that. Once again, I pledged to work harder to catch up with my increasingly fast-moving profession.

This left the last three suspects, the mysterious professor, but first, the odd couple, Wergeld and Fairchance. Unexpectedly, Holmes asked for them to come in separately, the widow first.

Mrs C. Fairchance

Mrs Clarity Fairchance was a fine, noble figure of a woman. Tall, spare and dressed in a dark, unfussy style. She was perhaps in her middle forties, her face was handsome, pale but unlined, giving the appearance of an ageless porcelain doll. Her eyes were a deep, dark brown, and this all added up to give her a rather stern appearance. It was impossible not to think of our own dear Queen when observing this lady, one also resigned to mourning in perpetuity.

"After previously showing little interest in socialising, what made you suddenly wish to attend this particular gathering at the Hall?" Holmes began, with little tact. "I know that you turned down several similar invitations when Harrison was newly resident here. What changed your mind?"

Mrs Fairchance looked visibly taken aback by Holmes' direct manner, and her face reddened as she replied. "You are very impudent, Mr Holmes, but in this case you are quite right. I live a solitary life, quite by choice, I must add. Ever since my husband passed I have felt no compunction to associate with the world, and I have no interests in its inhabitants. My husband left me his hard-earned, careful investments, which give me a modest, but comfortable income. There is also a summer house that I let from time to time."

"So, enter Mr Jude Wergeld." Holmes almost whispered the words. "And what do you know about your summer guest?" he asked, more brightly.

"I can see that you already know that it was he who convinced me to take up Mr Harrison's open invitation. He was charming, witty and very persistent, almost insistent. He said that he was from humble stock and had long dreamed of dining in such a place as Bedhurst Hall. But I appear to be telling my tale in reverse, Mr Holmes."

"Yes, do start at the beginning and please know that I appreciate your candour so far," Holmes replied, returning to his usual gallant and charming sincerity.

"It was only two weeks ago that Mr Wergeld knocked upon my door for the first time. He was smartly dressed, as you have seen, but he wore a great grey beard which he has since trimmed back somewhat. He said he was recently returned from the sea and desired a quiet place to spend the summer before returning to the Far East where he had several interests. He offered to pay for three months in advance, and I could hardly turn that down, could I?"

"Of course not," I said gently, before adding, "How did he learn about the evenings up at the Hall?"

"Well, he started attending church and had spoken to the vicar, several times. I suppose that is where he heard of them."

"And what of his character? Was he ever angered, or of violent temper?" Holmes asked.

"Not that I witnessed, but he was certainly physically strong. I once mentioned that a large tree branch had broken off in a storm and was obstructing access to the garden. He strode outside, hoisted it over his shoulder and carried it over to the shed, where he chopped it up as firewood. It must have weighed two hundred pounds, yet he lifted it as if it were a new-born baby."

"Most interesting," commented Holmes, leaning forward, his hands now together, fingers pointed and arched. "Has he received any visitors or communication, post or telegrams, while he has been at the cottage? Did he take a newspaper or write a journal that you knew of?"

"My, Mr Holmes, you do ask an awful lot of questions, I am very tired and my nerves are shredded by this terrible ordeal. However, I appreciate your good intent and will help as much as I am able. The answer is no, to all of your questions. I am sorry to report no visitors, mail or any behaviour that was other than helpful and courteous. He is a rough man by appearance, certainly uncultured, but always honest and straightforward with me. But, of course, I have to add a caveat, Mr Holmes. I have known him only a few weeks, so my opinion is of only limited value."

"Mrs Fairchance you have been an admirable witness and I thank you." Holmes gracefully dismissed the witness, rose and led her out gently by the arm.

Mr J. Wergeld

The mysterious lodger was the next to enter. Tall, well over six feet, he stooped to enter the parlour and stood obediently before us before Holmes offered him a seat. His face was browned by the sun and struck with deep heavy lines from hard weather and hard work. His features were squashed and indistinct, eyes deep set and dark from years of squinting at bright sunshine. This made it almost impossible to estimate his age, the ravages of years spent in harsh climates meant he could have been anything from forty to sixty. His hair started far back from his temples, a grizzled mass of grey and white swept backwards reaching well below his collar. He wore a thick, but trimmed, grey beard around a dark mouth, lips cracked and scarred by heat and drought. His clothes were simple but of superior quality, recently purchased and surely made to measure, considering the width of his shoulders and girth of his arms. He held his hat rather tightly, squeezing it out of shape with his enormous but stumpy looking hands.

"Mr Wergeld, good evening," Holmes began, for it was now after six. "Recently returned from the sea, a successful and profitable trip by the look of you. Decided to summer here alone before returning to whence you came. Please elaborate on what we already know, for your presence here as an outsider is going to be of considerable interest to the authorities and I will only be able to help you if your account is complete and honest."

Once again, Holmes' directness seemed to catch the witness unawares and Wergeld blinked in surprise, before quickly recovering with a barely concealed scowl.

"There is little more to tell. I grew up the East End and I did not have a bad life until cholera took my folks when I was but twelve years old. I spent the next four years in an orphanage before I left for the sea, learning my trade on various routes before settling down in the Far East in '48. I spent the next thirty years out there in Malaya, invested well in a rubber plantation, sold up and returned home. Well, it was home a long time ago, Mr Holmes. I have no family left here and no friends I care to seek out. It took only a few days to realise that there is nothing for me in England. Damn place is cold, unwelcoming and joyless."

"I was of a mind to return to the East on the first available passage but I heard, quite by chance, of a cottage for rent in a picturesque village just an hour north of London. I may not look it sir, but I do have some education and I have often entertained a fancy that one day I would write an account of my life, my struggles, my," here he paused, his gaze distant. "Ahem, my struggles and my eventual success."

"And you thought that a cottage in Bedden would be an ideal place for you to write this account," I agreed, approvingly. "Well, as an amateur writer myself, I have to agree that this is the perfect setting, both attractive and quiet, there is certainly little around here to distract a budding author."

"And what made you decide to leave this bucolic isolation and socialise with the landed classes up at the Hall?" Holmes inquired.

"Well, and this may well sound silly to the likes of you, but I have always hankered after attending a grand ball or feast at a real proper mansion or royal palace. Once I heard, at church, of Mr Harrison's monthly dinners and the open invitation he had given to my landlady, then I knew I finally had my chance. It may not be Windsor Castle, but it was more than I could ever dream of. So, I shamelessly spent every moment I could trying to persuade the Widow Fairchance to accept Mr Harrison's invitation, with myself as her guest."

The remainder of Wergeld's statement matched that of the other guests in almost every detail. Once finished, he waited, sitting bolt upright, until Holmes politely dismissed him, raising his substantial bulk and shuffling out of the room.

Prof. J. Seaworthy

Our final witness from the dinner party entered briskly and told his account with great energy and enthusiasm. Professor Jacob Seaworthy was an almost perfect witness, he confirmed the order of events, their timings and added many details and observations, even including a theory of how the murder might have been committed.

"Lianas!" he ventured, excitedly. "He grabbed a liana and strangled the poor fellow. Then he simply threw it into the fire, oh no that does not work, summer and all that, ah yes - he threw the liana back into the foliage. After all, what is it, a liana? Just more foliage to a searching police gentleman. Or, he buried it! Ha-ha! Have I got it Mr Holmes?" he positively beamed.

"Professor, you certainly have an inquiring mind," replied Holmes, "and your enthusiasm is commendable, although somewhat at odds with accounts of your character that I have previously received."

"Ah, Mr Holmes, I am a dry academic, more used to discussing Euclid than murder. I see a new puzzle rather than a dusty old equation of old. I cannot deny that it has, despite the sadness of the occasion, stimulated parts of my mind long laid dormant. I hope I have given no offence."

"Oh, far from it, Professor, an active mind is a disciplined mind," Holmes agreed. "However, I am sorry to say that I have to dismiss your theory, despite it being one that had also occurred to myself."

"Yes, I have to say that I also imagined this same scenario whilst in the glasshouse," I interjected. "But before I put my theory forward, I had to have a good look around and it was soon apparent that there were no lianas, or indeed anything similar, growing anywhere in the building. I even imagined the possibility of roots being used, but the ground was hard and undisturbed. There were no signs of anything having been dug up."

"Well said, Watson, so nothing was buried either. I need add only one thing. The ligament used was at least half an inch in diameter, no less. No root or tendril present here is of the correct size or strength to have been used in the murder. Nor has any carpet been de-threaded, no tapestry sliced, no human hair woven to produce the killing rope. It is none of these things. The method of murder is, so far, unknown to me." Holmes' eyes were cold and dark with steely determination.

I could see that Holmes' mind had moved on to other things and after a minute or so I apologised to Professor Seaworthy for my friend's sudden silence and said that he was free to return to the drawing room.

Seaworthy looked admiringly at Holmes, but said nothing. The Professor appeared to be strangely satisfied with himself. He rose, nodded politely to each of us, smiled, and left without saying another word.

Chapter Three - An Evening Inn

We sat in silence for a good twenty minutes. I dare not interrupt Holmes, he was totally motionless, in another place, analysing, calculating, speculating and deducing. He alternated between studying the police notes and staring into space. Although the only sound present was the tick of an ornate gilded ormolu mantel clock, I could somehow feel the pressure in the room steadily rising. It reached a crescendo when Holmes suddenly moved, reaching for a pencil and his sheaf of notes. He scribbled furiously for a further ten minutes, covering several sides of paper before calling loudly for a constable.

A moment later a young, fresh-faced lad appeared, his new uniform still slightly stiff from lack of wear. "Take this immediately to a post office. The details are all there, charge the wire fees to Inspector Gregson," he ordered. The young constable blushed but took the handful of sheets and left at speed.

"Are you planning to share your deductions with me, Holmes?" I asked, resigned to a negative response.

"Why, of course Watson. But not here and not right now. I must speak briefly to friend Gregson, then we shall return to the Inn for supper. I observed the local butcher leaving the Inn as we arrived and, judging by the fair being taken from his cart, I would wager that fresh suckling pig is on the menu."

Holmes did indeed speak to Gregson for several minutes and they agreed that the gathered witnesses could all return home. I overheard Gregson suggest that a plain-clothes man should be stationed by the outsiders' residences. Holmes agreed, rather reluctantly though, I thought.

We returned to the village in one of Harrison's dogcarts. The evening was warm and the sun had not quite set, its rays still sending out a warm golden glow that enveloped the trees and surrounding countryside. The hills and valleys appeared alternately pools of light and dark until we descended into tree-lined tunnels of darkness and finally into the village itself just as the sun dipped below the gentle hills.

An hour later, we were dining on delicious young pork with local vegetables, simple food but, in all honesty, as fine as many of the meals we were later to partake of in far more celebrated eateries.

"This is rather good actually, Holmes, don't you think?" I asked, trying to start a conversation.

"What was that, Watson?" Came the rather uninterested reply. "Oh, the food, yes, most pleasant, if a little plain." He returned almost immediately to his thoughts.

"Well, I am going to discuss the case, with myself if necessary, but please feel free to join in at any time," I declared, somewhat moodily. Holmes simply raised an eyebrow before continuing to poke at his meal, eating little.

"Is there anyone we can discount from suspicion? Or can we, at least, put them in some sort of order of probability?" I began, regardless.

"Starting from least likely, I would first suggest the vicar, he had no motive and he seemed to be a genuine friend of the victim. Then the Banks-Wells'. Again, there is no motive I can see, they already have considerable wealth and seem to lack any sort of ambition or imagination whatsoever. The Doctor and his wife do not seem capable of physically carrying out such an assault, neither the Professor. As for the Magistrate and his wife, I really cannot see them being killers, although I think we need to take a closer look at some of the Honourable gentleman's records, to determine whether he has ever crossed paths with Harrison in a legal capacity."

"The Professor seems to be a bit of an eccentric but otherwise harmless, hardly killer material," I continued. "Now we get to the ones that I believe demand further inquiry. The Colonel himself, of course, must be a suspect, he knows the house better than anyone else - but what does he gain from Harrison's death?" Then a sudden thought hit me. Embarrassingly, it was one that really should have occurred much earlier.

"Who stands to gain, who inherits the estate? Have the police located Harrison's will? Of course! Once we have the will we should have a much better idea of motive." I sat back, satisfied that I had made some progress, albeit by a somewhat circuitous route.

"Very good, Doctor, I commend you for finally imparting something of interest." Holmes finally broke his silence, rather acerbically. "A copy of the will has not yet been found in the house but we will have access to the original tomorrow when it arrives with Harrison's solicitor from London."

"I must also take issue with some of your reasoning. It is not generally a bad idea to rank suspects in order of probability, but only after you have gathered as much information as you possibly can. For example, you dismissed Wulf Fessington, but had you noticed his finger and waistcoat?" Holmes asked.

"No, I cannot say that I did," I replied, folding my arms, already resigned to the inevitable, but mild, humiliation that I knew would follow.

"The smallest finger on his left hand had a faint but visible band of lighter coloured skin where a signet ring had once sat. The third button on his waistcoat hung much lower than its companions, the thread having previously been stretched by the presence of a heavy gold Albert watch chain. What could these two observations imply?" he asked.

"That he had some sort of financial difficulties, and fairly recent ones at that, for the waistcoat has not yet been repaired." I was glad to add at least one observation of my own. "So, I agree, we cannot exclude him at this moment."

"Indeed, but I think you are probably right about some of the others."

Holmes was clearly enjoying this game of carrot and stick. I was more than happy to play along after seeing the manifest change in him, both mentally and physically, since leaving Baker Street.

"The Banks-Wells, unless actors of the highest calibre, have neither the wit nor the need to attempt such a complex crime. And as for the vicar, despite their well-known differences of philosophies, I have to agree with you, Watson, the friendship with Harrison appears to have been quite genuine and is backed up by all of the local witnesses."

"Unless we discover that he has unexpectedly left all of his estate to the church," I added mischievously.

Holmes smiled. "We will know for sure tomorrow."

After our meal, we retired to our rooms. We had secured adjoining rooms opposite a small upstairs communal sitting room. There we retired to have a last evening smoke, settling into the old but comfortable armchairs. As Holmes rubbed up some dark navy flake, I noticed an open file.

"Is that a list of the possessions found upon each member of the party?" I ventured, leaning forward to take a closer look. "Anything of interest?"

"There are certainly some points of interest." He handed me the papers. "But before I answer your question, cast your own eyes across the report from Gregson."

The report was simply a list of names, each followed a number of items. There was little of surprise to be found here, various keys, coins, handkerchiefs, watches and cigar cases on the men, jewellery, purses and embroidered reticules on the ladies.

"A strap of one of these reticules could have been used as a garrotte," I observed. "But, sadly, they would all be far too slim to be our culprit."

"Quite right, Watson, but there is no doubt that you are growing in ability, as you have inadvertently stumbled across the solution to an entirely different case that I worked upon many years before we met. You must remind me sometime to recount the story of the Brighton Heartbreakers. I believe you will, now, find the method of dispatch distinctly familiar."

"Other than that, there is very little of interest," I continued. "The vicar carried a small book of prayers and a rosary; the professor, a notebook filled with mathematical equations and a short pencil. Aha! What is this? It appears that you were quite right about Fessington. A chit from a bookie found in his pocket for five pounds, a wager on the Derby, the horse is Harvester. A good bet, from what I have heard, I have a little on him myself," I admitted, slightly embarrassed.

"Your knowledge of the turf may one day bring reward, but I fear that will not be today," Holmes chided, gently. "Does anything else not strike you as unusual?"

I flicked through the pages a second time. "Well, both Harrison and his friend the Colonel had almost nothing upon their person, just a couple of coins and rings, but that is hardly unusual as this was their personal residence, everything that they required would be close at hand, in fact I would suggest that it would be more suspicious if anything were to be found on them," I concluded.

"Once again, Watson, you sparkle with incandescent insights. But what about Wergeld, our visitor from far away climes?"

"Wergeld? He had little, a small bone-handled pocketknife, an old silver watch and chain, and a pouch of tobacco. Nothing unusual there, surely," I concluded.

"Not at first glance, but do you remember the murder scene, the tobacco on the ground?" Holmes took a deep draught of his pipe and exhaled, the coils, twists and turns of the smoke providing an elegant backdrop to his revelations. I nodded my confirmation and he continued. "I decided that this warranted further investigation, so I spoke to Gregson and he confirmed to me that the tobacco in the pouch was the same tobacco that was found in the glasshouse. But this was only the second most interesting fact that he shared with me."

"And the first? Come on Holmes, don't be a sphinx all the time," I implored.

"Wergeld's tobacco pouch was unusually large and contained at least eight or nine ounces of tobacco, dark and all recently rubbed up." Holmes sat back as if to let me absorb this revelation.

I thought a while before answering, slightly cautiously. "I am sorry, Holmes, but I don't see it. He is a sailor, they carry a lot of tobacco. They purchase it in bulk, often the cheapest available, for their long voyages. Surely he is just a creature of habit."

"Maybe if he were fresh off the boat or was living in less salubrious lodgings, but this is a man who claims an education and is staying here in a summer cottage while writing his memoirs. Why would he take a month's supply of tobacco, broken up and prepared to smoke, with him to a single evening's engagement?"

Chapter Four - A Silver Disservice

Tuesday 10th June 1884

The beds at the Inn were comfortable, so sleep came easily and after a dream-filled sleep I awoke, dressed and descended to the saloon bar for breakfast, only to discover that Holmes was already there supping upon a cup of dark coffee.

"Good morning, Holmes. I see you were up early. Let me see, by the look of your boots you have been examining the outside of the house and the gardens." I announced, rather pleased with myself.

"Quite right, Watson. And despite the local constabulary's best efforts, they haven't completely obliterated everything of interest."

I sat down and ordered rashers and eggs. "So, what did you find?" I inquired.

"Just what I expected. Nothing at all."

"Nothing?" I asked, rather surprised. "If you were expecting to find nothing, how is this of any help whatsoever?"

"Because, it confirms what we have been told. The windows and doors were all secured and there were no footprints in the flower beds, other than those of the gardener and these were faint and mostly obscured by the rain which fell the day before the murder."

"So, we can count him out," I agreed. "But what about the rest of the household, we have yet to hear from them?"

"Aside from the gardener there is Greaves the butler, two maids, a cook and a footman. A couple of girls and a lad from the village help out part time but none were present on the fateful night. We will interview the staff this morning. It is not a large household, so it should not take long, which is fortunate as I have to return to London this afternoon to follow up on some research."

"Sounds like you have other plans for me," I replied, as a large plate of bacon, eggs and local sausage was placed enticingly before me.

"Well, if you ever finish that feast, I would like you to remain here and keep an eye on things. Try to talk again to the witnesses, or, as we should start calling them, suspects. Make it seem casual, unplanned if you can. In a less formal setting they may be more open, forthright and willing to share. And, of course, make a note of any interesting or unusual behaviour."

I finished my breakfast and we took a police carriage up to the house. We arrived just as Harrison's solicitor was bidding farewell to Gregson. The Inspector held a manilla folder, which must be Harrison's will.

"Good day, Inspector," greeted Holmes. "I see from the brevity of your meeting that Harrison's solicitor had little to tell you."

"Quite right, Holmes," replied the tall blonde Inspector as we entered the house.

"Mr Williams, the solicitor for Mr Harrison, has supplied me with the original will," continued Gregson. "Williams was at pains to point out that he only met Harrison twice, once to draft the will and then again to sign it. He says that he knows nothing more of the matter and therefore begged that he could be excused to return to urgent business back in London."

"Most interesting," Holmes whispered, almost imperceptibly, before quietly adding, "I think I may have to pay another visit while in London later this afternoon."

We entered the living room, where Fauwkes was waiting, perched on a leather-backed armchair, leaning forwards in anticipation.

"The will itself is a simple document," the Inspector explained. "Apart from a generous donation to a seaman's charity, the entire estate of Mr James Harrison is to be left to you, Colonel Fauwkes."

Gregson waited for a moment to let this sink in. "Were you aware of the contents of the will, Colonel?"

"No, not at all. I had no idea." The Colonel seemed genuinely stunned and struggled to find words. "I knew he had no family, but I never expected - I never wanted, I certainly never asked," he stammered.

"Very good. Inspector, are the staff assembled for questioning, as I requested?" Holmes asked.

I think everyone present was surprised by this sudden change of tack, but Holmes had clearly already moved on from this revelation.

"Why yes, they are waiting in the kitchen. But do you not wish to pursue this matter further?" Gregson asked, subtly waving the will towards Fauwkes.

"Thank you, Inspector, Watson and I will be in the kitchen." Holmes smiled politely, left the living room and headed for the heart of the Hall.

"Well, Holmes, I thought there was more there to be investigated," I suggested, as we passed through the hallway and into the servants domain.

"Indeed there is, Watson, but not now and not here," he replied, enigmatically. "We have other business here to occupy us."

The kitchen was certainly light, a large range of windows illuminated a room painted white, giving the impression of almost clinical cleanliness. A large oven sat in a bricked arch at one end of the room and two white ceramic sinks lined the right hand side, just below the windows. A table for the preparation of food butted up to the white painted wall on the left. The black slate floor was a welcome relief from the, otherwise, uniformly bright decor.

The six regular staff were waiting patiently in a row. The Butler, two maids, the cook, footman and gardener. The interview was straightforward and surprising brief. The servants, apart from the butler, were housed in a separate building, about fifty yards from the main house, cleverly hidden by the slight drop behind the Hall. The maids and the cook were dismissed shortly after dinner. The gardener and the footman were already in their quarters, the footman waiting alongside the other guests' drivers for the order to take the guests home.

Holmes quickly established that each member of staff was alibied by at least one other, all within the servants' quarters. The maids and cook were still awake and chatting over a late night hot toddy in their small kitchen. The gardener, footman and the others were playing cards in the parlour. All were in the company of others until the alarm was raised.

As for the butler, Greaves, he swore that he was never in the glasshouse at all that evening but had left the dining room after serving the port and handed out cigars. The ladies back in the drawing room had confirmed that he arrived there not long after themselves and spent the next hour or so attending to their needs.

"Nothing to be learned there then," I declared, as we walked the short distance back to the Hall. Greaves followed a few yards behind. He was of medium height and carried himself well, his bearing a sure sign of his military past. He was perhaps in his late forties, but it was hard to tell as his face was mostly expressionless and ageless, his hair still thick and dark. His eyes were grey and seemed to stare mostly into the distance.

"Quite wrong, Watson," Holmes contradicted. "I learned a great deal though, sadly, I do not believe any of this new information will help us in our investigation."

"Come on, old chap, what on earth can you have learned?" I challenged.

"Greaves," Holmes turned to address the butler. "I take you are aware of the engagement between the footman and the maid, the younger, dark-haired girl, Mary, I think was her name?"

"Why, yes I do, but how could you possibly know, sir? They only announced it a week ago." He replied, quite stunned by Holmes' disclosure.

"I am afraid I have bad news for the poor girl. The marriage will never happen. I hope her friends will rally round to comfort her when this becomes apparent," Holmes declared, grimly.

"Holmes, whatever do you mean? This is really in rather poor taste, explain yourself," I demanded.

"Calm down, Watson, it is perfectly straightforward."

Greaves looked utterly bewildered, too shocked to speak. Holmes paused a moment before continuing.

"Did you observe the footman's shirt?" he began.

I nodded, "Yes it was rather dirty as I recall, but what of it? Nobody stays perfectly clean for long when dealing with horses and carriages all day. I just supposed that he had been working on a cart and wiped some oil on his shirtfront."

"So you did see it, Watson, but once again you failed to observe. What about the maid's dress?"

"What about it? I saw nothing unusual," I admitted.

"Two black marks on the back, matching those on the footman's shirt. One on each side, towards the top, where he had, well, I think you can imagine." For once, Holmes became rather sheepish, he was finally entering a field where he was far from being an expert.

"Blimey, you mean where he grabbed her-" began Greaves, suddenly reverting to his more earthy, non-commissioned tone.

"Tightly," I quickly interrupted. Greaves grinned while Holmes looked uncomfortable, I could swear that his face almost reddened.

"Most impressive Holmes, but why are you so certain that the marriage is doomed not to happen?"

"Because those stains were not oil. Greaves, have you recently cleaned the silver in the house?"

"Why, yes sir, less than a week past, in preparation for the monthly dinner, same as every month," Greaves replied.

"And did the footman participate in said cleaning?" Inquired Holmes

"No, it is not one of his duties. The maids and myself spent a whole afternoon at it. Hard work cleaning that much silver."

"I dare say it is, but if you now take an inventory I think you will find a good few pieces missing for, I fear, this is not the first time your footman has helped himself to a shiny treasure or two."

"So, the stains were?" I asked.

"Silver polish, Watson, distinct in colour and indeed smell. He had clearly been handling several recently cleaned silver items and his hands had picked up a residue. When cleaning large quantities of silver in a limited time, it is inevitable that some polish will be left behind. He had inadvertently, or carelessly, wiped this on the front of his shirt." Holmes finished with a flourish, drawing his hand across his chest, imitating the motions that the footman would have made.

"Well I never. Holmes, once again, I stand corrected, you have certainly learned a great deal, while I saw nothing." I admitted.

"Greaves, I suggest you wait until the rogue is out of his lodgings and then search his room with the aid of one of the local constables. Tell them to go easy on the poor maid as I am certain that she is blameless and completely unaware of her fiancé's nefarious activities."

Holmes dismissed a still visibly shocked Greaves, who turned and rushed back towards the servant's lodgings.

"That is one small crime solved, Watson, a nice hors d'oeuvres, if you will, but I now need to tackle the main course. I must bid you farewell, for now. I shall be back this evening, hopefully in time for an evening rendezvous at the Inn."

Holmes tipped his hat and set off towards the front of the Hall where a dogcart was waiting to take him to the station.

Chapter Five - Doctor Watson Investigates

It was only after Holmes had left, that I realised quite how vague the instructions he had given to me actually were. In truth, I was beginning to suspect that he may simply have preferred to visit London on his own and perform whatever research he intended without me to slow him down. It also occurred to me that, in the past, he had worked undercover, or in disguise, to gain information that otherwise would not have been available to him, so I resolved not to take offence or perceive any sort of snub. Holmes had developed, and followed, his own methods from long before we met and I was certainly in no position to question these in the light of his already formidable success.

Feeling a little more self-confident, I decided to head for the house to have a friendly talk with the Colonel, to see how he had adjusted to his nascent wealth. His reaction could be a useful clue as to any possible involvement in his friend's death. I prepared to report any unusual behaviour, which I knew would be of great interest to Holmes.

I entered the Hall, nodding to the reassuringly sturdy constable stationed outside the door as I passed by. The house was quiet and felt empty, the sparse style of decor only adding to the sense of sadness that now seemed to permeate its light, open spaces. The living room was empty, so I crossed back across the hall and through the parlour into the dining room. Finding this also unoccupied, I decided to take a quick look at the crime scene before venturing upstairs. I had begun to think that Fauwkes was not in the house at all, as I strode through the glasshouse full of its exotic flora, when I suddenly saw him, sitting on the very bench upon which his friend had been brutally slain.

He was sitting silently and unmoving, gazing out at the pleasant vista. A small cigar in his left hand had burned down to form a curving ash at least two inches in length. Some papers were lying on the bench next to him. I cleared my throat as I approached, causing him to stir and look round, the ash falling to the ground.

"Excuse me, Colonel, I didn't mean to startle you, my apologies," I said, gently.

"None necessary, Doctor. I must confess, though, that I was miles away, in a quite different place and time," he replied, with a weak attempt at a smile. "How can I help you?"

"I am just following up from yesterday's interviews," I said, trying to be as honest as possible. "Sometimes a witness will recall things later that they did not record in their earlier statements. Have you perhaps thought of anything else that might be of assistance?"

"I am sorry, but I cannot think of a single thing that occurred that evening that I have not already told the Inspector or yourself. There is, however, something that I have subsequently discovered that might have some bearing on the case." Fauwkes' pale face and black eyes spoke of exhaustion and sleepless nights.

"Please tell me everything, all information is useful, no matter how trivial it may at first appear," I replied, trying to quote Holmes as best I could.

"Actually, what I discovered is far from trivial, but I cannot as yet gauge its importance." The Colonel picked up the papers and gestured that I should sit beside him.

"After discovering the contents of Harrison's will, I was certainly shocked, but I soon realised that I had to pull myself together and start to come to terms with my new position and its responsibilities. So, naturally, I started to examine his papers to learn what I could about the Hall and its management. These were kept in a safe in his private office upstairs, in a room adjacent to his bedroom. I also wanted somewhere secure to keep the will, as it appears now to be the only copy. Harrison had always shared the combination with me just in case, he said, anything should happen to him. I now begin to wonder whether he did have some premonitory sense that his life was in danger. Anyway, I opened the safe and placed the will upon the topmost shelf and looked through the papers already there. This is when I made my discovery. You see, I knew that Harrison had various bonds and share certificates, which he kept in this safe, for he had shown them to me on several occasions, railway shares, government bonds and other investments from all around the world. However, this morning, when I opened the safe, many of these were no longer present. All of the government bonds and most of the share certificates were gone."

"That is most interesting, indeed," I declared, making notes with the short pencil that I kept in my inside jacket pocket. "When did you last see these documents?" I asked, desperately trying to imagine what Holmes would have asked.

"About six months ago, I think. Yes, I happened to be present when he opened the safe to take out some cash to pay the staff wages. I am sure that they were still there on that occasion. Whatever he did with them, I suppose I will just have to accept, move on and trust that he knew what he was doing."

"Thank you for your candour, I am sure this information will be most helpful."

It seemed to me that Fauwkes saw the loss of such valuable assets to be more of a point of interest than a personal financial loss. I had not considered him a serious suspect even before this and now I had even less reason to think him anything other than a grieving friend.

I thanked the Colonel and made my way back through the Hall and out onto the drive. I decided to walk the two miles into the village. I had no fixed appointments with any of the other suspects and, as I had the whole day to occupy, I thought a stroll would give me time to think about what I would ask, should I actually encounter any of them.

As I strolled down the road, through the arches formed by the overhanging trees, their branches hanging heavy with newly grown leaves, I tried to decide which of the suspects I should try to interview. I decided upon the Professor, Fessington, Wergeld and the Widow Fairchance, and rather than try to plan my questions in advance I would simply engage them in conversation and hope that, like Colonel Harrison, they proffered any additional information they possessed, voluntarily.

Happy with my simple plan, I upped my pace and reached the village in less than forty minutes. It was then that I realised that I had made an enormous error. I had singularly failed to ascertain the location of any of the suspects' residences. I stopped dead in my tracks and was fully prepared to have to walk back to the house to ask the constable, when I had a much better idea.

Before me lay the village green and on the far side was the Inn. It was a low, squat, sprawling building. It had obviously grown over many hundreds of years, each later addition butted up to its older neighbour, nothing quite matching but somehow all coming together to form a pleasing, organic and most importantly, welcoming tavern. This is where I would head first, after all it was now well past midday and a sandwich and glass of beer appealed greatly to me. And besides, if there was any local gossip to be learned, this would be the place to provide it.

I entered the public bar and was slightly disappointed to see but two other patrons, both aged, and I recognised neither. The landlord was his usual friendly self, so I ordered some bread, ham and pickles and sat at the bar, hoping to learn what I could from him.

"I do not mean to pry, but is there anything that you can think of that might help us regarding the terrible events up at the Hall?" I asked, quietly.

"Oh, I don't know nothing about that, I'm sure," replied the landlord, rather unconvincingly.

I pushed a sovereign across the bar for encouragement. The landlord, a Mr John Barnes, was local, born and bred. As I had previously learned, the Inn had been in his family for several generations. He took the coin and pocketed it without a word.

"Maybe the gentleman would be more comfortable in the saloon?" he hinted, with little subtlety.

He picked up my plate before I could reply and shifted it to the adjoining bar. I followed, passing back through the hallway and into the saloon bar on the opposite side.

"Well, what can you tell me?" I asked, completely ignoring the plate before me.

"There is much talk abroad regardin' the Hall. Talk of the master and his resident houseguest. Ungodly talk, but I pay no heed to such gossip. Mr. Harrison was a fine man, generous to the village and everyone in it. He revitalised Bedden, gave it its life back. He and the Colonel made this little place a heaven on earth for a brief time, everyone had work and a place to live. But there was always the talk."

"What talk was this?" I enquired, most earnestly.

"Bad talk sir, talk of improper behaviour between the men of the Hall. But I never gave it a second's thought, myself."

I was beginning to see the germ of a motive for the murder of Harrison that was entirely new.

"Was there any particular person in the village who was perhaps more vociferous in their condemnation of this alleged offensive behaviour?" I asked, carefully.

"Ha!" he exclaimed. "You'd be better off asking who was not offended. In public they were all in favour of the benefits Harrison brought them, but here, after a drink or two, the truth was very different."

"Do you think any of them would have gone so far as to actually act upon this ill-feeling?"

"I don't think so. Their bravado came solely from the ale and they knew that they could only suffer from such a terrible action. I have thought long and hard myself and cannot believe that any local could be responsible for this outrage. In fact, I now fear for the future of the village."

I finished my sandwich and, having obtained directions to where the Fessingtons and Mrs Fairchance resided, stepped outside into the warm sunshine. My head was slightly spinning, I could not decide if

I had discounted a number of suspects or discovered dozens of new potential murderers. I badly needed Holmes' counsel.

The Fessingtons had a large house at the far edge of the village. While it was considerably further from the Inn than Mrs Fairchance's cottages, I felt that the walk would help to clear my head. I passed alongside the well-kept village green and its charming duck pond, then continued until I joined the lane that lead north past various cottages and alms-houses towards the Fessingtons' villa.

After about ten minutes of good fresh country air, a gentle breeze and the warning sun, my mind had settled and I had reached a conclusion. I could now really appreciate Holmes' ability to stay calm and trust to logic and reason. My initial reaction to what the landlord had imparted had been almost entirely emotional - worry and panic. This had achieved nothing more than a spinning head and a rather childish impulse to reach out for my friend's help.

But now, after thinking the matter through logically, I believed I could, from the information provided and the evidence collected, dismiss this new strand of inquiry. Holmes was convinced that no one, other than guests and staff, had entered or departed the Hall on the night of the murder. I conceded that it was possible that a member of staff had let an assailant into the house through the back door used by the servants to access their accommodation. I would have to take this up with Holmes later, but as far as I could see, this would be a particularly difficult trick to pull off, as the servant's door enters directly into the kitchen where there was always at least one other member of staff present. And, in any case, the murder was committed in the glasshouse, which was locked to the outside, and was occupied only by our existing suspects.

Satisfied with my reasoning, I approached the Fessingtons' house in a confident mood. It was a good-sized, two-storey building built of attractive golden brown brick in the early years of the century. It was set back from the lane and sat before a fine garden full of young flowers, deep green shrubs and emerging roses. The entire front of the house was covered in wisteria, flowering abundantly in gorgeous hues of lilac and purple.

I knocked upon the door and was slightly surprised when Mrs Fessington herself opened the door.

"Good morning, I am sorry to call unannounced but I was wondering if I may have a brief talk with yourself and your husband?" I tried to be as polite as possible, as I was fully aware that, despite their earlier candour, they were under no obligation to help me in any way or even agree to speak with me.

"Why, Doctor Watson, of course, please do come in." Mrs Fessington broke into a wide smile, clearly pleased to be once more involved in the mystery. I was led through a tiled hall and into a smartly furnished sitting room. Wulf Fessington appeared, almost instantaneously, from the door on the far side.

"Doctor Watson, it is a pleasure to see you again. I must admit that I was reading in the garden and spotted you approaching. How can we help? Do you have any news?" He seemed just as eager for information as was his wife.

"It is still very early in the inquiry. I am sure that as soon as anything is discovered the authorities will inform you," I replied, trying to tactfully deflect their enthusiastic queries.

I did my best to extract any further information that they might have, but I was rather hamstrung by the fact that they seemed as intent on interrogating me as much as I was on questioning them. I struggled, initially, as I was not prepared to share our findings with them but then decided to change tack slightly and brought up the landlord's concerns.

"Harrison and the Colonel's private life is just that. Private," Wulf Fessington replied with unexpected but admirable defiance. "He that is without sin among you, let him cast the first stone," he quoted, sagely, from the gospel of St. John.

"Doctor Watson," he continued. "I myself am not without vice," he declared, waving away his wife's protestations. "I have lost a considerable sum through gambling. I have sought, and am now receiving, help and my wife is fully aware of the situation. I say this to you to prove my total openness and honesty and knowing that, as a Doctor, you will honour my confidence. I have paid my debts and, thanks to my loving Catherine, remain solvent and in work. You see, Doctor, I need you to know that, despite my shortcomings, I had no motive to kill my friend and had no way of profiting from this terrible crime."

I thought for a while before answering. "Thank you, sir. It is a brave thing to admit one's faults and failings so candidly."

I could not help but admire this man's courage and all thoughts of him being the killer fell away.

"I hope you continue to be successful in your recovery," I added, before making my excuses and leaving, content that I had reduced the pool of suspects by one.

Chapter Six - A Bad Night's Work

It was late afternoon when I reached the sprawling estate of the Widow Fairchance. The main house was set back from the road by about twenty yards, the front garden so overgrown that the property could easily have been missed altogether. The house comprised of a single storey, with a couple of attic windows poking out from behind the abundant clematis and wisteria, which clung tightly to the walls in a rather uncomfortable looking embrace. To the right was a large and ancient barn, almost fallen to ruin. From the front of the property, I could not see the summerhouse but, to be honest, from my position I could not determine exactly the full extent or borders of the property at all. The entire area was dense with excessive growth and the visible outbuildings were all in a terrible state of dilapidation.

I edged my way along the path towards the front porch and rapped loudly upon the dark wooden door. After a few minutes, the door opened, just a few inches, and I spied a white face and a single eye of the deepest brown.

"My name is Doctor Watson, you may remember me from last night up at the Hall. I am helping the police investigate the awful events of that evening. I am terribly sorry to trouble you, as I appreciate that you have been questioned already, but might I please inquire as to whether you have had any further thoughts or perhaps remembered anything that you have not previously recounted?"

I asked this question without lengthy introduction, in the deliberately straightforward fashion that I had learned from Holmes. The idea being that the witness would have no time to prepare a deceitful answer and would perhaps let slip a truth that otherwise, given time to compose themselves, might remain hidden.

"Of course I remember you, Doctor," Mrs Fairchance replied, quietly, as she fully opened the door and gestured that I should enter.

She led me through a dark hall and into an equally funereal parlour where she turned to address me, hands clenched tightly before her.

"I am sorry, but I really have nothing else to recount, I have told you all I know."

"Do you live here alone? Have you no servants? I asked, already suspecting that she had none, having answered the door herself.

"To be honest with you, Doctor, all I have is what little it takes to maintain this house. If I brought in outside help, I think I would wither and die from ennui. When my husband died, half of me left with him, quite possibly the better half. I live simply, waiting for the day when I will be reunited with him."

"You have my deepest sympathies, madam," I replied. "But did you not, earlier, state that Mr Wergeld had charmed you into attending the evening up at the Hall?"

"Oh Doctor, I am by no means perfect. He is indeed a charming man and I did agree to attend the dinner, although without any thought of impropriety. But that matter has now passed and I will no longer be troubled by Mr Wergeld."

"Why is that?" I asked.

"Because he has left, of course," was her startling reply. "Did you not know?"

After Mrs Fairchance had told me all that she knew, I quickly left the house. I was in a panic, how could this be? Had Gregson not insisted that the suspects, especially those who were not local, were to be watched at all times? I desperately needed to speak to Holmes. As I walked back into the village, I tried to imagine what my friend would have done in this situation.

What were the known facts? Well, Wergeld had left early that morning, before Mrs Fairchance had risen, and taken all of his possessions with him. Where could he have gone? If he was leaving for good, as he surely was, then he must have made his way to Bedford and caught a train from there. I realised that there were only two ways he could have made the six-mile journey - by carriage or on foot. I was certain that the police would have noticed if he had left in a cab, having somehow acquired one from somewhere in the village, so that meant that he must have walked. He would have probably set off several hours before dawn to avoid detection. It would have taken more than two hours, at a fair pace, to reach Bedford, but he could have still caught a train as early as seven or even six o'clock that morning. I sighed. He really could be a hundred miles away by now, or even already aboard a ship heading back east. That left just one question, but it was by far the most important of all. Why had he left in such a hurry at the dead of night? The answer now seemed obvious. He was making his escape.

The early evening sun had turned the centre of the village into a delightful bowl of golden-hued stone, umber thatch and a soft, mottled light, which reflected off the still waters of the pond. As I approached the village green, I spotted Inspector Gregson in conversation with a sturdy constable who sported great black mutton chops.

"Inspector, I have some urgent information," I announced.

"If it is regarding Wergeld, then we already know, Doctor," he replied with a deep sigh. "After having not seen him all day, supposing him to be inside the cottage, the constable watching over him left it until late in the afternoon before finally taking a look into his rooms. So, the villain has a good ten or twelve hour head start. I fear, Doctor, that we may have lost him for good, and with him, any chance of solving this confounded mystery."

"I have a terrible feeling that you may well be right, Inspector. He could already be at sea by now, or at least holed-up in London, Southampton or even Liverpool," I replied in agreement.

"Have you heard from Holmes? Although, I doubt that even he can help us now. Maybe he could explain why Wergeld killed Harrison and how he did it? I am certainly no closer to answering either of those questions myself," I admitted.

"I sent a telegram to Baker Street an hour ago, maybe somehow it will reach him, but I fear that this case will forever be a black mark against my name and that of the whole police force. The public do not like unsolved murders, particularly those of decent citizens, slaughtered in their own homes," sighed Gregson, morosely.

At that exact moment, a man on horseback galloped into view and thundered towards us, stopping abruptly just a few feet away in a cloud of dust and a hoarse bellow from a pair of exhausted equine lungs. A young man jumped down from the saddle and held out a sheet of paper.

"God's teeth!" swore Gregson, before quickly recovering. "It is young Holder, the lad I sent to Bedford with the telegram for Holmes."

"A reply sir, it came just as I was about to leave Bedford to return back here," said the youth. "I had just been giving Apollo, here, a treat for making such good time, when a man came runnin' out of the post office shouting and waving this message. I saw the first word - 'Urgent' - so I rode like the wind, made it here in no more than twenty minutes, I reckon."

"Excellent work, well done lad," replied Gregson, kindly, clearly impressed with the lad's riding skills. He took the telegram from his outstretched hand and replaced it with a couple of shillings. The now smiling Holder led his horse away, steam rising from his dark but slick flanks - certainly a fine beast and very aptly named.

"Urgent," Gregson read out aloud. "W and G return to London immediately (abbreviated) have JW under surveillance (again abbreviated) W bring SR. Well, I understand the first part of course but what is your SR?" asked Gregson.

"Service revolver," I replied, darkly. "Once again, I believe Holmes is several steps ahead of us all."

Chapter Seven - The Shipping News

Gregson quickly secured a light two seater Gig and we set off for Bedford as fast as we could. We just made the eight o'clock train and sat in nervous anticipation as the darkening countryside whipped past us. We arrived at St. Pancras almost exactly an hour later, and there, a realisation struck me. Holmes had not specified where we should meet him. Gregson agreed with me that we should head to Baker Street as that was from where Holmes had sent his message. We stepped out onto the Euston Road, hoping to find a cab in the growing darkness, when suddenly we heard a voice cry out.

"Ahoy! Ahoy! Over here!"

I looked towards the source and saw to my delight, illuminated by gaslight, Holmes waving from a four-seater carriage, just ten yards opposite. We rushed across the street and climbed aboard before setting off at a goodly pace.

"Time is now our enemy, gentlemen. We must find Wergeld before he leaves the country," Holmes announced. "I have learned much in a short time, but I have also had to rely on others to try to keep track of this miscreant."

"So you knew he was the guilty party before you left?" I asked.

"Not exactly, I still had several theories and suspects in mind when I left for London but, on the balance of available information, he was certainly the one who most attracted my interest."

"He is certainly an odd cove, that's for sure, but what made you suspect that he might be the killer?" asked Gregson.

"When a man lies once, he becomes a person of interest to me. When he lies repeatedly, he becomes a suspect. As a dear friend across the water once said to me, 'when you tell the truth, you don't have to remember a thing'. Wergeld lied and lied again."

"First, he claimed to have made his fortune in rubber in Malaya," Holmes continued. "As of this day, there are no rubber plantations in Malaya. Coffee abounds, and is far too profitable a crop to be replaced with any other in the near future."

"Then there is the matter of his name. 'Wergeld' or 'weregild' was the Saxon term for 'blood money', which was to be paid to the family of a murder victim. This may seem innocent enough in itself, but what if I were to tell you that not a single man in all England is known to have this for a surname?"

"A fake name, of course. It did strike me as rather unusual, but I just assumed it was foreign or perhaps from one of the more remote regions, such as Northumbria or Cornwall," said Gregson.

"I have no doubt at all that this name was not chosen at random," Holmes declared. "I believe it may contain a clue as to the reason for the murder itself."

"Blood money? I fail to see how the rogue made any profit out of this act," I said.

"Not quite, Watson. While the Wergeld is indeed, quite literally, a payment for a crime, I believe this man has, in his mind, made Harrison pay for a crime or injustice in a different, more deadly and utterly final way."

"What crime could this have been? I have to say that this case just seems to become more complex at every step, each time we answer a question, several more new ones spring up before us and take its place," sighed Gregson.

"Far from it, Inspector, the case becomes clearer by the hour. I need only a few more pieces to complete the puzzle, but I believe Wergeld himself is the only one who can provide these. We must find him quickly, if he leaves the country all may be lost."

"I thought you had someone watching him?" asked Gregson, his tension growing visibly by the second. He seemed to have aged several years in the past couple of days and he now appeared grey, drawn and haggard.

"I did, but the lad lost sight of him just after he reached the East End by cab. I should have put at least two boys onto him, Wiggins and another. See, Watson? Another foolish mistake, caused by inactivity of the mind!"

"But, surely, we have him, Mr Holmes," declared Gregson, brightening suddenly. "He is heading for the docks, I must get to a Police Station or Post Office, I will have fifty men on the docks within half an hour!"

"That's the spirit, Inspector!" laughed Holmes. "Cabby, take us to the nearest Police Station and quickly!" he commanded, banging his cane on the roof. "The Post Offices will all now be closed, of course. Now, Watson, please recount all that you have learned from your investigations today, back in the village. I can see from your expression that there is much to tell," he added.

Within ten minutes, Gregson had sent his message and we were rushing along Great Eastern Street, heading toward the docks. The mood had brightened considerably. Gregson was staring expectantly out of the window, while I was perched on the edge of my seat. Holmes sat silently, sphinx-like, his eyes peering into the middle distance, as I told Holmes every detail of what had occurred earlier in the day. Once I had finished, he made no comment but simply remained completely still, concentrating silently on thoughts I could not even begin to imagine.

"I have instructed my men to check the shipping agencies to determine which boats are leaving this evening. I have told them to drag the agents out by the scruff of their necks if they protest about the hour. We will soon know where he is heading." Gregson's face appeared keen and youthful once again.

We thundered down Leman Street, Holmes had promised the cabbie a sovereign if we reached the docks within half an hour and he meant to earn it! I am sure I saw sparks fly from where the metal rim of the wheels ground against the cobbles as we took a corner at a seemingly impossible speed. I feared the carriage would tip over, but the driver appeared to possess an almost unnatural skill in high speed driving, and kept us on the road and in one piece.

"My word, Holmes, I could quite believe that this cabbie was a chariot racer from ancient Rome in a former life," I managed to blurt out above the cacophony of clattering hooves and the iron-rimmed wheels flying over the cobbles.

Holmes broke, momentarily, from his apparent trance. He grinned, "Do you really think I chose this cab randomly? This is Bob Watkins, finest cab driver in London, ex-jockey and formerly employed as an escape driver by the city's most successful bank robbers."

A further lurch to the right pushed me back into my seat, where I remained, holding on to the window ledge as tightly as I could manage. It was with a sense of considerable relief that we finally reached the riverside, halted, and could step down from the still heaving cab and onto solid unmoving ground.

"The Malay Star and Contessa II are both scheduled to be leaving for the east this evening," Holmes announced. "But these are of no interest to us."

Holmes looked at our surprised faces. "Well, he is hardly going to return to a home that exists only in his own falsified history, is he?"

"It would have been remiss of me not to check up on which ships would be setting sail for the east tonight, but I believe he is heading south, towards Africa," Holmes explained. "There are three ships sailing for there, tonight. However, many more will be heading to the continent, aboard any of which he could reasonably find passage. We must not discount these vessels, as Wergeld may well take one of these to try to shake us off his trail and then change, once he arrives on the continent, for a longer haul vessel."

"That makes things much more tricky. In effect, we have to search almost every ship leaving port both tonight and tomorrow morning," Gregson replied, resignedly.

It was not long until the police began to arrive and in large numbers. Gregson and Holmes devised a search pattern based upon the shipping agents' information. Two police steam launches blocked the river about a mile upstream, so no vessels could slip by in the darkness. All ships bound either for the continent or Africa were thoroughly searched, Gregson even ordered inspections of those heading east, just in case Holmes was wrong about Wergeld's intended destination.

Wednesday 11th June 1884

Dawn broke in fine scarlet rays, and a bright blue sky slowly rose above London's stinking shipyards. Gregson sat upon a large iron capstan barking out orders to dark navy clad constables, Holmes was nowhere to be seen. We had found nothing. Wergeld was not aboard any ship that had set sail that night, he appeared to have completely vanished. I strolled along the riverbank feeling utterly useless in the face of such bustling industry.

"Watson, I am a fool, a blunderer and much worse!" Holmes had snuck up behind me and I flinched in surprise.

"Holmes, whatever do you mean?" I replied, quite perplexed.

"I have made a colossal error, one which I may not be able to repair. I have underestimated our quarry and that is unforgivable."

"Underestimated? How?" I asked.

"We have an image of our foe, Watson, but it is an image which was entirely constructed by the man himself. A sailor, a farmer, a decent, simple man. However, I now believe, in fact I am certain, that he is none of these things. After all, what do we really know of him, actual verifiable facts?"

"Well, erm, not much, I suppose," I struggled.

"Three things, Watson. One, he lied about his background, so we have no idea who he really is. Two, he ran from a murder investigation, a clear sign of a guilty conscience to most observers. And finally, three, if he is the killer that we suspect him to be, then he is a most clever and resourceful individual, as he has done away with his victim in a way that even I cannot currently explain."

Holmes looked at me directly, face to face, "Watson, this man is deeply intelligent and devious and has thrown us a blind. But I now see it. Gregson!" he shouted. "Bring me the records of boats leaving for Southampton and Liverpool."

I suddenly understood what Holmes had deduced. Wergeld had taken a boat, not to his final destination or even to mainland Europe, but to another English port, from where he would then catch an entirely different ship to wherever he wished to go. This, of course, brought up a frightening possibility. From whichever port he had landed at, he could have left for any one of a thousand destinations, far too many for the police to monitor. He had gone.

Gregson had passed on Holmes' order and now approached us.

"We'll soon have that information, Mr Holmes. On the down side, it will probably be largely guesswork and hearsay, as domestic routes are neither registered nor recorded. However, such trips are relatively rare these days, as the railways and canals transport the bulk of inland cargo. A passenger would certainly be noticed and remembered."

"Some good news at last, however small." I breathed on my hands to try to gain some warmth. The morning air was chilly, despite the bright sunlight.

"It occurs to me, that if we knew where Harrison himself had travelled to all those years ago, we might be nearer to knowing where Wergeld is heading. The two must surely be connected, now that we more than suspect him of being the killer. After all, from where else could they have known each other?"

"Once again, Watson, you cut through the gloom with your sword of light," smiled Holmes, kindly. "I am hoping to hear, shortly, a reply to an inquiry I made earlier today upon that very subject. There are many records for my allies to search through, but we should be able to ascertain the destination that both men set out for, sometime around 1848."

"Both men? You believe they might have travelled together?" asked Gregson.

"It is a possibility which I favour, and it would certainly aid us in our identification of the real Wergeld, but, of course, it is equally possible that they met each when they were both already overseas," Holmes replied.

"And from where did you divine the year 1848?" I asked.

"From Wergeld himself. It is the year he supposedly 'settled in the east'. The year itself is more than likely to be true, even if the location is a deliberate lie," Holmes explained. "This is a man of rare intelligence, he knows that the best lies always include some truthful details, it makes them far easier to remember."

Holmes then clapped his hands. "But now it is time for contemplation and refreshment. Inspector, will you join us for a breakfast at Baker Street? I can assure you that Mrs Hudson lays on a fine spread, which it appears you are sadly in need of. Besides, important information may have arrived in our absence."

Our return to Baker Street was considerably more civilised than our departure from St Pancras, and within an hour we were feasting on eggs and hot bacon washed down with strong coffee, courtesy of the inimitable Mrs Hudson. Once finished, Holmes and myself filled our pipes, while Gregson was treated to one of Holmes' Petit Upmanns.

The sweet smoke from my mixed Cavendish, allied with the crisp, intense scent of Gregson's Havana, managed to overpower Holmes' acrid black smog, for once giving the apartment a pleasant air, with curls and wisps of smoke picked out by the sunlight now streaming through the large windows.

"I have a question, Holmes." Gregson broke the silence, and the spell, by leaning forward and disturbing the gently swirling smoke. "What made you think that Wergeld would be heading south?"

"A fine and valid question, Inspector. I based this pronouncement upon something I had observed back at the Hall. You may remember the austerity of the decor, but what stood out to me was a small, but very noticeable, collection of African artefacts. There were seventeen small statues and four masks, all of West African origin. I learned more of their provenance earlier today, when I sketched a few examples from memory and presented them to an expert at the British Museum. This, along with what I had deduced from Wergeld's statement, gave a more precise direction to my subsequent investigations and narrowed the search for Harrison's mysterious travels down to a manageable area and timespan. West Africa, sometime between 1845 and 1850. Still a monumental task, but one I am hoping will shortly bear fruit. Once I have this information, I can move on to the final witness, confident that I have enough evidence to make them capitulate and give up the rest of the story. For, make no mistake gentlemen, there is much more to this tale than just a squalid, heartless murder."

I looked towards Gregson and he appeared just as surprised as was I at these revelations. Holmes had clearly been busy here in the capital. We smoked on in silence for a while until fatigue hit hard and I excused myself and retired to my rooms for a much-needed sleep. Gregson curled up on the couch under one of Holmes' enigmatic, unexplained, but beautifully embroidered oriental blankets - "a gift from an old client, from a rare case in which all parties prospered."

Just after ten o'clock, we were woken by the arrival of a telegram. Holmes was, of course, first to react and already had the paper in his hands by the time I entered the sitting room. Gregson sat upright, bleary-eyed, but expectant.

"Ha!" announced Holmes, "It is just as I thought." He handed me the telegram.

"1848, August, Borundia," I read aloud. "Just three words, but they do seem to confirm your theory old man. The date and the destination. Borundia, the small West African state. Hallo? Wait a minute." I paused to think. "The date, of course. It looks like you might have been right Holmes, 1848. That is the year Wergeld gave for his supposed resettlement in the east. It looks like they may well have travelled together after all."

"More detailed information will arrive shortly, I insisted that any discovery be sent immediately by telegram the moment it was found. We will soon have the exact dates that Harrison left England and arrived in Africa, along with the ship's name and, most importantly, its complete roster. We will know the real names of everyone who was aboard that ship, including, I now firmly believe, Mr Jude Wergeld."

Chapter Eight - The Ambassador

The ship's manifest arrived half an hour after the telegram. Wiggins handed the sheaf of paper over to Holmes who simultaneously slipped several coins and, rather unexpectedly, two notes into his dirty young palm as reward.

"Usual share rules, the notes are for the agents," Holmes instructed, seriously, before addressing the papers. "Good work deserves good reward, don't you think?" he declared.

"Yes, of course, but I cannot promise that we can cover such expenses, Mr Holmes," replied Gregson, sheepishly.

"Do not worry, Inspector, the work is its own reward, I rarely profit from my investigations," Holmes replied, his eyes fixed on the pages before him. I sighed and nodded in agreement, there was little chance of us ever prospering financially, mainly due to Holmes' unique way of charging or, rather, rarely charging his clients.

"It looks like we are in luck, gentlemen. The vessel was the packet ship, 'Africa Gem', the only regular mail and supply ship from London to Argentville, the capital of Borundia. A reliable and sturdy ship, by all accounts, but one with a passenger capacity of just thirty, ten in cabins with the remainder in steerage. Harrison is recorded as having travelled below decks, so I think we can assume Wergeld did likewise."

"So we have nineteen names to investigate," I stated.

"Fourteen," Holmes corrected, as he read further. "Five were women, and even better, Watson, we also have the ages of all the passengers. Two were under sixteen and can be discounted as being too young. One was just eighteen, so also very unlikely to have been Wergeld. Of the remaining men, six were thirty or over. My highest estimation of Wergeld's age is sixty, a thirty-year-old back then would be sixty-six now, so we can also reasonably discount these. That leaves just five names."

I could feel the intrigue and tension grow as Holmes whittled his way through the list. "A twenty year old would be now fifty-six, so we should prioritise the younger of the five remaining men, those closest to their early-twenties. That leaves just two names."

"Ha! Fortune is indeed shining upon us, Watson, for the final two names are Csaba Kovács and Thomas Shiner. Did Wergeld strike you as being particularly Hungarian? No, of course not, so we now finally have a name to investigate, one that may well be our quarry. Inspector, tell your men to stop searching for Jude Wergeld, we are now looking for a Mr Thomas Shiner."

"But where do we start, Holmes?" I asked. "Surely we know even less about this Shiner character than we did about Wergeld."

"Gregson, you must send a wire to the embassy in Borundia - ask them to search their records and interview their staff for any information regarding Mr Shiner." Holmes then turned to address me.

"You see, Watson, we have now gained three distinct advantages that we did not have previously. Firstly, tracking down information on a real man is far simpler than one whose very name is spurious. Secondly, Shiner does not know that we have discovered his true identity. This may give him a sense of impunity, making him feel relaxed and therefore slowing his flight. And thus, thirdly, I believe he will have, by now, reverted to using his real name. He believes it gives him anonymity and is, of course, an identity he no longer needs to fake. Not having to continually remember his false identity dramatically reduces the chances of him slipping up, making a mistake and revealing himself."

"And if this Thomas Shiner turns out not to be Wergeld?" I asked.

"Then we start again with a new theory. We should shortly be able to ascertain whether or not Shiner is in the country. If he has remained in Africa then, of course, this line of investigation would be spent. If he did indeed travel back to England in time to be present at the events of the past few weeks then he must surely be our man."

"Borundia is a small country," Holmes continued, "A French possession, I believe, is it not, Watson? Geography is more your territory."

"Yes, it is one of the smaller West African states and has been a part of France for at least two hundred years. I do not think it has ever been British, a fact that should aid us immensely, Holmes," I added brightly. "There cannot be too many Englishmen in the country and those that are there will surely tend to gravitate together in clubs and communities just as they do elsewhere."

"Very good, Watson, this should hopefully speed up the reply to Gregson's inquiries. What else do you know of the place?"

"Very little. The capital, and only sizeable town, is Argentville, on the L'Argenté River. I would imagine then that silver plays some part in the economy," I concluded.

Holmes ignored my attempt at sarcasm. "I must return to the city to pursue a lead that grows ever more interesting. Inspector, please report back here the moment you receive any new information. Watson will be here until at least lunchtime. Good morning, gentlemen."

Holmes had retrieved his hat, coat and cane and was through the door before I could protest. Gregson shrugged, smiled and bid me farewell. I sighed and settled down with my pipe to await further instructions. Within five minutes, I was sleeping soundly in my familiar chair, my freshly filled pipe lying unlit on the floor beside me.

The doorbell failed to wake me and only the hard rapping on the apartment door roused me from a deep sleep. The telegram was placed hurriedly into my hand and the boy seemed to vanish mere seconds after I had dropped him a shilling. I yawned and called down to Mrs Hudson for some coffee to try to revive my senses. The mantel clock informed me that it was nearly midday. I then, finally, examined the message.

It was from Gregson, "Ex Amb C J-B has info. TS well-known in B. Left Apr 1884 for Eng." The meaning was clear, at least the second part. Shiner had been in Borundia up until April this year, at which point he had returned to England. Holmes was right, he must be our man. The first half would take a little research, the former ambassador to Borundia was obviously the man to talk to, I just needed to look him up in Holmes' reference books.

It took less than ten minutes to identify Sir Christopher Janus-Bennedict, formerly Her Majesty's Ambassador to Borundia. From studying the short biography, it seems that there was an untold story, perhaps a scandal, behind his record of public service. Starting off in the Far East, he had quickly worked his way up to the lofty position of Ambassador to Sweden before being suddenly sent to Borundia, without explanation. Quite a fall from grace, and one from which he clearly never recovered, as he remained there for nearly twenty years, finally retiring from public life in 1880, some four years ago.

I left a note on the table for Holmes and replied to Gregson's telegram, telling him of my plans, in case he encountered Holmes independently. Feeling much more useful than I had before, merely acting as Holmes messaging service, I left Baker Street, hailed a cab and set off for the leafy north London suburbs and the home of the former British ambassador to Borundia.

After just over a half hour, I reached the house I was seeking. Built from sturdy red brick, and of fine proportions, the former ambassador's house was slightly conspicuous in the neighbourhood as it was considerably larger than those that surrounded it. Set amongst modest but very well kept gardens, it appeared the very model of a fine middle-class English house. I walked up the drive, the familiar and reassuring crunch of yellow gravel beneath my boots, and knocked upon the deep burgundy stained door.

A tall gentleman of about fifty years swung open the door. He was spare, balding and his large nose rather gave him the appearance of an elderly stork. By his manner and attire, I Immediately took him to be the butler.

"Good afternoon sir, how may I help you?" he enquired, staring down his long nose.

I introduced myself and explained that I had been sent by Inspector Gregson of the Metropolitan police on a matter of extreme urgency. The butler waited a few moments, then his head seemed to wobble slightly as he finally appeared to make up his mind. He gestured inside.

"Please come in sir, you can wait in the sitting room. I shall inform Sir Christopher of your presence." He led me inside the hall, which was festooned with all kinds of paintings, prints, textiles and artefacts, all of which appeared to be of African origin.

These items were almost universally bright and colourful, giving the hall an exciting, joyful atmosphere. The sitting room was, if possible, even brighter. Brilliant, red-painted walls had been covered with all forms of African paraphernalia. Paintings, masks, and coloured wall hangings seemed to cover every available inch of wall. I tentatively took a seat upon a familiar looking leather couch.

After several minutes, the door opened and in walked a figure that widened my eyes and made my jaw drop. Sir Christopher, as I imagined it had to be, held his arms wide open and bellowed a greeting in what I assumed to be a local West African dialect, "Jamm nga yendoo!"

Momentarily shocked, I simply blinked, open-mouthed, in return. Sir Christopher wore a one-piece kaftan, extravagantly embroidered and coloured with bright, geometric patterns. He was a little over five feet in height, with a surprisingly thick head of white hair. His face was deeply lined from years in the unforgiving African sun, but his blue eyes shone brightly with energy and his demeanour was one of a man many years younger than his sixty-nine years.

"Doctor Watson, please forgive me, I get so few visitors these days and I have always enjoyed a rather theatrical entrance," he grinned widely. "You say you are on a mission of great importance, please let me know how I can be of help?"

He sat down upon a rather garish chair directly opposite, one which appeared to have been tailored from zebra skin.

I explained the situation as simply as I could, emphasising the link to Borundia. After about ten minutes, I had shared all that I knew.

"First, please follow me." Sir Christopher suddenly rose and walked out of the room. I jumped to my feet and followed him swiftly through the hall and back towards the kitchen. He strolled confidently inside and stopped to observe the scene. A cook, two maids and a single unoccupied man were present in the kitchen. All were African, and all stopped and turned to watch us as we entered.

"Good day to you all, please carry on as usual," he signalled to his staff. "Kutu and Adama are general maids, Mandiki is the most wonderful cook I have ever encountered. Banta here is my Jack-of-all-trades, gardener, builder, plumber and confidant. A better group of help, no man could ever dream of." He raised his hands to encompass all of those before him.

"And yet, I have a problem, Doctor. One which, I am sure, the famed Mr Sherlock Holmes could solve in an instant or maybe his esteemed assistant could help me?"

Sir Christopher's tone had changed, subtly. It seemed that he was now demanding proof of Holmes' abilities and, by association, my own, before he would agree to help us.

"Sir, I am here on a matter of extreme urgency. A murder has been committed and we believe that you could be of material assistance to us in the investigation," I replied, firmly. "Furthermore, we do not perform upon request, ours is a serious business, sir."

"I do apologise, Doctor, I merely wished to see for myself the magic that you perform to solve the impossible." Sir Christopher blushed and appeared crestfallen.

"Well, I suppose it would not hurt to at least hear of your problem," I replied, realising that I had to keep this unpredictable character on my side. I silently swore that his knowledge had better be worth this charade. I knew for certain that Holmes would have refused to perform like this and would still somehow have left with all of the information that he required.

"Oh thank you, Doctor. Well, you see, the problem is really very simple. I am a lover of cheese and have been so long out in Africa, where it has been impossible to obtain anything other than the local bland goat or sheep variety. Now I am back home, I can indulge in the flavours of a hundred cheeses, all freshly imported from the surrounding counties. However, my enjoyment has been tainted by the loss of almost a quarter of my stock."

He paused, and then continued in a whisper. "Someone here, one of my servants, is stealing my cheese, and in large quantities. I dread to accuse any of my staff, but I know, deep down, that one of them must be the responsible party."

He looked at me with such a pitying face that I almost left the house there and then. The man was unstable and child-like, possibly suffering from a degenerative illness of the mind, yet I still believed he might have information of use to us.

I took a deep breath and looked around the room. I thought about Holmes and the techniques he would employ in a situation such as this. Observe, do not simply see. I looked carefully at each servant in the room and at their surroundings, then back at them again. Nothing, just normal people in normal clothes, I resigned myself to failure and the knowledge that I would never have even a fraction of the abilities of Sherlock Holmes. I turned towards Sir Christopher to announce my failure when something struck me, very faintly.

I smiled and suggested that we return to the sitting room. After we both sat down, Sir Christopher asked, "I can tell from your expression that you have an answer for me." He clapped his hands and beamed at me like an expectant child on Christmas morning.

"Oh please, Doctor, forgive my manners, you must have a drink before the great 'denouement'." He pronounced it in an utterly affected way, but I now had no choice but to play along.

I accepted the proffered brandy, which proved to be far finer than I had expected. Sir Christopher seemed to wink as I nodded in appreciation of the fine amber liquid. I was beginning to suspect that I was in fact watching an elaborate and deliberate act put on for reasons I had yet to ascertain. Again, I knew that Holmes would have seen straight through this charade, but I could work only with the modest abilities with which I had been gifted.

"The solution is actually extremely straightforward, sir," I began. "By observing the available evidence there can only be one culprit. I also believe that you are already quite aware of the identity of this thief, but I will come back to this point later." I tried to sound as authoritative as I could, and if I could also take some of the wind from his sails, then all the better.

"Your man of many talents, Banta, is wearing a dark brown leather belt. He is currently using the very last notch, a hole that has clearly been punched through long after the article itself was made. The other holes are uniformly sized and spaced, and all are lozenge-shaped. The last one is rough and more circular, the result of some quick work with a bradawl. It is also a good half inch further along the belt than the other holes, the result of a swiftly expanding waistline. The notch with the most wear from the buckle is actually the one two holes back, which shows just how quickly the owner has gained in girth. Only a major change in diet could cause such a weight gain. A large and sudden intake of rich cheese would be a definite suspect."

I waited for a moment to let this sink in, but then deliberately continued just before Sir Christopher could react. "This brings me back to my former observation. When a man quickly puts on weight, the fat accumulates mainly in two places - the stomach, as we have seen, and the face. While it is unlikely that you share Sherlock Holmes' ability to notice a weight gain of less than half a pound, I am very confident that anyone with functioning vision would notice if their close associate had gained at least two stones in weight. So, enough with this nonsense and tell me what you know regarding this case." I finished by rather theatrically draining my glass and placing it firmly back upon the side table.

The change in Sir Christopher was as surprising as it was immediate. His face relaxed, the colour seemed to drain from his cheeks and his almost permanently manic grin was replaced by a troubled frown. I almost believed, just for a second, that the bright colours surrounding me suddenly all faded at that exact moment. In front of me, aside from his unusual clothes, now stood a sober and serious looking man, the very image of a retired civil servant.

"Doctor Watson, I must apologise most sincerely for my behaviour up to this point. I cannot, at this time, fully explain the reasons behind them, but suffice it to say that there are other forces at work here in London that require me to be extremely wary of strangers. I have deliberately created this image of benign eccentricity and incompetence to keep away prying eyes and ears." He poured another drink for each of us and handed a glass to me, his eyes appearing to have now transformed into steel-blue sharpness.

"Doctor," he continued. "I am actually well aware of the work of Sherlock Holmes. The next time you call here, or indeed elsewhere, you might do better to mention his name or indeed your own, rather than that of the official police," he managed a weak smile. "If you had done so, I would have been far less suspicious. Does he ever really introduce himself as an agent of the police?"

"No, actually, he does not," I confirmed, my cheeks beginning to redden with deep embarrassment. It was dawning on me that I was actually dealing with a man whose intelligence was on a level far closer to Holmes' than to my own.

Sir Christopher seemed to sense my shame and quickly spoke.

"Doctor, please, we are all inferior intellectually when in the presence of the Holmes's. I have read your accounts and I have been singularly impressed with your own contributions to the cases, despite your constant literary self-deprecation."

I wondered, briefly, as to why he had mentioned 'Holmes' in the plural? I was sure that it was not a mistake, but Sir Christopher continued with hardly a pause, giving me little time to dwell on the matter.

"I was ambassador of Borundia from 1860 until 1880, for my sins. You see, I had previously held a similar position in Sweden, a great honour indeed. A major indiscretion with a minor prince led to my downfall and subsequent relegation to Borundia as a punishment, or at least so they thought." He smiled, without guilt, throughout this admission.

"I felt particularly aggrieved, as I have always acted first and foremost as an agent and informant for England, using my influence, position and even my proclivities only in the interests of my Queen and my country. Despite my fall from grace, I still had some supporters back here in England who aided me throughout my time away. When I returned, I was swiftly re-employed in a role that more suited my abilities, but my public disgrace was never lifted as it continues, sadly, to provide the greatest cover one could ever wish for."

"A man of my, leanings, is always somewhat of a target and a liability. I could be bitter over my treatment, but I choose to continue to serve my country because I believed it was the right thing to do then and I still believe that it is, even now." His face was proud, defiant. "I am also a man of some means, Doctor, I have never needed to take up the salary to which I have been entitled to at any of my appointments."

"But, yet again, I digress. Let me continue. Of course, I felt pretty dreadful about my new posting at first, but I soon discovered that Borundia was a wonderful place in which to live and work."

He paused to refill his glass - I politely declined, but took out my notebook and pencil as I hoped he might, finally, be close to imparting something relevant to the case.

"The country is poor, of course, but there is no starvation and little disease," he explained. "The river creates a fertile valley with plenty of good land for farming, we were actually exporting food by the time I left. The biggest irony is that despite the name of the capital, and indeed the major river, no silver has ever been found anywhere in the country. The local saying is that there is 'less silver here than in a pauper's cutlery drawer'. It is all a myth built upon the observations of some of the first European visitors. Upon navigating the river upstream they observed that the 'sunlight shimmered upon the surface of the water like liquid silver.' And from such a story, a thousand fruitless treasure hunts were launched."

"Every year, a handful of prospectors would arrive. Despite the warnings of both officials and locals alike, they would head off into the wilderness clutching worthless title deeds sold to them by unscrupulous dealers back in Paris or London. Some returned exhausted after a few weeks but most were never seen again."

"Those that survived to return attempted to find employment to pay for their passage home. This was always difficult as the only work available was manual and the pay barely enough to feed and house them. The French ones sometimes found work with the military, which gave them a chance of an eventual return home. We did what we could for the British, but we had few resources and no money to speak of."

"But Borundia is a small, tight-knit country, Argentville even more so. Half of the population knows each other personally, and all of the Europeans know each other intimately. I arrived in 1860, full of trepidation and ignorance but, within a few weeks, I had come to realise that I was living amongst the most friendly, peaceful and generous people I have ever encountered. I soon found that my hitherto essential talents for duplicity and covert activities were now worthless here. People meant what they said and did what they promised, without exception. Life was difficult but simple, if you worked hard, you could enjoy a basic, but fulfilling, existence. I settled down and slowly forgot all about London and its eternal political machinations."

"I was soon on first name terms with most of the British community in Argentville, but was only on passing terms with Harrison and

Shiner. Having arrived some ten years previously, they had bucked the trend and managed to scrape a living up in the mountains, returning every few months with a bag or two of semi-precious stones. They were conspicuously guarded about the location of their camp and never allowed anyone to travel back with them."

"This all changed after a few years. They had saved enough to buy a small house and, more importantly, a relatively modern fishing boat. This enabled them to finally earn a decent income, by local standards, and were soon employing several locals to keep up with demand. Within six months, they had moved to separate lodgings, mainly because Shiner had become engaged to a local girl, Sarah Hardcastle. She had lived her whole life in Borundia and remained even after the deaths of both of her parents. She had a small inheritance and lived simply, teaching at the local school. Remember, I was still fairly new to the country at this point and most of this information came to me from other sources, much of which I learned well after the actual events."

"Now we enter a slightly murky period. The known facts are few and what follows is all I know for certain. Shiner and Hardcastle were married in September 1852. Just over a year later, in December 1853, the new Mrs Shiner was dead, lost in an accident whilst out walking along the coast. Harrison left Borundia for good, three months later. Shiner stayed but he was now a broken man, a hard drinker and an occasional troublemaker. His business remained successful, run now by a hard-working group of local men, so he still had a regular income, although most was lost either on drink or the paying of fines for his various misdemeanours."

"Over the years, less and less was seen of Shiner until he finally sold his business and villa and moved into an old farmhouse in the interior where he remained, living mostly alone for the remainder of my appointment and beyond. That is the absolute limit of my knowledge on the subject." Sir Christopher let out a little sigh and sat back, relaxing as if a weight had been lifted from him.

"Thank you, Sir Christopher, for such a detailed and candid account. I must be honest with you and admit that I will have to think for a while about the possible implications of what you have shared with me. I see one obvious possibility, but it seems to ask as many questions as it answers, and then there is, of course, the long period of time between these events and the present. I think I should return to Baker Street and try to get a message to Holmes."

I looked down at my record of the meeting and saw that I had covered maybe half a dozen pages in hastily scrawled notes.

"Doctor Watson, it has been a genuine pleasure to meet you. I hope that by opening myself up and laying the intimate details of my life before you that I have gone at least some way to make up for my initial misrepresentation, rudeness and obstruction. I sincerely hope that we meet again, in fact it may already be fated," he finished, enigmatically.

"Thank you, Sir Christopher, I am certain that the information you have provided will be of great use to our investigations. And on a personal note, I honestly believe that you have served your country with selflessness and great dignity."

I shook his hand warmly and left the singular residence to find that he had kindly, and somehow without any obvious communication with his servants, arranged for a Hansom to be waiting right outside. I smiled as I climbed aboard, Sir Christopher was clearly a man of many talents and one that I sincerely hoped to meet again.

Chapter Nine - Setting Course

I reached Baker Street just after half past two, ran up the stairs and burst into the sitting room. I was surprised to see Holmes sitting in his chair, smoking an unfamiliar looking briar.

"Watson, you look flustered," he stated. "Please sit, relax, take a brandy. Fill your pipe and tell me all that you have learned. I see that your visit to Sir Christopher has yielded much that is new to you, please recount all, spare no detail."

I spent the next half hour going through everything that had happened since I received the telegram from Gregson. At certain points, I swear that I could see Holmes nodding in agreement or raising an eyebrow, most notably when I mentioned Sir Christopher's unexpected use of the plural of 'Holmes'.

Once I had finished, I looked expectantly at Holmes for his response. He put down his pipe, arched his fingers and his eyes glazed over as he entered a state of deep thought. After a minute or so, he responded.

"Watson, you have done remarkably well. You might have learned more, but you failed to press for the gossip and conjecture surrounding Mrs Shiner's unfortunate demise, as there would surely have been at the time."

I sighed, resignedly at the compliment swiftly snatched away.

"But, Sir Christopher has, without a doubt, supplied us with the motive for this crime," Holmes continued. "The murder itself was simple revenge, Watson. What is less simple is that which remains to be determined, what made Shiner believe that Harrison was responsible for his wife's death, why it took so long to take his revenge, what suddenly prompted him into committing the crime and how was it carried out?"

"These are all questions that I rather thought were better left to you, Holmes," I replied. "And anyway, where have you been all morning?" I asked, somewhat churlishly.

"I have paid a visit to Harrison's solicitor, a Mr Caerwyn Williams, we saw him briefly at Bedhurst Hall. I was never entirely satisfied with Mr Williams' behaviour. He was evasive and appeared overly keen to leave Bedhurst as soon as possible, somewhat unusual behaviour from someone who had serious and continuing obligations regarding Harrison's estate. He also held the only copy of Harrison's will, something that seemed to genuinely surprise even Fauwkes."

"And what have you learned?" I asked, tapping out ash and refilling my bowl.

"That solicitors are intransigent to the point of deliberate equivocation, even when threatened with obstruction of justice. Even a telegram, sent by our old friend Lestrade directly from Scotland Yard, failed to elicit any information which he had not already divulged."

I could sense Holmes' obvious frustration and inwardly resigned myself to a long, painful afternoon in the bad company of an irate Holmes. However, as he relit his briar in a cloud of questionable aromas his mood seemed to brighten.

"As I was making no headway, I decided to return at a later date, preferably with the backing of the authorities, and transferred my energies to the more urgent matter at hand, that of the apprehension of Thomas Shiner. I met up with Gregson at Scotland Yard to see if the regular police had made any progress in tracking him down."

"Gregson had not been idle and had wired every major port to be on the lookout for Shiner, hoping that he had indeed reverted to using his real name. There had been a couple of promising looking leads but they were soon discounted and it was certainly looking pretty bleak for a while. But, sometimes, simple hard work is more effective than deductive reasoning."

"In a short period of time, we had assembled an enormous amount of data regarding the schedules of ships bound for West Africa from all British ports. We had now also added those from the major European ports. This was the point at which I realised that we were approaching the problem from completely the wrong way. It was an error which may have already cost us our quarry, although Gregson still holds out hope that if Shiner does reappear in Borundia, the French authorities may agree to his extradition. I am more doubtful, as without a confession we would be hard pressed to convince a judge here, or more importantly in France, that we have enough evidence to be reasonably confident of getting a conviction.

Remember, Watson, we still have no proof that Shiner is guilty, we cannot even say how he committed the murder."

"But what of the testimony of Sir Christopher?" I interjected.

"Hearsay, conjecture and gossip," Holmes waved a hand, dismissively. "That is how it would be labelled in court. No, if we do not get him before he leaves the country, then I truly believe we shall have lost him for good."

"But wait a minute, Holmes, what error is this that you refer to? I can see nothing that we could have done any differently."

"The most efficient way to locate Shiner is not to start from his last known location." Holmes ignored my look of dissension and continued. "No, we should have begun at his expected destination and worked backwards. Once I had realised this, I swiftly determined that there were only six ships leaving English or European ports headed for West Africa in the next two days. We are watching all of the local ports closely but simply do not have the resources to stop and examine every vessel heading across the channel. There are four ships planning to leave from the continent, one from the Low Countries, one from the south of Spain and two from Marseilles."

"I think you are onto something here, old chap. The Low Countries are the closest to England, which would allow him to attain some level of safety as soon as possible. Conversely, southern Spain would mean a shorter sea voyage. Marseille is a large port and easily reached within forty-eight hours. When do the ships leave?"

"Very good, Watson. Valencia is scheduled to leave in about," he checked his watch, "fifteen hours, so we can certainly count it out. That leaves us with Marseilles, the first ship leaving from there has a similar issue, but the second is a definite possibility and, finally, the Dutch port of Flushing."

"And when is that ship planning to leave port?" I asked, excitedly. "And why on earth are we sitting here smoking when we could be on Shiner's trail?"

"Eight o'clock tomorrow evening, after the stand of the tide. The second boat from Marseilles will leave about an hour later. The reason we are still here is that we have yet to determine which route he will be taking."

"That is as maybe, but would we not be better off being rather closer to one of these two possibilities, across the channel, at least?"

"I appreciate your enthusiasm, Watson, and I have, of course, booked us passage upon a fast steamer to Calais at seven this evening. But we still have some time before we need to depart and new information could arrive at any time."

I left for my room, packed a small bag for the journey and returned to the sitting room to see Holmes grinning broadly, brandishing a fresh telegram.

"It is Marseille, Watson. News from Gregson, he has managed to contact the captain of the ship in Flushing. He states, categorically, that no passengers are allowed on his ship. He transports building materials and fertilizer, has a spartan crew and confirms that he has no space above or below deck for any additional voyagers. In fact, now that he is aware of the situation, he has promised that he will detain anyone asking for passage and even return them to England for us, if requested."

"Well, maybe he will do the job for us," I said, hopefully.

"I fear Shiner is far too intelligent to fall into such a trap, however convenient it would be for us all. He would make discreet enquiries first and then head south as soon as he discovered that passage aboard this vessel was impossible."

"So, either way, he will have a large head start on us," I replied, glumly.

"Which is of little matter, as the ship, *Le Hêtre Pourpre*, will not leave Marseilles until ten tomorrow evening. Our paths will converge at that point and at that time, at the absolute latest," Holmes corrected.

"But what then?" I demanded. "We cannot arrest him in France, we have no authority to detain him, let alone force him to return to England."

Holmes did not reply, as he was furiously scribbling onto a sheet of paper. He opened the door and shouted for Mrs Hudson. When she appeared, he offered her the paper and instructed her to have it wired to Gregson, immediately. He then rushed to his room and stuffed a few items into his overnight bag.

"Come, Watson, we must be in Marseille as soon as we can." He was smiling and his eyes shone like sunlight on polished metal.

"You have a plan, don't you Holmes?" I barked, as we rushed out of the apartment.

"We may yet bring Shiner to justice in England, but now we must hurry," was his short reply.

Chapter Ten - Across The Channel

We quickly found a cab, rushed across town and within an hour were comfortably ensconced in a South Eastern Railway first class carriage. Green fields and orchards slowly replaced the dark gloom of London as we sped through the aptly named 'Garden of England'. Holmes was silent throughout the journey, which allowed the gently rocking carriage and the metronomic sounds produced by the rails to coalesce and ensure that I was soon in a deep sleep.

The early evening sun was still warm and the sky a deep blue as we arrived at Dover station. I yawned and followed Holmes out of the carriage. We made the steamer with minutes to spare and spent most of the crossing admiring the sun slowly sinking towards the diminishing white cliffs behind us. I found something to eat and washed it down with a swig from my hip flask. I offered the flask to Holmes, who shook his head silently. When he finally spoke, it was only to confirm our ongoing travel plans.

"We will arrive in time to catch the 9.30 train to Paris via Lille. I have wired ahead for rooms close to the station, but we will not be settled much before two in the morning. You would do well to get as much rest as you can, Watson, tomorrow will be a very long day."

We arrived in the dull, grey port of Calais just after nine o'clock and walked the short distance to the station in the dying rays of the sun. We found an empty first class carriage and were soon underway on the Chemins de Fer du Nord, trundling through the darkening, nondescript, flat northern French countryside. I expected a repeat of the silence that had marked the entire journey so far, but suddenly and unexpectedly, Holmes began to speak.

"Watson, do you know the best time of day to burgle a house?" he asked, quite seriously.

"Well, I don't know," I stammered. "Perhaps midnight? No, later, maybe two or three, the early hours I would say."

"Certainly the most common response, but quite wrong, of course. Why on earth would you try to gain entry to a property at the exact time when you can almost guarantee that the occupants would be present?" Holmes was clearly enjoying imparting this little lesson upon me.

"Well, yes, I see that now," I admitted. "So, if I reason correctly, then sometime during the working day would be better. At least then the man of the house would likely be absent."

"Much better, Watson. Mid-morning or mid-afternoon would be my choice. Those are the times when the staff are most likely to be running errands and also the times when deliveries are made and tradesmen tend to call."

"The greatest house-breaker I ever knew," continued Holmes, "was a man named Finch. He would arrive at his intended target in the middle of the day dressed as a common workman. He would carry a six-foot ladder and a bag full of tools. His genius was not in employing any great skill or knowledge, but in learning how to use regular, innocent-looking, everyday tools to gain access to his victim's abodes. If questioned, he always appeared to be a genuine tradesman, no lock-picking tools, jemmies or such-like were ever to be found upon his person. He also limited his activities to maybe once per month so the regular authorities were never even close to ever apprehending him."

"But, I take it, from your intimate knowledge of his methods, that you were the one to finally bring him to justice," I responded, somewhat less than convincingly.

"Stow you cynicism, old chap," Holmes smiled, most surprisingly. "I certainly confronted old Finch and indeed eventually convinced him to retire, but not until I had employed him in a capacity that earned him the greatest payday of his life, not to mention aiding in the recovery of the greatest piece of art ever created."

"Why, that's incredible Holmes," I spluttered. "You have to tell me more," I demanded, but I had already seen the change in his expression, he would elucidate no further, at least not on this day.

I settled back and tried to attempt some deduction of my own as I lit a small cigar. Holmes was already sucking on one of his awful pipes, this one so black, I could not even determine whether it was a briar or a clay.

I thought for a long while, but having singularly failed to add anything to what we already knew, and still having no idea as to what Holmes was planning, I gave up and decided to simply enjoy my smoke. My mind drifted from the real remembered rooms and gardens of Bedhurst Hall to the imagined sun-bleached coast of Borundia. From the mixed collection of characters that we had interviewed, to the poor victims of this egregious affair.

The change at Gare du Lille was smooth and simple, despite the major construction work that was still underway at this time, and we were underway upon the second leg of our journey within half of an hour. Holmes had spent the intervening time in the telegraph office, writing furiously right up until the moment the train began to move. As the whistle blew, he rushed out of the little office, sprinted along the platform to the carriage, pulled at the door handle, opened it and jumped aboard in one fluid movement. Throughout this incredible display of agility, his face remained as calm and unmoving as ever, not a flicker of excitement or a bead of sweat crossed his stony visage. He sat down without a word, studying what appeared to be several telegrams, just a selection of those that he had somehow arranged to have delivered to various points along our journey.

Stuck for anything else to do, I spent the next three hours or so attempting to determine a method of capturing Shiner that would be both practical and above all, legal. I knew that Holmes had a plan, but I could not fathom what it might entail, or if we really had any chance of success in the twenty-two hours or so that we had left before the *Hêtre Pourpre* departed for Africa.

Thursday 12th June 1884

We pulled into Gare du Nord not long after one o'clock. We shuffled wearily off the train and along the deserted streets to our nearby hotel. It was a grand old building, but I had little interest in its aesthetics at that point. We headed swiftly to our rooms and once there I merely washed the accumulated grime of travelling from my hands and face before falling into bed and almost instantaneously into a much-needed sleep.

Holmes had calculated that the quickest route to Marseilles would necessitate us catching the six o'clock train the following morning. This meant that I had slept for barely three hours when I was awoken by the knock of the liveried young man delivering my pre-arranged breakfast. I ate and dressed hurriedly, before settling the account and meeting Holmes outside, where he had already acquired a carriage for the three-mile journey across town to the Gare de Lyon.

While buying tickets, I also bought, rather on impulse, a guide to the French railways. I wanted something to read on the journey and, despite it being in French, I believed I could make at least some sense out of it with what little I knew of the language. Holmes was again sending and receiving messages right up until the guard's whistle. Once aboard, we found a quiet carriage and settled down for the long journey to Marseilles. We would not arrive until after four in the afternoon but, being unable to act in the meantime, I could see no way that any plan of Holmes', no matter how ingenious, had any chance of success. The man himself sat in silent contemplation, a state I was already beginning to find singularly annoying. His eyes were half-closed and I could now observe how dark and fatigued they appeared. His face was even paler than usual, clear evidence that he, as I had suspected, had not slept at all the previous night.

"Holmes, you look dreadful, try to get some sleep. We have a ten-hour journey ahead of us and you cannot affect events until we arrive. In addition, I am certain that some rest would actually improve your faculties and greatly improve your chances of solving this entire mystery." I tried to make this last point as forcibly as I could, hoping to appeal to his sense of logic.

"In many ways you are indeed correct, old chap," Holmes replied, in unexpected agreement. "I shall indeed attempt a short repose."

He sat back, closed his eyes and folded his arms. Within a minute, he was breathing slowly and deeply and giving all the signs of being asleep.

I sighed, shook my head and picked up my guidebook. How he could simply switch off like that astonished me. I read for the next few hours, slowly working my way through what I could understand of the book. I knew that the French railways had begun rather slowly, a direct result of the aftermath of defeat in the Napoleonic Wars, but had grown exponentially over the next fifty years, until their scope rivalled the best of the rest of Europe. As I struggled to understand the current ownership structure of the various regions and routes, we sped past small villages, fields of wheat, grapes and livestock then, later, through forests that seemed to stretch for dozens of miles.

I learned that the railways south of Paris were now known as the PLM, the original name, 'Chemins de fer de Paris à Lyon et à la Méditerranée', having been deemed rather unmanageable. The line we were travelling on, Ligne de Paris-Lyon à Marseille-Saint-Charles, was the major artery south from Paris and, as such, was always busy, as was evidenced by the crowded lower class carriages, even on this early train.

I must have dozed off shortly after these rather insignificant revelations, and the book fell onto my lap. It might be of some interest to know that this very same guidebook was used on several further adventures over the following ten years or so, and became an essential item to take with us whenever we crossed the channel.

The train stopped for coal and water at Lyon, where many passengers disembarked, only to be replaced by a similar number of new travellers. The hustle and manic activity lasted for about half an hour, before we finally departed upon the last leg of our journey.

It was now afternoon and I could feel the temperature begin to rise steadily as we steamed south towards the Mediterranean. By three o'clock, it was so warm I had to remove my jacket and slide open a window to allow a cooling breeze to enter the stuffy cabin. It was only after I had let in the fresh air that Holmes finally stirred. He opened his steely grey eyes and stretched his back and arms.

"Watson, you were quite right. The rest has invigorated me and refreshed my mind," he declared. I was not entirely convinced that he had actually slept at all, but at least he was resting.

"By the height of the sun and the growing heat, I would calculate that we are no more than an hour from Marseilles," said Holmes, looking out of the window. "Now it is time to let you know exactly what each of us must do once we arrive."

Chapter Eleven - Marseilles

We left the warm shade of the carriage and stepped out onto the platform into bright sunshine and a veritable wall of hot air. I loosened my collar and tie while Holmes appeared not to notice the heat at all. Once outside the station building there was at least a gentle sea breeze, which made the atmosphere more bearable. Holmes, yet again, headed for the nearby post office to send and receive his secretive correspondences. I was under strict orders to head for the port itself and find a restaurant or bar from which I could observe the ship upon which all of our hopes rested.

The *Hêtre Pourpre* was moored on the Quai du Port in the shadow of the Fort de St Jean and its massively imposing bastion walls. The stroll from the station in the late afternoon sun had left me sweating profusely and I was heartened to discover that locating a position to keep a watch on the ship would not be a problem. I was spoilt for choice, as there were dozens of bars, most with tables outside on the quay itself, lined up along the front of the harbour. I chose the least grubby-looking, about fifty yards from the ship herself. I ordered a tonic water, sat in the shade of the hostelry frontage and tried to cool myself down.

The *Hêtre Pourpre* was the second of three similar looking working ships, sturdy and simple three-masted barques that required the minimum number of crewmembers, making them the workhorses of the oceans. The ship to the rear of the three was currently unloading and there was much activity both on the quayside and on the boat itself. The two other ships were less frantic, but men were boarding and leaving both at regular intervals. I had to take great care not to become distracted by all of this activity lest I miss our quarry slipping quietly aboard. He knew that he was a wanted man so he may well have been taking precautions to avoid being too easily identified.

Despite my determination to concentrate on just the one subject, I could not avoid speculating about Holmes' plan. To be entirely honest, I was rather disappointed by my friend's scheme. I had expected something ingenious or elaborate, but his instructions had been simple. Watch the ship and observe Shiner embarking. Continue observing closely to ensure that he does not jump ship as part of some sort of ruse or blind, and await Holmes' arrival.

I had almost finished my second tonic water, wishing dearly that I could have added to it something rather stronger, when I saw a figure approaching from the direction of the Hotel de Ville. His height and broad shoulders made him immediately prominent. Despite the heat, he wore a long coat and a wide-brimmed hat that hid most of his face. However, there was no doubt in my mind that this was the man that we had chased across half of Europe. He carried a large leather bag with his huge right hand and had another slung over his shoulder. He kept to the shade of the bastion wall as much as possible and, once level with the *Hêtre Pourpre,* he dashed towards the gangplank with a surprising turn of speed for one so large. In a few seconds, he was aboard and quickly vanished below deck.

I continued my vigil until the sun began to set. The solid harbour walls seemed to soften as the light took on a gentler, golden hue. I was certain that Shiner was still aboard, from my viewpoint nobody of his size could have left the ship unobserved. I stood up to stretch my arms and legs and, once seated again, I was shocked to see Sherlock Holmes seated in the chair directly to my right.

"I take it from your calm demeanour that Mr Shiner is safely stowed aboard and waiting below decks for his ship to sail to safety."

He even had a drink before him and, to my great chagrin, his appeared to be have within it, a full complement of gin.

Holmes looked at my resentful expression and laughed. "Come on Watson, old man, you have done a grand job and you certainly deserve this."

He waved his hand and the gruff barman, who had been standing patiently in wait behind us, placed a drink, identical to Holmes', before me.

I could not help but laugh along with his little joke, "Holmes, I will never entirely fathom you."

I gratefully took up the glass and made a toast. "To success, and hopefully to justice." Holmes raised his glass in acknowledgement.

"But, I have grave concerns, Holmes. He is aboard ship and will shortly be leaving, probably never to return," I said, with a sigh. "What can we do from here?"

"From here?" He replied. "Nothing. But we will not be here for long, Watson, for we shall, shortly, also be on board the *Hêtre Pourpre*."

Holmes smiled broadly at my shocked expression but refused to add any further information, despite my myriad questions. He simply sat back and sipped at his drink until the sun set below the western harbour wall and the crew of the *Hêtre Pourpre* began to cast off her ropes.

"Now, Watson."

Holmes leapt up, picked up his bag and strode quickly towards the ship. I hurriedly followed and we just managed to slip aboard before they raised the gangplank and cast off the final moorings. I noticed a crewman nod, knowingly, to Holmes as we passed and I realised that this was also a part of his plan, but to what end? Were we to sail all the way to Africa in pursuit of our quarry?

Holmes held a finger to his lips to indicate silence as we entered the ship and passed through the quarterdeck. We slipped by several closed doors before descending a set of steep steps and continuing to the end of a narrow corridor. Holmes opened the grim looking door and we stepped into a very rough looking, and smelling, cabin. There were four bunks but, in the darkness, none looked comfortable or indeed particularly clean. Two small portholes on the left side might let in some light during the day but the cabin was now almost completely dark, only a small oil lamp hanging from the ceiling offered the dimmest of illumination.

"Perfect," announced Holmes, against all of the available evidence.

"Forgive me, but are we really to spend the next several weeks in here?" I asked, not even attempting to hide my despondency.

"Hold hard, Watson. We shall not be here long, one night, maybe two but, for now, it is ideal. Well away from the rest of the crew and their singular passenger," Holmes reassured, as he played with the lamp, finally managing to increase its flame to a more reasonable level.

I looked around the sparse cabin. It was actually not as bad as I had first feared. The bedding on the bunks was old but appeared to have been recently laundered. The floor had been scrubbed and upon it, I noticed a trunk and some canvas bags. I opened one, cautiously, but to my relief, it contained bread, ham, cheese and fruit. The others contained blankets and also, to my delight, several bottles of French wine and even a local brandy.

"No reason for you to suffer whilst we are secreted down here, Watson," grinned Holmes, sitting down upon on a low bunk. He took out his pipe, filled the bowl and lit it, while I prepared some sandwiches and poured red wine into a pair of white enamel mugs. I sat upon the trunk and ate the simple fare most gratefully. The excitement and expectation of the day had made me quite forget that I had eaten nothing since early that morning. Although I spared no time in finishing off my bread, ham and cheese, Holmes merely picked at his repast, preferring to smoke than take on what was, by now, much needed sustenance.

"Eat up, old chap, you have not eaten since, well since I have no idea," I admitted, worriedly. "Did you even take breakfast this morning?"

"Watson, fear not," he replied in his usual dismissive fashion, "My mind is nourished by cogitating upon the one puzzle that remains in this case. But, I will finish this one sandwich, to satisfy your paternal concerns. But not until I have finished this pipe." He puffed deeply and defiantly. Holmes' great intellect could sometimes be matched by his childish intransigence.

"Very well," I sighed, refusing to rise to his bait. "So, if you will not eat then you can at least answer this question," I responded. "What are we doing here? What can we possibly achieve hidden away down here on a ship heading for West Africa? I will not be ignored now, Holmes, I demand that you tell me your plan."

I was, by now, hot, tired and frustrated.

"I have travelled the entire length of France with hardly a word from you, let alone the slightest hint of an explanation. I have carried out your orders to the letter, without a word of complaint, despite having not a single clue as to your intentions. And now? Now, I am holed up in the bowels of an ancient barque, heading off towards the Atlantic."

Holmes grinned, most infuriatingly. "My plan? It is simple, Watson. Tomorrow we visit Shiner's cabin and interview him. I have only a small hope that he will confess, but he might at least confirm that which I have, so far, ascertained."

"Well, if you persist in this fashion, I will have no choice but to take heavily to drink to pass the interminable time."

I picked up the bottle and emptied its remaining contents into my mug. I took a long draught, appreciating, for the first time, that the wine was actually rather good.

"Watson, my dear old friend, please forgive me my obfuscations. The truth is that all of my plans have been enacted and the traps that were set have now been sprung. We are now at the mercy of time and fate. I am optimistic that we will meet with some success tomorrow, but I fear it will not be the end of the matter, this mystery still has some way to go," he concluded, ominously.

I sighed and took another swig. "I plan to soon be asleep, leaving you to your eternal, and possibly infernal, thoughts."

"Very well, but before you do pass out from imbibing all of this Provencal wine, perhaps you would like to hear about one of my very earliest cases."

My mood changed in an instant. Up until this point, Holmes had barely mentioned anything of his life before we met, and had never discussed his earlier cases.

"Of course, Holmes, I wish, dearly, to hear of all your cases, as knowledge of the earliest of these will help me to understand more your methods and their development."

"Very well." Holmes refilled his pipe and, once again, brought it to life. I noticed that he had eaten barely a third of his sandwich, but chose not to comment. After all, I was far more interested in hearing an account of one of his early cases than I was in admonishing him for not following my medical advice.

Chapter Twelve - The Croxham Church Mystery

"In March of 1875, an unusual message was delivered to my Cambridge college rooms," Holmes began, now wreathed in cinereal smoke.

"It was from an acquaintance of a friend from university, one whom I had aided the previous year, when in a particularly difficult situation. The note was signed by a Nathan Coverdale, who resided in the nearby village of Croxham."

"The village of Croxham lies to the south of Cambridge, just to the west of the Gog Magog Hills. It is a small village with only one notable, indeed unusual, characteristic. Most of its residents are Catholic and have always remained so, in secret when their religion was suppressed during the Reformation and, latterly, quite openly. It was, therefore, one of the first parishes to allow a Catholic church to be officially re-established following the Catholic Emancipation Act of 1829. In reality, all that the existing Norman church, St. Sebastian's, had to do was to change its official title as it reverted back to its original status."

Holmes drew upon his briar, a faint glow rising in its depths, and continued.

"The message read:

'Dear Mr Holmes,

I am very sorry to trouble you. I have been recently informed of your great success in the matter of Master Trevor's difficulties, and the help that you provided him in his hour of need. I am also most desirous of your skills to aid us in unravelling a great and impenetrable mystery. I have recently lost my father to a most terrible murder. The police appear to be quite confounded and show no signs of being able make any progress, let alone actually solving the case. I implore you to come to Croxham and investigate. I have some small funds available and will happily offer them to you in exchange for your time and expertise.
Most sincerely yours,
Nathan Coverdale.'"

"I have to admit, Watson, as to being flattered by the reference to the previous year's events. I was also young, confident and not one to shirk a challenge. The wording intrigued and challenged me - 'a great and impenetrable mystery.' I replied by return and the next day I was in a dogcart on my way to Croxham."

"I met Coverdale outside his family house, a large, sprawling Tudor mansion of warm red brick, sculpted hedgerows and walled kitchen gardens. He led me inside where he recounted his tale."

"Coverdale's father was the local landowner and, as such, was the wealthiest and most powerful man in the village. He was also the local magistrate and a Deacon at the church. The village had been the very picture of harmony until the local priest, Father O'Rourke, an old Irishman, much beloved of his parishioners, passed away. His replacement was far less successful; an unsympathetic and distant man, qualities that failed to enamour him to the local parishioners."

"The final straw came when Coverdale's father found large discrepancies in the parish accounts, Father Jeremiah Arthurs was stealing from his own parishioners. Coverdale senior was furious and made no secret of what he had discovered. He planned to confront the nefarious priest and stormed into St Sebastian's to have it out with him, one to one. He marched down the central aisle, but he never made it any further, as he suddenly let out a short cry and fell to the ground. He was found with a massive and terrible wound to his head, he had been killed instantly by a huge blow with a blunt instrument."

"Well, surely, the priest was the main suspect, he had motive and opportunity," I interjected. "Hardly a difficult case for you, Holmes." The wine and food had greatly improved my mood and I was listening intently.

"Except for one thing, Watson," Holmes replied. "The priest was, at that time, hosting a choir practice in the upper level of the church in front of the organ. Amongst his choristers was Coverdale Junior, along with eight other witnesses."

"To make things even more complicated, Coverdale Senior had been followed into the church by two villagers, concerned that the irate magistrate might take matters into his own hands. Their testimonies confirmed that the events had occurred exactly as described and eliminated the possibility of an assailant having entered or left the church in the moments before or after the crime was committed."

"Then the criminal must have entered by a side door. Come on Holmes, most churches have at least half a dozen ways in or out," I countered, quite unconvinced.

"All of the other doors were locked and the keys were all found upon the priest himself. There was no other way in or out of the church. I know what your next question will be, Watson, but the villager that remained let nobody in or out of the church, not even the priest, until the authorities arrived. The building was thoroughly searched but no trace of any third party was ever found."

"Then I can see no way that the crime could have been committed." I paused. "Unless. Wait a minute. Unless there was, in fact, no crime at all. Perhaps Coverdale's shouting had caused a piece of ornamental stone to come free and fall, causing this terrible injury. It may have then rolled under a pew and been hidden from view or shattered into dust upon impact and not been noticed."

"What a wonderful suggestion, Doctor, and one which may, one day, solve another mystery, but not this one."

Holmes appeared, for once, genuinely impressed by my thinking, but swiftly continued.

"Once Coverdale had finished his story, I headed for the church to see if any clues had been missed by the police. Unfortunately, as the grass outside had been trampled on by so many comings and goings, I could not confirm whether a third party had or had not entered or left the church. Similarly, inside the building, any trace of an attacker was long gone, hidden by the stomp of honest, but inconvenient, police boots."

"My next move was to interview Father Jeremiah himself, the chief suspect of Coverdales, both Junior, and indeed, Senior. I met up with him at the old vicarage, which had, naturally, become his residence. He was a short man, thin of hair but with keen, piercing blue eyes. He sported a pencil thin moustache below a long, sharp nose. Upon his black waistcoat he wore several button badges, a silver cross, the 'agnes dei' and, more unusually, a scallop shell."

"He was, as expected, rather reluctant to speak with me, a young man without any accreditation to the official police, but he did at least confirm a few suspicions and deductions that I had made."

"I think that you had, at this point, determined a reasonable theory as to how he had committed the crime, something to do with those badges," I suggested, as I topped up my mug, by now thoroughly enjoying my evening.

"Quite right, Watson," Holmes confirmed. "But then I made an error. I rather goaded him, by suggesting that the police would surely soon arrest him, at least for theft and fraud, if not for the actual murder of Coverdale Senior. This made him quite irate and he fairly threw me out of his home, but not before making it clear that all of the relevant bookkeeping entries were made, not by himself, but by the Parish

Treasurer. There was no proof, at all, that he was involved in, or aware of, any malpractice."

"So, you had to determine how the murder was committed and prove who was responsible or else the priest would walk free," I stated. "How did you do it?"

"I met up with Coverdale Junior and arranged to join him and the police Inspector inside the church in an hour's time," Holmes continued, as usual, ignoring my request for a quick solution. "I instructed Coverdale that he must convince the police to also bring along the priest, Arthurs, and a couple of burly constables. I then headed back to the church to test a theory."

"I was waiting at the end of the central aisle, just before the chancel, the transepts to the left and right of me, when the small party of four entered. I observed that Coverdale had, indeed, persuaded the Inspector to bring Arthurs, along with a single constable."

"I was not at all disappointed, Watson," Holmes stressed, "as this proved a new theory that I had been aching to test in a real life situation. I had discovered that asking a figure of authority for assistance is an unexpectedly complicated affair. If you do manage to convince them to provide any level of aid at all, then you have already been successful, but usually what is then provided falls well short of what was requested, required or, indeed, promised. The solution is to always deliberately request aid in a quantity far in excess of that which you actually require."

"Holmes, you are addressing a Doctor, and a military Doctor, at that. What you had 'divined' is something that we learn within the first few months of study."

I could not help but laugh. Holmes was certainly a genius, but he was far from being an expert in all areas of life.

"Back in India, if a commander needed an additional company he would start by asking for a division," I added. "But please continue, old chap, the culmination of the case in a church, how singular."

Holmes continued, unperturbed by my red-cheeked interjection. "They approached me, but when they were perhaps fifteen yards from my position, I called on them to halt and come no closer."

"'What is the meaning of this, young man, explain yourself. I have taken a great risk in bringing Father Jeremiah here, against his will,' barked the Inspector. He was a bright man, maybe five and thirty years of age. We worked together on a few occasions hence, I always told him that he was wasted in the Fens, but he had no desire to move to Scotland Yard."

"I began, 'The events that occurred here, on that fateful afternoon, were tragic and possibly unique. I will now explain exactly what happened. Father Jeremiah, maybe it is now time to confess?' I asked, calmly. He said nothing, but his head appeared to drop as if he had recognised what was to come."

"I continued, 'The Magistrate, Coverdale, stormed into the church, demanding answers regarding the missing parish funds. Seconds later, he was dead. He was alone on the church floor, yet he was found with a terrible wound to the head. No one left the scene, no weapon was ever found. How had he been killed and who was responsible?'"

"'Well, get on with it for G… for … just, please, get on with…' spluttered the Inspector, angrily."

"But before he could finish, I cried out, 'Now, Mrs B, just as we practiced!'"

"Three of the four faces before me were frozen in shock, the other, Arthurs, dropped his shoulders in resignation."

"A slight swish was heard and then suddenly an object swooped down from high up in the rafters. It shimmered in what little, dull light was able to enter the church. A brass object, twenty inches high and maybe eight wide, swung down towards us. It rushed through the air, gaining speed as it approached. Just as it seemed it would smash through us all, as if pins in a game of bar skittles, it suddenly accelerated upwards and away behind us."

"Those standing before me watched, transfixed, as the brass container swung back again, but this time it passed far overhead. It swung back and forth several times more, rising each time, until it settled to a regular, gentle pendulous swing, close to the roof beams above us."

"'What on earth is that?' demanded the Inspector."

"'That is the murder weapon,' I declared. 'Gentlemen, may I introduce Botafumeiro Junior, and its controller, the indefatigable Mrs Branch.' I pointed towards the balcony where a well-dressed, middle-aged lady in blue waved back, enthusiastically."

"I looked out upon three open mouths and one which quivered. 'Let us retire to Father Jeremiah's house and I will explain all.'"

"Once settled within Arthurs' living room, I began my explanation."

"'When I arrived here this morning, I thought that this was a murder, terrible and vicious, a thing of pure evil, perpetrated to hide a theft of the worst kind. But what little experience I have so far gained, has shown me that nothing is ever quite as simple, or straightforward, as it may first appear.'"

"'I will begin by explaining the technicalities concerning the death of Mr Coverdale, Senior. Arthurs was conducting choir practice up in the attic choir at the back of the church when in raced Coverdale. Arthurs' reaction was two-fold. Firstly, as any good teacher would have, he instructed his students to remain in place and not turn around and peer over the balcony to observe the commotion that was occurring below. Secondly, he pulled the ropes that released the object which swept down and inflicted the mortal injuries upon Mr Coverdale, below.'"

"'My suspicions were first raised by the badges which Father Jeremiah wears upon his waistcoat. The scallop shell is well known as the symbol of the 'Camino de Santiago', a pilgrim trail that runs from Paris to Santiago de Compostela in northwest Spain. He was very reticent when I questioned him, but he did confirm that he had spent some time in Spain and admitted that he was aware of the Camino.'"

"'The most striking feature of the cathedral of Santiago de Compostela is "Botafumeiro", a huge brass censer, weighing over two hundred pounds, which is swung on ropes from the upper dome of the cathedral. It is quite the spectacle, I have been told, and one that I, one day, hope to experience at first-hand.'"

"'Once this idea had formed, I returned to the church and examined the roof to discover that Father Jeremiah had constructed a replica system, almost identical to that in Spain, but on a much smaller scale. A large brass ring was attached to the highest point of the ceiling, directly above the chancel and from this hung the censer on one central rope. The censer's height and angle was controlled by four guide ropes, one at each cardinal point. As it had yet to be used during a service, the lateral guide ropes were still tied up, hidden from view. The censer itself was sitting on a ledge above the choir, also unseen, but connected by the main rope to the brass ring. This rope hung down over the choir loft, sadly, just within touching distance of Arthurs as he rushed forwards to view the scene below. One good yank was enough to dislodge the brass thurible and send it on its way, swinging down towards poor Mr Coverdale.'"

"'It was while I had been examining the swinging censer and its guiding ropes that I realised that I was not alone in the church. The inimitable Mrs Branch, here, was by the altar replacing the wilting flowers. She was most keen to aid me in my investigations and indeed volunteered to be my assistant in the demonstration that we have just witnessed.'"

"'So, you are saying that when Coverdale roared into the church, Arthurs released the swinging censer, which struck him with a lethal blow?' asked the Inspector, still struggling with the concept."

"'Yes, Inspector, and if you care to examine the censer you will find dried blood and hair coating one side, there is no doubt that this is the instrument that caused the death of Mr Coverdale,'" I concluded."

Holmes sat back, contentedly, and took a deep draw upon his pipe.

"Wait a minute, Holmes," I declared. "This all seems rather unlikely, old chap. Arthurs somehow set up this killing machine in advance of being caught out? It is just not possible, he would have had to have worked out the swing, the height and all of the other variables, just the timing itself would have been horrendously difficult to calculate. What if Coverdale had been two feet to the left or the right? The censer would have passed harmlessly by. Moreover, how did he even know when Coverdale was approaching? No, Holmes, I am sorry but this just does not make any sense."

"Well I am glad to see that your sense of reason is still functioning Watson," Holmes replied, with a smile. "I promise you that everything happened exactly as I have stated, but you are quite right. There is still more to be revealed. Pray, let me continue."

"We were in the priest's home. I poured a large brandy and placed it into Arthurs' quivering hands. The more I examined this case and the deeper I probed, the less straightforward it had become. But I now believed that I had a theory which explained all of the facts."

"'Father Jeremiah had replaced a much loved and respected priest, one who had served the parish for many years and was considered to be more akin to family than pastor for most of his flock. Arthurs lacked the charm and personality of his predecessor and was struggling to be accepted. Then he had an idea. He had seen, and been mesmerised by, the legendary swinging thurible of Santiago de Compostela. He determined to recreate the spectacle in Cambridgeshire, thus endearing himself to his own parishioners and maybe also to those further away. He meant to make St Sebastian's a place of pilgrimage.'"

"'But to achieve this goal, first he needed money. A two hundred pound brass censer was well beyond his financial means, so he resorted to taking from the parish funds. I am certain that he believed that he would soon be able replace the stolen money once the flying censer was up and running.'"

"'When he heard Coverdale screaming and shouting, as he rushed into the church, Arthurs panicked and released the rope. Did he mean to kill Coverdale, or just slow him down? That will be for a jury to decide. But either way, a man was killed and justice must be done.'"

Holmes sat back having finished his account of the case and took a long draw upon his pipe.

"So, what happened to Arthurs?" I asked. "He was clearly misguided in taking the money and the attack upon Coverdale was, at best, reckless, and at worst? Well, he must have known that had the censer hit its intended target, there was a very good chance Coverdale would have been killed. Still, I am not convinced that he deserved the rope."

"You are quite right, Watson," Holmes replied after taking an unexpected bite from his almost intact sandwich. "He did not deserve a capital sentence. He was found guilty of manslaughter, as it could not be proved that he had intended to kill his victim. The charge of theft was dropped for lack of evidence. He received ten years hard labour but, sadly, this turned out to be a life sentence, after all. He had a weak constitution and conditions in the prison were extremely poor. He was dead within three years of entering Bedford Prison."

"But the case did confirm an essential tenet of detection as well as deduction. Always examine, thoroughly, the entire scene of the crime and its surroundings, and never, ever, forget to look up, Watson!" He exclaimed. "It is the one place that is almost always overlooked. Not one member of the police took the trouble to tilt their heads backwards - if they had, they would have seen the unusually large censer hanging in a most unexpected place."

"If they had simply lowered the censer, and examined it, they would have seen the gore and surely solved the case themselves from there."

I sighed. Holmes' criticism of the regular police was often harsh but in many cases entirely justified. I looked at my watch and saw that it was approaching midnight.

"Nearly twelve," I said, gesturing with my watch towards the bunks. "Time for me, at least, to get some sleep."

"Of course, old chap, please excuse me," Holmes said as he rose from the bunk to allow me access to the berth directly above. I lay back and only briefly saw Holmes sit back down and continue to smoke before, exhausted and rather full of wine, I drifted off to sleep.

Chapter Thirteen - Adventure at Sea

Friday 13th June 1884

The gentle rocking of the calm early summer seas ensured that I slept long and deeply. I eventually stirred, to see Holmes pacing up and down the small cabin, still dressed and showing no signs of having taken any rest, whatsoever. I climbed down, filled a bowl with water and washed my face and hands as best I could. My head was still dull from the previous night's indulgence and I was in no mood for any strenuous activity - at least not until I had eaten whatever I could find leftover from yesterday. A quick breakfast of bread, salted ham and cheese, though becoming unwelcomely familiar, gave me energy enough to face the day and, after filling and lighting my morning pipe, I began to feel much more my usual self.

"So, what now, Holmes?" I asked. "I do not look forward to spending the day stuck down here, it is already getting warm and I fear that in a few hours the heat will become unbearable."

"Fear not, Watson," he replied, enthusiastically. "I believe that our little spell of confinement is shortly to end." He checked his watch. "We should expect a sign at any moment."

No sooner had I pulled on my boots, than there was a loud rapping at the door. Two sharp knocks, a pause and then a further three in quick succession.

"The signal?" I asked, quite unnecessarily.

Holmes quickly opened the door, to reveal a scrawny man with skin as hard and brown as a walnut. He turned without a word and scampered back up the corridor. Holmes quickly and silently followed, and I tried my best to keep up. We emerged upon deck, where both Holmes and I squinted in the bright sunshine for several minutes until our eyes had become more accustomed to the morning sun.

The ship was in full sail, a white arrow speeding through the deep blue ocean. A few hardy seagulls still sat upon the masts or circled close by. All around was the usual bustle of sailors going about their work, constantly moving, pulling at ropes, adjusting the trim of the sails, shinning up and down the rigging.

Then I spotted a lone figure who was clearly not involved with the working of the ship. He stood motionless, his back turned to us, staring out to sea. A large man, broad shouldered and tall, his enormous hands resting upon the ship's railings. There could be no mistaking the giant silhouette. Standing just ten yards before us was the man we had sprinted across half of Europe to intercept. Somehow sensing that he was being watched, he slowly turned to face us.

"Mr Thomas Shiner. How delightful to see you again," announced Holmes, with exaggerated politeness.

"You!" he cried.

Shiner lurched forward, his fists tightening into massive balls of flesh and bone. He looked as if he were about to strike, when he suddenly stopped and took a step back. A smile appeared upon his crackled brown face.

"Well, if it isn't my old friends Sherlock Holmes and Doctor, I am sorry, your name has slipped my mind." His grin was perhaps more menacing than the snarl it had replaced.

"Watson," I replied, automatically.

Holmes ignored me and waded straight in.

"Thomas Shiner, I believe you to be directly responsible for the death of Mr James Harrison, late of Bedhurst Hall. Can you venture any mitigating circumstances that we are unaware of, or was it murder, plain and simple?"

"Mr Holmes, Doctor *Watson*," he replied. "We are on board a ship heading to Borundia. You have no jurisdiction here. Come to think of it, you have no jurisdiction anywhere," he laughed. "Even if you had a dozen constables hidden in the bows of this ship, they could do nothing. We are far away from England and its pathetic rules and social graces. No, Mr Holmes, I am, and shall remain, a free man, never to see England's cold and dull shores ever again."

He produced a battered and scratched pewter flask from his jacket, twisted open the bayonet cap, raised it in salute and took a long swig.

"God bless the *Hêtre Pourpre!*" he shouted. "And all who sail home on her," he added with a snarl.

I noticed that several of the crew had stopped working and were quietly moving to surround the three of us. Two men approached slowly from somewhere towards the front of the ship, they both wore caps and had an air of authority about them. In his state of gloating mirth, Shiner noticed nothing and continued to goad Holmes and myself.

"But no hard feelings, chums, I promise that I will to show you around Argentville when we arrive. It is a quiet sort of place but I know where we can find some, *entertainment*," he bellowed with laughter.

Holmes then spoke. Quietly and precisely. "And what exactly is it that makes you think that you are on board the *Hêtre Pourpre*?"

Shiner stopped, confusion spreading across his large face. "Of course I am, don't be stupid. I boarded last night, met the captain and spent the evening here, drinking with the crew. The name is painted on the stern, clear as day. Ha! Your silly games will not work on me Holmes," he snapped, regaining his composure.

"Let me introduce you to the captain of this vessel." Holmes gestured towards the two men wearing caps. The older of the two stepped forward. "This is Captain Robert Irons, commander of the British merchant ship *RMS Ania*."

"Thomas Shiner," The bearded captain began. "I have received information that you are a dangerous man and wanted for serious crimes back in England. As captain of this vessel, my word is law and for the safety of my crew, I order you to be kept locked in a secure cabin, below decks, until we arrive at our destination. There, I shall hand you over to the appropriate authorities." The captain made a gesture and four large sailors approached Shiner.

"Alright, I want no trouble, but I do need answers," he stammered. "What is going on? How have I come to be aboard this ship? Where then are we headed? Kidnap is illegal and will not be easily explained away when we reach port."

"There was no kidnap or coercion involved, because none was necessary," explained Holmes.

Shiner's shocked and confused expression closely matched my own. I craved answers every bit as much as did Shiner.

"Explain yourself, stop talking in circles, man," growled Shiner.

"You were not taken from the *Hêtre Pourpre*. You never even stepped foot aboard that ship."

"But I saw the ship's name, I spoke to her French captain on board!" Shiner cried.

"It is amazing what one can accomplish by telegraph, with the aid of the local police, a sign painter along with two vessels and their crews," Holmes replied.

It began to dawn on me what Holmes had achieved. All of those scribbled messages sent back and forth from telegraph offices throughout the length of our journey from London to Marseilles. What he had contrived and produced was spectacular.

"I have a few contacts in the south of France, some of whom are in the local police force. I imposed upon these to aid me in my plans. They arranged for a sign painter to come to the dockside and temporarily cover up the name *Hêtre Pourpre* upon the back and sides of the ship. This name was instead to be painted upon another vessel, one berthed close beside it. It took a little persuasion, but we eventually managed to arrange for a suitable ship to be moved into position, directly behind the now anonymous, *Hêtre Pourpre*. Upon this second vessel was painted the name, *Hêtre Pourpre*. This is the ship that you boarded. It was relatively easy to arrange for the French captain to greet you here and show you to a cabin filled with hospitable sailors, before returning to his real ship for her voyage to Africa. I take it that you enjoyed the evening and forgot all of your troubles in good company and free flowing rum."

"So here we are," Holmes was now in full flow, "upon the barque *RMS Ania*, heading for Southampton. No laws have been broken, you stepped aboard this ship of you own free will. We should arrive home in ten days, all being well. There you will be handed over to the authorities."

"Well played, Mr Holmes," Shiner sighed, pragmatically. "Well played, indeed. Except for one thing. You still have absolutely no proof against me. If you had, I would have been arrested long before

I left the village. I shall serve my time quietly in the brig but I will be a free man in ten days, mark my words."

Shiner was led, uncomplaining, below decks and Holmes and I joined the captain in his quarters.

"I apologise, Watson, I haven't officially introduced you to our host. Captain Irons, this is my colleague, and confidant, Doctor John Watson," introduced Holmes.

I shook Irons preferred hand, warmly. "Honoured to meet you, sir. I am only beginning to understand the complexities of Holmes' plan but I can already clearly see that you have been a major part in bringing it to fruition. I must thank you for all of this hard work, your officers and crew, also. It was surely a herculean task that you performed in transforming this ship to a passable facsimile of the *Hêtre Pourpre*."

"Our part was fairly straightforward, to tell you the truth," replied Irons, handing a tot of rum to each of us. We were now sat at a well-worn, but freshly scrubbed, wooden table in Irons' cabin. It was light and airy, the panelled walls covered with prints and photographs of ships and seascapes from around the world. It was a welcome change from the bowels of the ship where we had spent the previous night.

"An officer of the local police approached us yesterday asking if we were prepared to be a part of a plan to capture a dangerous criminal and bring him back to England. I immediately agreed to cooperate of course, partly out of a sense of duty, but also, I have to admit, because it sounded like a real adventure, something we are all too lacking in, these days, on our travails across the oceans," Irons smiled, widely.

"All of the hard work and preparation had already been taken care of," continued Captain Irons, "A couple of locals quickly repainted the ship's name, and the real captain of the *Hêtre Pourpre* had already agreed to come aboard to play his part. After that, all I had to do was to provide a few crewmen and a large quantity of rum to keep Shiner occupied for the evening. Once again, this was not my idea but came directly from Mr Holmes, here. His eye for detail is really quite incredible, he even stipulated that the cabin where Shiner was to be entertained should face the sea rather than the dockside so there was less chance of him observing any activity which may have raised suspicion. Of course, after an hour or so of drinking with my men, he was quite oblivious to any comings or goings so it was perfectly safe for you both to come aboard."

"Well I never, Holmes. This is still a remarkable achievement, all arranged by telegraph and whilst on the move between towns and, indeed, countries," I added, with huge admiration.

"It was not a complicated scheme, really. I deliberately kept it as simple as possible, as I had to be able to communicate the plan quickly and accurately over a long distance," explained Holmes, as Irons offered us his oilskin pouch and we gratefully filled our pipes.

"Firstly, I contacted Gregson and asked him to wire the police in Marseilles to explain the situation and to introduce myself officially.

I then sent word to my contacts in the city, who located the *Hêtre Pourpre* and arranged the sign painters."

Holmes paused as he tamped down the broken flake into his pipe and lit it with a long cedar wood cigar match.

"My contacts then joined forces with the local police to find a suitable vessel heading for England that would cooperate with my scheme. Here, we were extremely fortunate. We found, in Captain Irons, both a patriotic champion of justice and a willing collaborator, one prepared to go as far as to relocate his vessel directly adjacent to the *Hêtre Pourpre;* a generous act which increased our chances of success, exponentially."

Holmes toasted the captain with his glass of rum. I then raised my own and was joined by Irons, grinning as he held the orange mouthpiece of his brown-stained meerschaum between his teeth.

We spent the next few hours in pleasant conversation before partaking of a light lunch. Irons then excused himself and returned to his duties, while a crewman showed us to the cabin where we would be spending the remainder of the journey. While not quite as fine as the Captain's berth, it was infinitely better than our previous billet. Our belongings were already there waiting for us, so I took the opportunity to retrieve my notebook with the intention of writing up the case so far.

"I think I will find a quiet spot of shade on deck and catch up with my notes," I announced. "But before I do, Holmes, now that we are alone, I would like to you ask a question that has been troubling me."

"Of course, do go ahead, old chap," replied Holmes, as he rooted around in his overnight bag.

"I cannot believe that all of these people and agencies have acted in such an amenable way purely out of sense of justice. I am concerned that you have had to expend a considerable sum in arranging this scheme. I know just how much you desire a righteous outcome to this affair, but surely not at your own personal cost. I cannot see Gregson and Scotland Yard covering such expenses and unless you have some sort of prior agreement with Fauwkes, I am fearful that you will be considerably out of pocket."

Holmes stopped rummaging and faced me, a sincere expression upon his face.

"I care not for money. I have no interest in gold, jewels or any other trinkets. Justice is all that I seek, that is my treasure and my reward. In the past, I have been well compensated from cases where my clients have been wealthy. Similarly, I have also solved cases without charging at all for my services. In future, I may charge a fixed fee, but for now I am happy to invest not just in justice but also in my reputation which, as a doctor, you know to be priceless."

Holmes recognised that I was not entirely satisfied with his answer, but before I could speak again, he added, "Less than fifty pounds,

Watson. The total cost of this adventure. Including train fares, telegrams, accommodation and all payments to those who made the enterprise possible. I consider it money well spent and that must be an end to it," Holmes finished, defiantly.

"Very well, Holmes, you are quite right. It is not my place to judge what you do with your own money. But I do hope that you are amply and justly rewarded for your largesse in a future case."

I spent the remainder of the day catching up with my writing and did not see Holmes again until we joined the Captain and First Officer for dinner. The food was far better than I had expected, or indeed felt we deserved. Holmes had revealed earlier that Captain Irons had steadfastly refused to take any payment for his help or for our passage back to England. His hospitality was extraordinary and, at length, we found ourselves smoking dark Sumatran cigars, sipping rum and listening to a succession of increasingly hilarious anecdotes, recounted by Wilson, the First Officer.

During a pause while Wilson went below deck to find more rum, the Captain asked a question that, in truth, I should have already asked Holmes.

"So, what happens when we reach Southampton? Shiner is adamant that you have no proof that he is the killer. How long can the police, realistically, hold him?"

"That is a question that troubles me deeply, Captain," replied Holmes. "I have one last line of enquiry to follow when we reach

England. I am hopeful that it will increase my knowledge of the background to the affair but, even with this information, I fear we may have no real case against Shiner unless he confesses. The truth is that we still do not know exactly how Harrison was killed and, until we do, we cannot prove that Shiner was the one responsible. I doubt we can persuade a judge to keep Shiner in custody for much more than forty-eight hours."

"We may be able to engineer some extra time if we can keep him at sea whilst Watson and I land first," added Holmes. "If you are willing to spend a couple of days at anchor off the south coast while we make our way to London, we might just be able to gain an advantage," he suggested.

"Of course, Mr Holmes, we are in no rush to reach Southampton, nothing on board is perishable and we carry precious little mail these days. Shiner's room has no windows and he is no sailor, so I doubt he will even realise that we have stopped, let alone what we are planning," replied Captain Irons, smiling broadly.

Buoyed by the Captain's continued cooperation, we retired for the night and took to our bunks in good spirit. The days that followed passed in pleasant regularity. We were spared the worst of the Bay of Biscay's malevolence and made good time as we headed north. The good weather and calm seas continued for a week. The spell of wind and rain that then followed was bearable as it persisted for just two days, before passing and being replaced, once more, by blue skies and smooth glassy seas.

Chapter Fourteen - Return to Baker Street

Monday 23rd June 1884

We reached the south coast after ten days and, as promised, the Captain dropped anchor a couple of miles out from Southampton. Aided by two crewman, we took the ship's dinghy, raised its small canvas sail and headed towards the port. After two hours of unsteady progress, trying to remember my summer sailing lessons when just a boy, we slunk into the harbour and within half an hour, we were on a train speeding towards London. I must admit that it felt good to be back, both upon dry land and in familiar surroundings.

We arrived back at 221B Baker Street just after midday and it was a joy to be able to change clothes, bathe and take a light luncheon. Mrs Hudson seemed pleased to see us, but Holmes was his usual brusque self. The woman has the patience of a saint, I made sure that I thanked her profusely.

After we had eaten, Holmes sat down at his desk and quickly wrote two messages, which he handed to Mrs Hudson.

"Take these to the post office as quickly as you can," he ordered, with an off-hand gesture.

She gave him a stern look and stood unmoving.

"Please, Mrs Hudson," he added with a sigh. Mrs Hudson tutted, but took the missives with her as she left the room.

"What now, Holmes?" I asked. "Should we head to Harrison's solicitor to see if we can persuade him to reveal what it is you believe him to be hiding?"

"I fear that we may have but one chance with Williams. We must have every possible advantage on our side before we confront him, and even then we cannot be certain that we will be able to persuade him to break what I believe to be a solemn oath sworn to Harrison under very different, and indeed very difficult, circumstances."

"I understand your reasoning, Holmes, but what more can we possibly bring to bear against this man? You have admitted, yourself, that even a direct plea from Scotland Yard had no impact upon him."

"I have had much time to contemplate this case, Watson, and I have come to certain conclusions. I feel I am closer now to having the armoury required to breach Williams' defences. He is clearly a fine man, steadfast and with the highest of morals. He will not divulge what he knows unless we can convince him that it is the right, proper and just thing to do."

"So, what exactly are we waiting for?" I demanded, growing impatient with Holmes' continued obfuscation.

"Not what, old friend, but whom," Holmes answered. "We await two people. Gregson will represent the law, armed with whatever legal precedent he has managed to uncover. The other will be Fauwkes, Harrison's closest friend and, indeed, heir. I wired him as soon as I realised that he may well be the key. As the beneficiary of the estate, he must surely have a right to see the genuine will made by Harrison."

"Genuine will?" I asked. "What on earth do you mean? Do you not believe that the will supplied and acted upon by Williams is the real thing? Is it a forgery? This opens up an entirely new aspect to this case. And I thought it already complicated." I could not help but let out a small, exhausted sigh at this point.

"Yes, Watson, the will that we saw was a fake, but everything contained within it were the express wishes of Harrison," Holmes replied.

"Now I really am lost, Holmes," I said. "If it represented the exact wishes of Harrison, how can it be a fake?"

"That is exactly what we need to ascertain, Watson, and we shall have only one chance to succeed."

Chapter Fifteen - Legal Arguments

Much to our considerable annoyance, we were unable to arrange a meeting with Williams for that afternoon, and in addition to this ill fortune, Fauwkes was not able to leave Bedhurst Hall until the following day. Thus, the meeting with the reluctant solicitor was set for ten o'clock the next morning. We passed a frustrating evening, neither one of us being able to settle down or take our mind off our forthcoming appointment. I tried reading, but could not finish a single paragraph without being distracted by thoughts of Shiner, Harrison, wills and murder. Holmes just sat and smoked in silence.

I tried to think through the remaining unknowns in the case. We were certain that Shiner had murdered Harrison in revenge for the death of his wife. What we did not yet know was as follows:

What had changed to make Shiner believe that Harrison was responsible for his wife's death, after all Harrison remained in Borundia for three months before leaving?

Why did it take over thirty years for Shiner to take his revenge, what had he suddenly learned?

How did Shiner kill Harrison, leaving no murder weapon?

Until we learned the answers to these questions, we would have no chance of making a case against Shiner. In my mind, I repeatedly turned over the events of the previous days but failed to make any further progress.

"I agree with you, Watson, it is a most intriguing and difficult affair," announced Holmes, suddenly.

"Why yes or, rather, what?" I spluttered, before smiling. "Of course, Holmes, you are quite right, after all, what else would I be thinking about? I do not think I have turned one page of this book in the past hour. Even I, with what little skill I have, would have observed this."

"I think I may have whittled it down to just two questions Holmes," I said, glad of any conversation, no matter how repetitive. "What made Shiner believe Harrison had killed his wife, and how did he then murder Harrison?"

"Shiner had plenty of money, so he was quite able to have pursued Harrison when he left Africa, but he did not, he remained in Borundia for another thirty years. If only half of what I have heard about Shiner's character is true, then there is no way that he would have let Harrison get away if he had even the slightest suspicion that he was responsible for his wife's death. Therefore, I think we can assume that Shiner had not the merest inkling of Harrison's involvement in his wife's death until shortly before he sold up and left Borundia."

Happy with my reasoning, I treated myself to a small cigar from my silver and leather case. I offered one to Holmes, but he was content with his pipe.

"You see a little further, Watson, well done. But we must wait until tomorrow for the answer, I hope, to at least one of your questions."

Holmes returned to his pipe and did not speak again that evening. I took Holmes' silence as an excuse to take an early night, but soon regretted it, as I signally failed to fall asleep.

Tuesday 24th June 1884

I woke early but was not in the least surprised to find Holmes already sitting at the dining table, drinking coffee and thumbing through the morning papers.

"Good morning, Watson," he declared with surprising alacrity, considering that he had probably barely slept, if at all.

"I hope you have the strength to see the day through, old man," I replied, before tucking into Mrs Hudson's wonderful rashers and eggs.

I hoped that Holmes would take my hint but, as usual, he ate little, preferring strong coffee followed by an even stronger bowlful of tobacco.

We finally departed Baker Street at nine o'clock and headed for St Pancras. There we met up with Fauwkes and shared a cab to Williams' offices in Pimlico. Waiting outside was Gregson, punctual as ever, holding a brown leather portfolio.

"We have done what we can, Holmes, but short of charging him with obstruction of justice, we have little left with which to threaten him,"

Gregson announced soberly. "And if we tried that, he would probably just laugh in our faces."

"The battle is not yet lost, Gregson," Holmes smiled. "We must be positive, if he even so much as suspects that we hold a weak hand, then we will undoubtedly lose." Holmes' optimism was as unexpected as it was encouraging.

We were shown into Williams' office. It was that of a typical London solicitor, large and airy, with a substantial partner's desk situated in front of a wide bay window. The walls on one side were lined with leather-bound legal publications, rows of green, red and black volumes filled shelves from the floor to a height of well over six feet. On the opposite side was a fireplace surrounded by fine Italian marble. The mantelpiece held a gold ormolu clock and several framed photographs of grey men in dark clothing. On the wall above the fireplace was a pair of dark and rather dreary landscapes. Williams rose as we entered and gestured for us to sit.

"Gentlemen, welcome. I am Caerwyn Williams, solicitor and executor of the will of the late Mr James Harrison of Bedhurst Hall. Mr Holmes, a pleasure to see you again," he introduced himself with a humourless smile.

He momentarily appeared flustered as he realised that there were only three chairs available before his large desk, but before he could speak, Gregson declared, "Please do not concern yourself, Mr Williams, I am more than happy to stand."

I thought this was quick thinking by Gregson, his large looming frame could be a useful way of applying subtle, indirect pressure upon the recalcitrant solicitor. At the very least, it would help to counter Williams' own ploy of keeping his back to the light to help mask his facial reactions.

Williams was a man of below average height and slim of build. He wore a fine quality black suit with a stiff high-collared white shirt. His black tie was fixed with a large gold stud. Across his waistcoat was a gold watch and chain. This hunter bore the engraving of a compass and square, which matched the masonic badge upon his lapel. His hair was greying and swept back from the temples. He had a smallish face and nose but his eyes shone brightly with intelligence or defiance, perhaps both.

Holmes began immediately, "Mr Williams, we have no time to waste. Since I was last here, circumstances have changed materially. We now know who killed Harrison, and why he was killed. We have a man in custody and are close to being able to bring charges. It is time for you to divulge all that you know. I understand the difficult position that you are in, but surely, you must wish to see that justice is done for your client. Sharing with us what you know may well be the difference between Harrison's killer being convicted and him walking free."

"Mr Holmes, as far as I am concerned, nothing has changed. I wrote up the will of Mr Harrison and he signed it. That is the sum total of my knowledge in these matters. No amount of pleading, or indeed threatening," he gestured towards Gregson standing menacingly behind us, "will change that."

"Again, I do appreciate your position, but let me explain to you what has occurred since we last met," insisted Holmes.

Holmes then proceeded to recount all that had happened since we left London in such a rush, almost two weeks earlier. He described how Shiner had left Bedden in the middle of the night and how we had pursued him across France, finally catching up with him in Marseilles. He then told the solicitor all that I had learned from Sir Christopher Janus-Bennedict, the friendship that had grown between Harrison and Shiner, their life in Borundia and, finally, Shiner's marriage to, and the subsequent death of, Sarah Hardcastle. At this point, I thought I saw a look of sadness cross the face of the otherwise stoic solicitor.

"So, you must now be as convinced as we are of Shiner's guilt. I beg you to lift your shield and share with us what I know you to be holding back."

For a moment I thought Williams was about to break, but he simply sighed and slowly, sadly, shook his head.

"Mr Williams." Holmes now spoke with increased volume and vigour. "I have not yet introduced our companion, here, for I thought to spare his involvement if at all possible."

Holmes waved towards Fauwkes who had, so far, sat in silence.

"This is Colonel Ephraim Fauwkes, the inheritor of Bedhurst Hall and what remains of James Harrison's wealth."

Williams, for a moment, looked unsettled but quickly recovered.

"Well I am delighted to meet you, Colonel," he managed, uncertainly.

"I choose my words with great care, sir, when I state 'what remains' of Harrison's wealth," Holmes continued, with great authority. "For we have proof," Holmes pointed back towards Gregson and the brown leather valise that he carried, "that a substantial part of Harrison's estate has been misappropriated and that you are directly responsible."

I tensed up as I realised that this was Holmes' bluff, his one chance to make Williams give up the secrets that Holmes was convinced were being deliberately kept from us. If Williams demanded proof of these allegations, then the game would be up, for we had only Fauwkes' word that these missing bonds had ever existed at all.

Williams sat, wide-eyed with shock, but said nothing.

"Must I invoke the law and bring in the authorities?" Holmes demanded, slowly, in a low, quietly threatening tone.

"Mr Holmes, please... I cannot." Williams begged, in a whisper.

Suddenly, Holmes' entire demeanour changed. When he next spoke, it was in a far softer, more conciliatory tone.

"Mr Williams, may I speak to you alone and in confidence for a moment?" he asked, gently.

Holmes turned to face us. "Please leave us, quickly now," he urged.

We rose swiftly and left, Gregson followed by Fauwkes and then myself. Holmes closed the heavy oak door quietly but firmly behind us.

We waited outside for nearly half an hour before the office door finally opened and out strode a purposeful-looking Holmes. He swept towards the front door, dismissing our questions with a wave of his long, thin hands.

"Not here, gentlemen," was all that he said as he left the building, encouraging us to follow.

Once back inside the waiting four-wheeler, Holmes finally broke his silence.

"Inspector, I thank you for your time. Your very presence was, just as requested. I ask that you be at Scotland Yard tomorrow afternoon, where I hope to be able to put our final case to Shiner."

He then turned to Fauwkes. "Colonel, we will drop you off at your hotel and I ask that you are also present tomorrow. We will call for you on our way to Scotland Yard."

Despite the perfectly understandable protestations from Gregson and the Colonel, Holmes refused to elaborate and the journey soon descended into silence.

Chapter Sixteen - Discussions and Truths

It was late in the afternoon by the time we had delivered Fauwkes to his hotel in Mayfair, having earlier dropped off Gregson at Scotland Yard. We paused briefly at a post office, where Holmes sent off yet another of his mysterious telegrams, before we finally arrived back home at Baker Street.

We took an early supper, during which Holmes signally refused to answer any of my questions, insisting that he would be more forthcoming once we had settled down to smoke. With impatience growing inside me, I carelessly overfilled my briar and failed to light it with a taper, before finally giving in to frustration.

"For heaven's sake, Holmes," I snapped. "We have aided and accompanied you wherever and whenever called upon, surely the least you can do is share with us what you have discovered."

"You are quite right, old friend. I shall tell you what I have learned today," Holmes replied unexpectedly.

"One should never interview a witness or suspect in the presence of the official forces. I thought Gregson's presence might convince Williams to reveal what he knew, but it proved the exact opposite and almost cost us everything."

"What do you mean?" I asked. "I thought that your bluff was successful only because Gregson was there to back it up."

"Far from it, the bluff would have worked far better without Gregson's physical presence. It was only when I made to speak with Williams in confidence that he finally felt he could safely reveal all that he knew. I have been a fool, Watson. I should have realised that I was asking Williams to risk his very livelihood if he admitted, in front of a police officer, what I suspected to be true."

"Of course, we had backed him into a corner and he was in an impossible position," I agreed. "But one thing still bothers me, Holmes. What made him so reluctant to share the truth with us, why was he so loyal to Harrison? It seems rather strange considering that he claimed to have only met him on two occasions."

"Williams put himself at great risk in acting as he did. This I could deduce without knowing the exact reasons behind his actions. There are but few circumstances where one might be expected to act in such a way."

"The first is fear. Was Williams being coerced? This theory, once thoroughly investigated, proved to be without merit. There is absolutely no evidence that Williams has been swayed by any outside influence."

"The second, and far more likely answer, is loyalty. But this would surely necessitate a pre-existing connection between Harrison and his lawyer. As you say, Watson, Williams claims to have met Harrison only twice."

"So, Williams lied then, they knew each other far better than he had claimed?" I suggested.

"Maybe, or maybe not," Holmes countered. "There is one possibility that allows both theories to be true. We saw it in Harrison's possessions and again upon Williams' very person today."

"But Harrison had nothing upon him, just some coins and rings..." I stopped for a moment as realisation set in. "Rings! I will wager that at least one was Masonic!" I declared.

"Just as was the badge upon the lapel, and the engraving on the pocket watch of Williams," nodded Holmes, drawing deeply upon his pipe.

"Masons. Well that would certainly explain his reluctance to share with us what he knew. It could also explain how a mere two meetings could lead to such a level of loyalty."

I was beginning to feel a little less excluded from Holmes' reasoning and hoped that he would now be more predisposed to share with me more information on a regular basis. It was terribly frustrating when he chose, as was often the case, not to share what he had divined until the absolute last possible moment. I rose and poured two brandies before sitting back, emptying, then repacking, my pipe and lighting it, this time with far greater success.

Holmes took a sip of brandy. "Thank you, Watson," he said before leaning back into his seat. His slight frame, with his knees pulled up, seemed to make the back of his chair loom ominously over him like a large and dark tombstone.

"Williams is indeed a loyal man, but also honest and moral to such an extent that he was almost mentally torn in two by the task he had been asked to perform. You remember when I stated that the will was a fake?" Holmes asked.

"Yes, but I still cannot fathom how you came to know this to be the case, or why a fake will could still contain Harrison's exact wishes? What would be the point? Why would someone create a fake will that does exactly what the testator intended all along?"

"It may make more sense, Watson, if you knew that the author of the real will and the fake were actually one and the same," declared Holmes, a little theatrically.

"Harrison? You mean to say that he wrote both wills? But why? Wait a moment, I do have an idea." A theory was slowly forming in my mind, but coming in and out of focus, failing to settle clearly. "What if he wanted to hide the destination of some of his estate?" I speculated.

"Watson, bravo, you are so very close to the answer. Let me help you from this point onwards," Holmes offered, supportively.

"You are quite right in what you suggested. Harrison did wish to leave some of his estate to a person whose name he did not wish to be publicly known. If this beneficiary were to be revealed, it would have placed them both at very great risk. Knowing what I do now, I can certainly state that this person's very life would be in peril if their name were to have been discovered."

"Harrison came up with a quite brilliant plan," continued Holmes. "Simple, but ingenious. What he needed most was a solicitor of unswerving loyalty with an unyielding sense of justice. In Williams, he found both qualities. He had to convince the solicitor that it was morally correct, and in the true spirit of justice, to produce these two wills which hid the mysterious inheritor and then to act upon each one in turn in the event of Harrison's death."

"Once he heard about Harrison's untimely demise, Williams quickly acted upon the original will. He transferred ownership of the shares and bonds over to the secret beneficiary before destroying this first will and heading to Bedhurst Hall bearing the second will. By definition, in every legal sense, this subsequent will has to be considered a fake, a forgery. This explains why Williams could not admit the truth before an official agent of the law."

"This also explains," I added, enthusiastically, "why there was no copy of the will up at the Hall, it had to be kept in London with Williams or the plan would not work."

"Exactly, Watson. Williams produced the second will, signed, dated and witnessed. No one suspected anything was amiss, and they never would have if Fauwkes had not noticed that the bonds and shares had recently been removed from Harrison's safe. This was, of course, because they also had to be in London with Williams for the plan to succeed."

"But we are not yet finished, there are still questions, Watson. Some, I already have the answers to but others, I fear, may never be fully explained without the direct cooperation of Shiner himself. That cooperation may be gained or lost depending on how we proceed."

"One question I do have is this, how on earth did he convince Williams to act in what is, by any definition, a criminal manner? Harrison must have sold him a compelling tale, indeed. I understand how the Masonic connection might have secured Williams' loyalty once he had agreed to this scheme, but what could have possibly made him consent to risk his career, and indeed liberty, for a virtual stranger?"

"This, my dear friend, is where, sadly, I have to end our discussion, for now. I have certain facts now at my disposal, but I cannot share these with you, or anyone else, until at least tomorrow."

Holmes saw my face fall and quickly added, "Watson, please do not be disappointed. If I cannot share what I have discovered, then I can at least try to explain the reasons why." Holmes scraped out the detritus from his pipe into the fireplace and laid it down.

"You are certainly familiar with the term 'the element of surprise'. It is widely known and yet its legitimacy and effectiveness does not diminish, no matter how widely it is disseminated. But I have made a deeper study of its effectiveness, specifically when used during the process of interrogation, and have made several salient observations."

"Firstly," continued Holmes, "the effect is much greater if the subject is taken completely unawares. There should be no build-up, no knowing glances from the interrogator, no little hints that 'we' know something that 'he' does not. Secondly, the sense of surprise must be complete and genuine. I have made a small study of reactions in both face and body to different situations and stimulations. It surprised me how much a hardened criminal can divine from the faces and demeanour of those questioning him. Therefore, it is essential that nobody in that room is aware of what I intend to reveal. Even if it gives us but a single additional percentage of advantage, that might be just enough to make the difference between Shiner talking or remaining forever silent."

"Another question yet to be answered is, of course, what made Shiner act now, suddenly after thirty years?" Holmes added. "This is a question, I believe, that only Shiner himself can answer. I have some theories in mind but can, so far, find little data to support them."

"I take it that you have a plan for tomorrow. It is, after all, the last day that Shiner can be kept incarcerated without charge," I reminded Holmes.

"Tomorrow afternoon at three o'clock, we shall meet up back at Scotland Yard. Our old friend Lestrade will escort Fauwkes, yourself, and I to a final interview with Thomas Shiner. He will subsequently be either charged with murder, or set free. Which outcome it is will depend entirely on us."

"And what about Gregson?" I asked. "Surely he will want to be there at the dénouement."

"The good Inspector will be there in good time. He is, even now, engaged upon a mission of vital importance to our cause. If he succeeds, we have a chance, if he does not then we will almost certainly fail. It is that simple, old friend."

The evening dragged slowly on. Holmes removed to the writing desk and sat scribbling for hours, although he seemed to cross out, angrily, at least as much as he actually put down upon the paper. The evening was warm, so I opened the bay windows to let in some much needed air. I smoked cigars and tried to read, but I could not take my mind from the case and tomorrow's meeting, upon which so much weighed. My head was full of questions. Uppermost of these was one, which I had stupidly neglected to ask Holmes, 'who was the mysterious beneficiary of Harrison's will?' It had slowly become clear to me that this was the key to this entire sorry tale. However, Holmes was unwilling now to add anything to what he had already revealed or answer any more questions until the next day. I reluctantly gave up on gleaning any more information out of him that night and instead spent a couple of hours working on my own notes before finally retiring to bed.

Chapter Seventeen - A Taste of the East

Wednesday 25th June 1884

I spent a fitful night and dawn could not arrive soon enough for me. I rose, washed, shaved and was delighted to find that Mrs Hudson had already risen, so I was soon enjoying a wonderful hot breakfast. It was only then that I heard an unexpected sound and I stood up and looked towards the sitting room.

There, curled upon his chair and still wrapped in his mouse coloured robe, was Holmes.

"A coffee please, Watson, if you don't mind," he asked, casually.

"Please do not tell me you have been here all night," I sighed. "Holmes, this is not healthy behaviour. One day it will start to affect your mind, you know. You are abusing your greatest gift."

"Stop nannying, Watson, there is work to do. I need to visit Lestrade to make final arrangements for this afternoon's gathering. You can join me or remain here until I return," muttered Holmes.

"Of course I will accompany you, I think I will go mad if I am stuck here for much longer. This adventure has recently seen its pace rather slowed," I smiled.

We left as soon as I had finished my breakfast. Holmes had taken nothing other than strong, sweet coffee, but I had given up trying to convince him to eat. The case would be over by this evening, one way or another. After that, my concern for his health could once again become a priority.

We travelled to Scotland Yard in an open cab, the morning was already warm and bright, making the trip comfortable, despite my stubbornly silent companion. We met Lestrade at ten and he seemed less than convinced by Holmes' very basic instructions.

"So you want to talk to Shiner, I understand that, but I was hoping that there was a little more to your plan than just that," he sighed. "Just yourself, Doctor Watson, myself and a constable?"

"Your most stoic constable, Inspector, it is essential that he is as inscrutable as he is sturdy," corrected Holmes.

"Very well," Lestrade agreed, without enthusiasm. "Constable Barnes will be ideal. He has no discernible facial expressions and he is as strong as an ox."

"You also insist that Colonel Fauwkes should wait in my office, under no circumstances can we allow him to be observed by Shiner. What about Gregson? What have you done with my man, Holmes?"

"The good Inspector should be back with us, just in time. When he does, please arrange for him to be shown to the meeting room. There he will wait outside and be joined by Colonel Fauwkes. This is where we must have an agreed signal to inform those of us inside the room that Gregson has returned and that all is well. I have arranged with Gregson that he feign a commotion outside, similar to a prisoner shouting loudly in complaint. The key words are to be 'I never drank the communion wine'."

Lestrade laughed. "Well that, at least, I agree, is a good plan. I think we can be fairly confident that no one else will shout those exact words in the corridor while we are interrogating Shiner."

"Indeed. Nevertheless, this will be my cue to begin my final assault and one last attempt to break Shiner. I just hope it will be enough."

I was not used to Holmes sounding so apprehensive, it was becoming apparent how finely balanced this case had become.

Holmes declared that all was now prepared and that we should retreat for an early lunch. Surprisingly, he also asked Inspector Lestrade to join us, as our guest. We left Scotland Yard and headed north. We walked for a good half an hour before turning down a decidedly unwelcoming looking alleyway. Hanging outside an anonymous looking grey fronted building was a Chinese lantern. Holmes rapped upon the windowless door and after half a minute it was opened by a young Chinese lady.

"Mr Holmes, please come in," she said with a broad smile. "We have your favourite today, roasted duck."

We passed through the door and into a beautifully decorated restaurant. We were led to a table and sat surrounded by paintings and statues that were completely alien to me, but seemed to fit perfectly within these surroundings.

We were happy to let Holmes order the food and were soon thoroughly enjoying our meal, even if we were not always entirely sure what it was that we were eating. I was simply happy to see Holmes eat anything, even if he was, for the most part, just picking idly at his food.

"So, what brings you here, Holmes, not that I mind?" asked Lestrade.

"I helped the family a few years ago and acquired a taste for the food at the same time. I find it relaxing here," replied Holmes.

The other clientele, of which there were few at this early hour, were all oriental except for one man sitting in a dark corner, hunched up, seemingly in an attempt to hide his large physique. I could not make out much detail, but he had light hair and an impressive moustache. Although he never mentioned him during our visit, I am certain that Holmes had chosen this specific place to eat in order to observe this man rather than to share its cuisine with Lestrade and myself.

We left an hour later with Lestrade singing the praises of this newfound eatery. It had proved a pleasant diversion but we were now heading back towards Scotland Yard and the final chapter of this story.

Chapter Eighteen - The Small White Room

Lestrade and Holmes had ensured that Shiner was the first to arrive. He sat in a simple chair before a plain wooden desk. Constable Barnes was seated to his right, Shiner well within grasping reach of the burly policeman's oversized arms. They had been left alone for around half an hour, hoping that this may disconcert Shiner.

We entered in the order that Holmes had dictated. First Lestrade, then myself and finally, a few steps back, Holmes. The interrogation room was simple, about fifteen to twenty feet square with plain, whitewashed walls. Apart from the ones occupied by Shiner and Constable Barnes, there were three sturdy wooden chairs set a few feet from the desk.

"Why, Mr Holmes, Doctor Watson. It is a genuine pleasure to see you both again," grinned Shiner, seemingly unperturbed by both the location and our attempts to unsettle him.

Holmes took the central seat, directly opposite Shiner. I sat to Holmes' right, Lestrade on his left.

Holmes' introduction was blunt and direct.

"Mr Shiner. Do you not think it is time to end this? Make your confession, tell your tale and maybe the courts will be lenient. If you are truthful with us right now, I will do all that is in my power to ensure that you receive a fair sentence. If you share everything with us right now, I believe that you may be spared the rope. If you persist in denying what we know for certain to be true, then I will not be able to help you."

"Mr Holmes," began Shiner, slowly. "I am an old man now. Whether it is prison or the rope, it makes no difference to me. But then again, I have no fear of you, Mr Holmes, as you have nothing on me. I am an honest man and you have no case against me," he snarled.

"We know all about your relationship with Harrison. Your voyage to Africa to seek your fortunes, your travails and misadventures. We know that you failed to match his success and returned to England with little to your name, whilst he lived a life of luxury in a country mansion. Surely, you were jealous and wanted to punish him?" Holmes accused.

"Oh no, Mr Holmes, not at all. For, as you know, Harrison had long ago left Africa before he made his fortune. Why would I be jealous? I have heard he made his money honestly, through his own hard work, and good for him." Shiner smiled through gritted teeth.

"So, what made you return to England, if not jealousy or revenge?" asked Holmes.

"Like I have always said, I missed the old country, I wanted to see home one last time. However, I soon realised that this country was no longer my home. It had changed, or I had had changed, does not really matter which. So I left."

"And where were you planning to go? Back to Borundia? Strange, as I have received information that you sold your business and property out there before you left," countered Holmes.

"Ah, your information is not entirely correct there, Mr Holmes. I did indeed sell the old fishing business and I also sold some land, but I did not sell my farm. What I sold was a piece of land on the coast overlooking the mouth of L'Argenté River. I had spent every penny I had in acquiring it, knowing that one day this piece of strategically important land would be worth a great deal. It took nearly twenty years to be proved right, but I finally sold it and for a very good price. This enabled me to return to England and rent a house for the summer. But I am far from penniless, Mr Holmes, for I still own the balance of what I was paid for the land along with my homestead back in Borundia. I will certainly enjoy using the former to employ a lawyer to sue you all for assault, false imprisonment and more."

The air was charged with tension. I had not expected Shiner to be such an intelligent and eloquent opponent. I had forgotten that he had acquired the beginnings of a good education before fate stole away his parents. This was no ordinary seaman adventurer made good we were facing, but a cunning and dangerous snake of a man.

"You are right, of course, Mr Shiner," Holmes continued. "We know that you have money. We know that Harrison had money. But we also know that this whole affair was never about money."

"Very well then," Holmes continued after receiving no response from Shiner. "I shall give as fair and accurate an account of the background to this case that I can, from what we have ascertained. Please correct any inaccuracies, if you will, and afterwards, I will ask you to fill in such parts of the tale that remain unknown to us."

Holmes proceeded to recount the tale that Sir Christopher Janus-Bennedict had shared with me in his eccentric house nearly two weeks ago. He put significant stress on Shiner's short and tragic marriage and Harrison's subsequent return to England. Shiner sat unmoving, his eyes fixed upon Holmes throughout the course of his account.

"Once you were back in England, you headed straight to Bedden. You knew that the best place to mingle with the villagers, whilst avoiding direct contact with Harrison, was at the church. You could be confident that, as an avowed atheist, Harrison would never attend, leaving you free to inveigle your way into village society and convince the Widow Fairchance, firstly, to rent you her summer house and then to finally accept her long-standing invitation to visit the Hall. That is where you confronted Harrison and that is where you killed him."

"Revenge was the motive. Revenge against Harrison for the death of your wife." Holmes sat back in expectation, but Shiner's expression had changed not one iota.

"Tell me," said Holmes, after a short pause. "Do you think Harrison was aware of your presence in the village? Did he suspect something was amiss? You couldn't risk a confrontation in public in front of witnesses, so you conceived your fiendish plan."

"And what a plan it was. You knew that Harrison would be shocked, confused and suspicious if you arrived at the Hall as yourself, unannounced and out of the blue. But I am not sure that he recognised you at all, a harmless old sea-dog accompanied by a local widow. Thirty years, and the addition of a thick beard, meant that Harrison had no clue as to who was his latest dinner guest. After all, he had entertained many and varied personalities over the years. You were not even the only newcomer at the table, Professor Seaworthy was also there for very first time."

"You spent the evening trying to fit in as best you could, until the gentlemen retreated to the conservatory to smoke. This was a tradition that was well known to the people of the village and thus was something that you had become well aware of, long before your visit. You had also learned that this arboretum was lush and maze-like, so you simply followed Harrison, watched him sit down at the bench and waited for the right moment to strike. From what we have heard from the witnesses, I do not believe you allowed him to plead his case or even speak a single word to defend himself. You killed him right there, instantly, in cold blood."

Shiner remained still for a minute and then slowly a smirk began to cross his grizzled face.

"You have been busy, Mr Holmes, Inspector." He nodded towards Lestrade. "I again state that I am guilty of no murder. However, as you have worked so hard and been *oh so very clever,* I shall answer some of your questions," smiled Shiner, sarcastically.

"I did pass Harrison deliberately in the village on several occasions to see if he would recognise me. The first time, I looked away as we got close, but the next time I looked him straight in the face. He did appear to react slightly, at first, but he said nothing. I tried for a final time the following day and this time he paid me no heed at all, I expect he thought me just another labourer passing through the village. I had to trim the beard a bit before persuading the widow to take me up to the Hall, but I was now confident that Harrison would not recognise me."

Shiner all but spat out the name of his former friend. His sardonic smile remained, while his ice-cold eyes stared unblinking at Holmes.

"But that is all you will get out of me regarding that evening. I was simply a guest at a dinner in a house where a man died." Shiner sat back, seemingly content with his unassailable position.

"I have no wish to go over events that occurred after you murdered Harrison," Holmes quickly responded. "I am only interested in what happened beforehand, many years beforehand."

"What happened to your wife, Mr Shiner?" Holmes demanded, leaning forwards, his hard grey eyes boring into Shiner. "What makes you think that Harrison was responsible for her death?"

Shiner's rictus grin vanished, instantly, leaving only a face so barren and devoid of feeling that I felt physically cold in its presence.

"Very well. I will tell you my story. Then, perhaps, you will see that justice has been served in this matter and let me leave this place, to live what remains of my life in peace," declared Shiner, his vacant mask slipping just an inch to reveal a speck of pain in those colourless eyes.

"We were as close as any two friends could be. From the moment we met on board the 'Africa Gem' we were inseparable. He was a shy and sensitive man, I am more open and gregarious, but somehow we seemed to find a common middle ground. We lived, laughed, drank and sinned together. We were both chock full of dreams and ambition, but we also knew how to work hard. Borundia was not quite the land of plenty we had imagined it to be. It was soon apparent that there were no fortunes to be made there. I was all but ready to leave after only a few months, but Harrison persuaded me to stay. We had found a small deposit of semi-precious stones, enough to make us comfortable, if we invested well, but to nowhere near the levels of which I had dreamed."

Shiner's reminiscences seemed to soften him and he was now visibly more relaxed.

"As you know, we bought a boat and became fisherman, at least for long enough until we could afford to employ a crew to do the work for us properly. We returned to our mining and within a year had made enough from both concerns to buy ourselves plots of land in Argentville. There we each built a house, alternating between working on our plots and the mine in the hills."

"Things changed in 1851, when I met Sarah Hardcastle. It was love at first sight, I can tell you gentlemen. I took one look at her beautiful face and knew that she had to be mine. I spent the next six months in pursuit of her and she finally agreed to be my wife, we wed the following year."

"Was the marriage a happy one?" asked Holmes. I could tell that he was keenly absorbing every word and subtle inflexion.

"As happy as is any, Mr Holmes," snorted Shiner, in reply. "She was a great beauty, but also an independent, almost wild, soul who needed taming occasionally. But I provided well for her, she could have no complaints."

I tried hard to stop the anger rising inside me. The man was clearly a brute and a bully. I was beginning to wonder whether his whole friendship with Harrison might have been rather more one-sided than he had described it.

"How did she die, Mr Shiner?" Holmes asked, gently and sensitively. Even a monster such as this must have been terribly injured by such a huge loss.

Shiner hesitated for a moment before shaking his head, presumably to clear it, and replying.

"It was December of '53. She was walking by the coast. She liked to walk along the cliffs in the evening. They say she lost her footing and fell. Those cliffs are sixty feet high and the sea below is the

Atlantic. Even that far south, the seas in December can be treacherous, and the rocks below..." Shiner's voice faded to a whisper. "They only found a few scraps of her clothing, covered in blood. The sea took her, what was left of her, after the breakers and the boulders had finished their foul work."

If it had been any other man, I would have been aching with sorrow and sympathy at hearing such a tale, but knowing Shiner, as I had come to, I reserved my pity for that poor woman alone.

My next thought was much darker. Had she not fallen but jumped, to escape her beast of a husband? I could hardly bear to imagine the abuses and deprivations he may have inflicted upon her to make her take such a course. I pledged there and then, that if this proved to be the case then I would finish the job myself if Shiner avoided justice in the courts. I was, by now, biting my lip to stay calm.

"I am sorry for your loss," said Holmes, with much more sympathy than I could have mustered. "Then what happened? What led to Harrison leaving?"

"Well, as you can imagine, I was hit hard by the loss of my Sarah. I took heavily to drink. To be honest with you, I had always enjoyed a drink, but for the next few years, I drank to such excess that I could do nothing else. I hardly even noticed that Harrison had left to return to England. I just picked up the earnings from the fishing boat once a week and spent the next seven days drinking the profits away."

"The next thing I knew, ten years had passed. Gone in a flash. I was so shocked that I decided then and there to give up the drink for good. I realised that I was no longer a young man and, in any case, the profits from the fishing boat were no longer enough to both carry out badly needed repairs and also keep me in drink. So I killed two birds with one stone, so to speak. I hiked back up into the hills and re-opened our little mine. It was deathly hard work for a while. I was awful sick as the alcohol left me but up there I had nothing to turn to, so I slowly recovered my health along with my wits. After six months, I returned to Argentville, sober and carrying a sack of gemstones. I fixed up the boat and had enough left over to buy a second."

"Over the next ten years, I bought eight more boats, until I controlled most of the local fishing fleet. I was fair to my men, mind, I always paid them, even in the lean times. They reciprocated by working hard and soon I had spare money to invest. I began buying up plots of land overlooking the mouth of the river. Harrison had often recounted stories of great wars and naval battles, and he had always stressed the importance of high ground overlooking strategically important sites. What could be more important than the mouth of a country's major river?"

"By 1875, I owned the entire coastline, three miles either side of the mouth of L'Argenté. I was aware that many in the town thought me quite mad but I was prepared to wait for my investment to bear fruit. In the summer of 1880, I received a letter from Paris, inquiring as to the availability of my land. Six months later a similar one arrived from Vienna. By the end of the following year, I had received offers from seven different nations, but being a patriotic man, I was still holding out for the one offer that I valued above all others. One from Her Majesty's government."

"I had heard nothing by the middle of '83, so I decided to act. I grabbed several of the more incendiary offers and posted these to London. This finally spurred them into action and I duly received an offer that was acceptable to me. Although it was far from being the highest bid, I was happy that Britain would now become a major influence in the country."

"I will never know whether it was coincidence or divine providence, but if I had not been taking such an interest in world affairs at that time, then I would never have seen the newspaper that changed everything."

"Please continue, Mr Shiner, your account is vital to this whole affair," Holmes said quietly.

"Some months previously, I had begun to have papers delivered from London to aid me with the sale of my land. I posited that if I had more knowledge of world politics and events then I could gain a higher price for my land. As I have just explained, this certainly worked out in my favour. However, it was while idling through one of these that I saw something that chilled me to the bone."

"It was a photograph, one of those new halftones. They had only started appearing a few years earlier, before that, we had to put up with sketches or vague, blurry images. But this picture was clear. It showed a successful businessman celebrating the opening of a railway line back home. I very nearly turned the page over, but something about him made me stop. It may simply have been the novelty of the photographic image, but I slowly began to realise that I actually recognised the face. It was James Harrison. I quickly read the article, which confirmed Harrison's identity and went on to describe, in some detail, his great success and wealth. I will admit that, at first, I felt a certain sense of pride that my old friend had been so successful, but then I noticed something in the picture."

"Pinned upon his jacket's right breast pocket was a brooch. It was made from gold and inlaid with diamonds. It was a fine piece, indeed. It was also the most valuable and treasured possession of my late wife, Sarah. It had belonged to her mother and her grandmother before that. She had always worn it with pride."

Shiner paused.

"She was wearing it when she left to take her walk, on the night she fell to her death," he growled.

His words seemed to echo like thunder around the small white room.

Chapter Nineteen - Witness

This revelation left me reeling, but Holmes rather seemed to take it all in his stride. I looked to Shiner and back to Holmes, wondering who would speak next.

It was Holmes who, finally, broke the silence. "So, you took this to be proof that Harrison had, in fact, murdered your wife and stolen her most precious possession. He then made off with the proceeds of his crime while you were too intoxicated to notice, let alone, even care."

"Once you saw this picture, you swore revenge and, using the proceeds of the recent sale of your land, tracked him down to Bedhurst Hall. The rest we already know."

Holmes paused and then I heard the sound of a commotion outside the holding cell. The voices were rather indistinct but I could just about make out the words 'drank' shortly followed by 'communion'. Gregson had returned, and he had been successful.

Holmes resettled himself in his chair before leaning forwards.

"Mr Shiner, I give you one final opportunity to confess. Tell the truth, admit that you killed Harrison. Otherwise, what is to follow may cause you far more harm than any custodial sentence," he implored.

"There is nothing more that can now be done to me, Mr Holmes," replied Shiner. He then leaned forward, as close to Holmes as the desk between the two men would allow.

"You have lost, Mr Holmes. Let it go and, for God's sake, it is now time to let *me* go!" he growled.

"Very well," replied Holmes, in a low, resigned whisper, which was quickly followed by a loud bark. "Gregson, bring in the witness."

Shiner's face appeared momentarily puzzled and he muttered, "What witness?" as the door opened and two figures entered the room. One was the tall light-haired Inspector. The other was completely unfamiliar to me.

She was a lady of late middle age, perhaps even approaching sixty. It was difficult to put an exact age to her, as she held an ageless grace and skin which hardly carried a line, even after so many years. Her long hair was mostly white, but still retained a slight hint of the original blonde. She wore it tied back and swung down low, behind her, in the fashion of a much younger woman. She wore a black skirt and smart jacket over a plain white blouse.

The effect of her presence upon Shiner was extraordinary. His puzzled look continued for a moment but then his eyes widened and his mouth began to open slowly. He seemed to be attempting to speak but no sound emerged. His jaw hung open. His lips quivered, shortly followed by his hands and soon, it seemed, his whole body was shaking.

Gregson finally broke the silence. "Gentlemen, may I introduce Mrs Sarah Shiner, née Hardcastle."

"But how, how?" stammered Shiner, his face now deathly white, despite its years of exposure to the harsh African sun.

"Please, let me explain," declared Holmes, as I rose and offered up my chair to Mrs Shiner. She sat down silently and looked directly at her husband with a calm, emotionless face. As I moved to stand behind her, I glanced over to see Lestrade, whose shocked expression showed that he had been kept as much in the dark about this development as had I.

"I approached this case as I would any other," began Holmes. "I looked for all of the available evidence and followed whatever clues I could find. While others were making assumptions, I simply stuck to the facts that were known."

"The unusual activity surrounding Harrison's will gave me our first clue, although the full truth behind it did not come to light until the very end of the case."

"Although this was all completely unknown to you, Shiner, it seems that Harrison made several changes to his will shortly before he was killed. This made me wonder if he had not already suspected that somebody in the village might have wished him harm. This made the presence of the newcomers into the village of even greater interest. It took a relatively short time to exclude most of the other suspects, which left us with only two realistic possibilities. Professor

Seaworthy, despite having lied about everything from his profession to his very name, seemed an unlikely candidate, due to his supposed old age and slight frame."

Holmes subtlety waved away my exclamation of surprise at this revelation, before continuing.

"However, all of this speculation was soon rendered obsolete by the abscondment of 'Wergeld'. He had realised how close we were to identifying him as the main suspect, so he chose to leave as soon as darkness could provide him with the cover he required."

"Before we chased you the length of France, we had already uncovered your true identity and Doctor Watson, here, had determined much of your life in Africa. But despite the rapid linear course we were taking, my mind was constantly drawn back to the matter of the will. It was clear that something was wrong, but it was not until we returned to England with you as our guest, that I could finally put all of my efforts into solving the problem of the legacy."

"I was certain that Williams, Harrison's solicitor, was deeply involved and after expending a huge effort persuading him of the essential nature of his testimony, and swearing to keep his name out of the official reports, he finally acquiesced."

Holmes voice cut through the atmosphere like a blade of the brightest light. All but one of the faces of his audience was open with surprise and incredulity. Only Mrs Shiner sat expressionless and unmoved as Holmes continued.

"The tale he recounted was one of desperation, betrayal, violence and duplicity, but also one of friendship, hope and love."

"Poor Mrs Shiner suffered terribly at your hands. You, sir, are a drunk and a bully, a man who thrives on inflicting violence upon those physically weaker than himself. Harrison may have been your friend at first, Shiner, but after many years of suffering your behaviour, he began to detest and fear you in equal measure. Your arrogance and inebriation hid these simple truths from you. If you could not persuade, you would threaten, and after a while you could no longer tell the difference between the two."

"Harrison had formed a close friendship with your wife, one to which you, in your myopic state, were completely blind. He knew how you had abused her, mentally and physically. How you beat her and shouted at her all manner of foul abuse. She would run to him in tears and beg his help to rid her of you, once and for all."

"But Harrison was no murderer, no cold blooded killer. Beneath your cruel, drunken exterior he could still see his old friend, the one with whom he had shared so much hardship and eventual success. He deliberated and schemed until he came up with a plan that would both save his friend and punish her tormentor."

"Once again, as with all great plans, simplicity was the key factor. Mrs Shiner had to disappear in a way that would be both convincing and plausible. Harrison knew that to make the plan practical and believable he must utilise all of his local knowledge, while also encompassing Mrs Shiner's existing habits."

"Harrison knew well that Mrs Shiner walked along the cliffs most evenings and this gave him the germ that became the heart of his stratagem. He created a model, some of Mrs Shiner's clothes hung upon a frame of dry sticks and twigs. To this, he added some stones, for ballast, lightly attached with fine twine. As a final touch, he cut his hand with his belt knife and added a goodly amount of blood to the clothing. He then took this model up onto the cliffs and awaited Mrs Shiner."

"Once she had had rendezvoused with Harrison upon the cliffs, the pair hid and waited until dusk. From his years in the fishing trade, Harrison knew exactly when the fleet would set sail for a night's fishing. When he spied the small boats closing in on their location, he hurled the model into the ocean. The watching crews must have gasped in horror as they saw the familiar figure of Mrs Shiner tumbling from the cliffs into the ocean below. As expected, the waves crashed the fragile structure against the rocks and the thin wooden sticks inside were snapped and crushed. The remaining clothing was therefore freed to churn in the wash until, eventually, parts of it washed up upon the rocks and shore, to be found the following day."

"Once completely dark, but before the fishermen could return to raise the alarm, Harrison led Mrs Shiner back into town, disguised beneath a hooded cloak, and onto a boat that he had arranged to set sail that very night. As a token of her gratitude and affection, she had presented to Harrison her family brooch, which he wore with pride, once he had left Africa for good. She landed in Spain ten days later, and from there, journeyed on through Europe and back to England."

"After changing her name, Mrs Shiner found work at a girl's school in Northumberland, rising from teaching assistant to head of year and eventually taking over as headmistress. Once Harrison had returned to England and made his fortune, he reconnected with Mrs Shiner and they secretly remained in contact until his untimely death. Somehow suspecting that his end might be near, he had changed his will to ensure that a substantial legacy would be left to Mrs Shiner. Not willing to expose his dear friend's new identity to the possibility of revenge by her husband, he concocted an elaborate scheme of creating two subsequent wills that would ensure that she would receive what he had intended, but in total secrecy."

Holmes was clearly approaching his final pronouncement, but he was suddenly silenced when Shiner, who had remained quiet for the duration of Holmes' discourse, let out a pitiful scream and fell forward, head first, onto the desk. I quickly moved forwards and gently lifted his head. His eyes were half-open, but his face had tightened into a lop-sided expression of agony. He shook for a moment and then he stilled. The left side of his face hung down, his limbs had lost all of their strength. He slumped back into his chair and slipped slowly to the floor. I instinctively called out for help, but I already knew there was little that could now be done for him.

"What is going on?" demanded Lestrade, in a fluster.

"A massive stroke," I replied. "We need to get him to a hospital."

Gregson opened the door and shouted for help. Lestrade stood up and hovered above me. Holmes sat and watched, one eyebrow slightly raised. But amongst all of the commotion, one thing sticks in my memory more than anything else. As all was noise and chaos around her, Mrs Shiner rose and slowly, but gracefully, glided out of the room, her fixed expression never changing.

Chapter Twenty - Broken Flake

Monday 7th July 1884

Shiner clung onto life for a further five days but eventually passed away without uttering another word. A coroner's court subsequently determined him to have been responsible for the death of Harrison and the case was thus officially closed. Holmes kept his promise to Williams, who entirely escaped mention. Somehow, he also managed to spare us from having to justify our, legally rather dubious, capture and imprisonment of Shiner.

We left the court in mixed spirits. I was happy with the outcome, natural justice had, after all, prevailed. But Holmes was agitated, unsatisfied that after so much work his quarry had escaped facing judgement in a court of law."

"Holmes, old boy, you won. You should be happy, or at the very least, satisfied. The villain is no more. We were as sure of his guilt as anyone could ever possibly be. So what if God has taken him before the hangman? Surely, it makes no difference," I insisted.

"Yes, I suppose, on that point, you are right, dear Watson. But I cannot help but feel that Shiner may have taken his secret to the grave."

"What secret? Surely, we know all that we can possibly know about this affair," I replied.

"Not all, Watson. How did he kill Harrison? That is his secret and one which I am no closer to solving than I was on that first day when I arrived at Bedhurst Hall."

"It is over, Holmes, does it even matter?" I asked.

I have decided not to record Holmes' exact response, suffice it to say, that he disagreed.

Chapter Twenty One - The Pigtail Twist

Tuesday 22nd July 1884

Two weeks had passed since the Shiner case had been closed by the courts. Holmes had kept himself busy with chemical experiments and the writing up of copious notes regarding this and all of his other recent cases, but the frustration at not being able to completely solve the crime hung over him like a dark cloud, threatening, at any moment, to become a storm.

The summer evening was warm and we had opened wide the bay window to allow in some cooling fresh air to compete with the swirling smoke of our pipes.

"Look Holmes, you must stop obsessing over this case. It has gone and anything you might now discover can no longer have any material impact," I declared.

"You are quite right, Watson, yet an incomplete case is anathema to me." Holmes tapped out the detritus from the bowl of his dark dank pipe into the fireplace.

"Why don't you try some of this?" I asked, offering Holmes my leather tobacco pouch. "I picked it up at H&S in Bedford."

Holmes took a chunk of the dark, hard-packed plug tobacco and nonchalantly rubbed it up in his hands. He then packed his pipe, lit it with a single match and puffed away, contentedly.

"This is very good, Watson. Dark and cool, just like the weather this evening," he smiled. For all of his machine-like qualities, Holmes could, on rare occasions admittedly, relax and act like a normal human being.

I let out a short chuckle in response and picked up my new briar, which I had acquired at the same time as the plug tobacco. I examined the fine brown and gold swirls of the bird's eye grain and contemplated what a small thing of beauty had been hand-carved from the fifty-year-old root of a Mediterranean bush. I broke off a piece of plug, rubbed it up and half-filled my virgin briar. As I put the remainder of the tobacco back into its pouch, an amusing thought struck me.

"Well Holmes, it appears that, for once, this tale will not have a twist in it," I grinned.

Holmes smiled in agreement and took a deep pull upon his pipe. Suddenly his eyes widened and he slowly removed the stem of his pipe from between his lips. His mouth remained open for a few seconds and I could see that he was formulating a new theory or idea, right in front of my eyes.

"Are you alright, Holmes, you look suddenly troubled?" I asked, as Holmes stared blindly into the distance, his mind fully occupied with this new deduction.

"Ha! Watson, yes, that's it!" he suddenly exclaimed. Holmes then began to laugh. He laughed long and loudly, his whole body shaking.

"Whatever do you mean? The solution? You have it?" I stammered.

"Not I, old chap, you," Holmes finally replied, once he had regained control over his convulsing body. "You have cracked it! Well done Watson," he laughed.

"What on earth are you talking about, Holmes? What have I cracked? As far as I can see, I merely made a rather poor joke."

"Ah yes, but your little pun has finally showed me exactly how Shiner committed his evil act. And once again, of course, it was simple but brilliant," Holmes explained.

"What did we find at the murder scene? On the ground surrounding Harrison?" he asked, still grinning widely.

"Let me see. There was a cigar, a sprinkling of ash and some dark flakes of tobacco," I replied, still completely unaware of where Holmes was heading.

"Yes, dark flakes and, in addition, an oily residue was found upon Harrison's neck. Do you not see it yet, Watson?"

"No, not at all," I sighed, as I took another puff upon my pipe.

"What did Shiner have upon his person when he was examined at the scene?" Holmes demanded, with growing excitement.

"He did have a pouch filled with an unusually large amount of rubbed up flake tobacco with him, as I remember. But how could he have killed Harrison with a large leather pouch full of broken flake?" I asked, incredulously.

"Because it was not rubbed up flake, Watson. It was a pigtail twist!" Holmes declared, loudly.

I struggled for a moment but then I saw it clearly, as if I was a packhorse whose blinkers had been removed from their eyes.

"Pigtail twist? Well, yes, that might work," I speculated.

"Pigtail twist is, as you know, Watson, a form of tobacco rolled, pressed and packed until it forms a rope which is then curled into a ball or cylindrical shape. It is an ideal way of keeping tobacco from drying out over long periods of time. One can also break off small pieces and chew these. This makes it particularly popular with sailors, where smoking by the crew is forbidden on many vessels."

"Shiner had eight or nine ounces in his pouch when we examined it," Holmes continued. "This would have formed a length of 'rope' of perhaps forty inches or more, easily long enough to strangle a man, and strong enough, too, if doubled up."

"Dear God, Holmes, you are right. The tobacco noose might just have had sufficient strength to commit the terrible act before, presumably, snapping and scattering those flakes upon the ground. It would also leave a dark oily residue upon the neck of the victim."

"And then came the most ingenious part," Holmes added. "He then simply pulled apart the 'rope' until it became just a pile of loose flakes lying innocuously within his leather pouch."

There followed a long pause. Once the shock of Holmes' revelation had sunk in, I finally broke the silence.

"What an incredible and singular murder weapon. It seems Shiner was indeed a most creative thinker despite his evil nature. I can see why the police underestimated him."

"Indeed, he was a man born with a fine mind, who would have had a bright future had his life developed differently. Instead, he drifted through life using his physical size to bully those closest to him into meek acquiescence and turning to drink when things went against him. Yet, despite years of abusing himself thus, he somehow retained his brilliant mind and planned and executed this most imaginative and daring scheme. I may abhor the man and his actions but I must admire the mind that created such an accomplished stratagem, one that very nearly confounded the local police, Scotland Yard's finest and even myself."

I inwardly smiled at Holmes' self-defined investigative hierarchy. Of course, he was being completely dispassionate in his assessment of the abilities of each group, but it was still amusing to hear him place himself at the very top of such a pyramid.

"Holmes, we must now inform Gregson and Lestrade, I am sure that they would be keen to hear the final piece of the puzzle," I suggested.

"Oh, I don't see why we need to do that, Doctor," my old friend grinned. "After all, the case is officially closed, what good would it do now? And think about it, Watson, would the avid followers of your accounts of our cases not be delighted to be able to read the final problem solved exclusively in your own words?" Holmes replied, with the merest hint of sarcasm and a definite twinkle in his eyes.

"Oh my goodness," I suddenly spluttered. "I have just remembered something ghastly. On the day that I made my investigations in and around Bedden, I visited Colonel Fauwkes at Bedhurst Hall."

"Yes, I am aware of your visit, your work showed some promise," Holmes replied, in a manner that I took to be encouragement.

"Well, somehow Wergeld's, or rather Shiner's, pouch had been left out on a table in the entrance hall," I said, rather sheepishly.

"What of it?" Holmes asked, without enthusiasm.

"Well, I had run out of tobacco and here was a pouch full of it, maybe as much as nine ounces. It was just sitting there, slowly drying out now that it had all been rubbed up. It was just going to go to waste, I concluded, so I took a little, maybe an ounce, no more, and refilled my own pouch. I thought it could not do any harm, could it? But, Holmes, what have I done?" I asked, with a feeling of rising panic.

"Ha-ha!" Holmes laughed, loudly. "Watson, not only have you destroyed vital evidence, you have smoked part of the actual murder weapon!"

Seeing Holmes howling with laughter quickly eased my concerns and I could now see the situation for what it was, absurd, bizarre, but also darkly comical. I was soon laughing along, heartily, with my friend.

Once I had recovered enough, I rose and poured two large brandies. They were not the last we enjoyed that evening.

Epilogue - Wednesday 23rd July 1884

The very next day, the weather changed. The rain returned and London became, once again, a grey and miserable place. Holmes lasted another few days before the black fog of ennui returned to weave its evil way into his very being. He sat motionless in his chair, legs pulled up underneath him, wrapped in his fawn dressing gown. On more than one occasion, I saw him staring at the black leather-lined box that still sat, untouched, upon the mantel.

The memories of the previous weeks' excitements were slowly fading, so I did my best to record what I could during the following days, my note keeping having been sporadic and irregular at best.

A week had passed since that wonderful evening when we had talked and laughed and taken too much brandy. I was sitting at the writing desk, turning my notes into the most complete account of our adventure that I could. Holmes was in his chair, staring at a fixed point somewhere in front of him.

Without a word, Holmes suddenly rose from his seat. He walked purposefully towards the fireplace and stretched out his right arm towards the mantelpiece. My heart sank, as I knew exactly what he intended. I have rarely felt such utter sadness.

His outstretched hand opened to pick up the leather and Macassar wood box. His fingers touched the top of the small case. I sighed and slowly shook my head in quiet despair.

Holmes' hand was stilled by a sudden sound. From downstairs came the familiar sound of the doorbell and, with it, the promise of a new adventure.

The End

A Ball of Pigtail Twist
Picture used by kind permission of Gawith Hoggarth & Co Ltd, Kendal

Acknowledgements

I would like to thank the following, without whom, this book could never have existed.

H & A, Mum, Dad, James (Harrison), Chick and Waleria (Babcia). Tom Shiner (the polar opposite of his literary doppelganger, a finer chap was never made). Dominic Selwood and Robert Rankin for their great encouragement. Dom and Al at H&S. Daiva & Giuseppe. Steve Emecz and Rich Ryan at MX Publishing for having faith in me.

Finally, Sir Arthur Conan Doyle and his good friends, Doctor John Watson and Mr. Sherlock Holmes.

Also from MX Publishing

MX Publishing is the world's largest specialist Sherlock Holmes publisher, with over a hundred titles and fifty authors creating the latest in Sherlock Holmes fiction and non-fiction.

From traditional short stories and novels to travel guides and quiz books, MX Publishing cater for all Holmes fans.

The collection includes leading titles such as <u>Benedict Cumberbatch In Transition</u> and <u>The Norwood Author</u> which won the 2011 Howlett Award (Sherlock Holmes Book of the Year).

MX Publishing also has one of the largest communities of Holmes fans on <u>Facebook</u> with regular contributions from dozens of authors.

www.mxpublishing.com

Also from MX Publishing

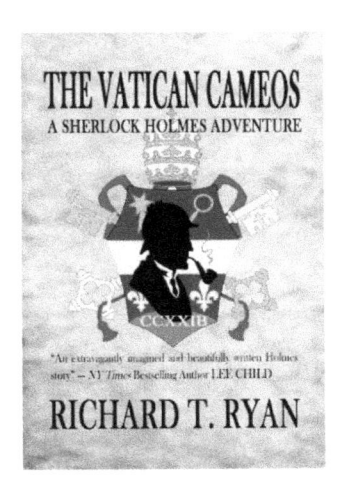

THE VATICAN CAMEOS
A SHERLOCK HOLMES ADVENTURE

"An extravagantly imagined and beautifully written Holmes story" – NY Times Bestselling Author LEE CHILD

RICHARD T. RYAN

When the papal apartments are burgled in 1901, Sherlock Holmes is summoned to Rome by Pope Leo XII. After learning from the pontiff that several priceless cameos that could prove compromising to the church, and perhaps determine the future of the newly unified Italy, have been stolen, Holmes is asked to recover them. In a parallel story, Michelangelo, the toast of Rome in 1501 after the unveiling of his Pieta, is commissioned by Pope Alexander VI, the last of the Borgia pontiffs, with creating the cameos that will bedevil Holmes and the papacy four centuries later. For fans of Conan Doyle's immortal detective, the game is always afoot. However, the great detective has never encountered an adversary quite like the one with whom he crosses swords in "The Vatican Cameos.."

"An extravagantly imagined and beautifully written Holmes story"
(**Lee Child**, NY Times Bestselling author, Jack Reacher series)

Milton Keynes UK
Ingram Content Group UK Ltd.
UKHW020644220124
436466UK00019B/865